Right Here,
Right Now

Right Here, Right Now

HelenKay Dimon

KENSINGTON PUBLISHING CORP.
http://www.kensingtonbooks.com

BRAVA BOOKS are published by

Kensington Publishing Corp.
850 Third Avenue
New York, NY 10022

All Kensington titles, imprints and distributed lines are available at special quantity discounts for bulk purchases for sales promotion, premiums, fundraising, educational or institutional use.

Special book excerpts or customized printings can also be created to fit specific needs. For details, write or phone the office of the Kensington Special Sales Manager: Kensington Publishing Corp., 850 Third Avenue, New York, NY 10022. Attn. Special Sales Department. Phone: 1-800-221-2647.

Brava and the B logo Reg. U.S. Pat. & TM Off.

ISBN-13: 978-0-7582-2223-7
ISBN-10: 0-7582-2223-8

First Kensington Trade Paperback Printing: March 2008
10 9 8 7 6 5 4 3 2 1

Printed in the United States of America

To my husband, James, for the support,
the cross-country move,
the opportunity to write for a living,
and everything else.

Acknowledgments

This book survived a cross-country move, a drastic career change and an illness that refused to go away or respond to medication. I have never been a big believer in the "this book wrote itself" philosophy, and this one proves I was right. Think of this as the miracle book. The one that somehow got written despite the universe's attempts to the contrary. And, for that I owe a huge "thank you" to several folks, including my editor, Kate Duffy, who gave me the time and much needed direction on this book, Kassia Krozser and Mica Stone who listened to my complaining, and Wendy Duren who read the initial draft and, as always, saw where it went off track and gave me a gentle shove to get it moving in the right direction again. Thank you all.

Chapter 1

"This isn't working."

There they were. To Gabrielle Pearson the phrase stood second only to "It's not you, it's me" as the most lame male excuse on the planet for cutting out of a date before the dessert menus hit the table.

Gabby glanced around the upscale restaurant looking for reinforcements. If anyone heard Reed Larkin's big kiss-off over the rumble of conversation and clanking of silverware, they were not letting on. No one held up a roll ready to lob it at Reed's fat head. A shame, really, since his over-inflated ego made it the perfect target.

"Gabby? Did you hear me?" Reed asked with his suddenly not-so-kissable mouth turned down in concern.

"I'm not deaf. I was thinking." Thinking that a woman never had a vial of strychnine when she needed one.

He frowned. "I was—"

"It's interesting, don't you agree?"

He switched to squinting. "You lost me."

"Obviously."

She lowered her fork to the white tablecloth, but not before toying with the idea of stabbing Reed smack in the center of his perfectly angled chin. One hit of the sharp prongs and no woman would ever be lured in by his inviting, sexy smile again.

"I'm talking about your timing, Reed. You waited until you were done with your meal to make this announcement. You skipped the appetizer course and choked back your undercooked steak without taking a breath." Now she knew why.

Reed was a man on the run.

The big weasel.

Here she had thought tonight, formal date number nine, might be *the* date. The one to capture all the heat pulsing between them with a bedroom ending. Hell, she'd be lucky to get cab fare out of him now.

Reed took a long swallow of water.

When he didn't choke, Gabby cursed life's unfairness. "I'm assuming I'm the part of the relationship that's not working."

"Look, it's not you. It's—"

Oh, no, no, no. "Don't finish that sentence."

If he continued down that road, the half of the salmon filet she had managed to swallow would make a repeat performance all over his expensive navy suit. Tempting, but not going to happen.

"What's wrong with you?" he asked as if he actually did not know.

"Just don't." She pointed a finger in the general direction of Reed's heart to back up her threat.

Those ice blue eyes that were so attractive up until five minutes ago blinked several times. "Gabby, we should—"

"Stop talking before someone loses a body part." Her gaze dropped to her fork. "Preferably you."

The sexy sparkle behind his eyes faded. For the first time since they sat down to eat, Reed's usual assurance slipped. Nice of him to show some reaction.

She learned long ago to control her emotions. To keep her reactions neutral and her anger at bay. No matter how fast that ball of anxiety started spinning around in her gut, she held it all in. Forced her outside to defy her insides.

She had been through far worse than a broken relationship, weathered much and never broken. But something about the silliness of the scene, of Reed cutting her off at the same time she mentally planned his seduction, broke open the dam inside her and sent anger spewing in every direction.

Her chest clenched as her cheeks grew hot. Her jaw pulled tight enough to make her back teeth ache.

Pissed. She was down-to-her-bones pissed. A new sensation and one she chalked up to a building of stress unable to find any release. One that refused to go away quietly.

If Reed intended to hand her a relationship pink slip, then she planned to give him an ending to remember. "Tell me something."

He smiled at the older couple sitting at the table next to them. "Sure."

"Where did it go wrong for you?"

Their relationship hadn't taken any wrong turns for her. They had cruised along just fine with her getting more interested and attracted every single day. Then the waiter put the entrees on the table and everything went to hell.

"The 'it' is . . . ?" he asked.

"For a smart guy, you seem to be experiencing some trouble with small words."

He stopped glancing around the restaurant and focused on her instead. "Talk slow and I'll try to keep up."

"Fine." Actually, the scene was anything but fine, but she clearly did not get a vote. "Us. You and me. The relationship. Since we never even had sex, I mean."

He clamped his lips together. "Is this really necessary?"

Definitely. "Maybe there's something you forgot to tell me? You know, about your preferences and such."

Color rushed back into his cheeks. "Wait a damn second."

"We've gone out. Had a good time. It's called dating, in

case you didn't know." This anger thing felt good. Freeing. Rather than fight it, Gabby let it flood through her.

"Well . . ."

"The next step between normal, healthy adults would have been sex." The step she had been imagining ever since he walked into her favorite morning coffee shop about a month before, forgot his wallet, and borrowed money and a seat at her table.

As if she needed another reason to give up caffeine.

"So?" She balanced both elbows on the table, blocking out the low rumble of conversation from the other diners. Dropping her voice down to a conspiratorial whisper, she asked, "What was it?"

Reed tugged on his ear in a nervous gesture she might have found endearing on another night, in another situation. Not on this one.

She leaned in until only her fury separated them. "Not the kissing, because that was good."

Okay, the lip action had been *great*. Score one for the tech nerd with the linebacker shoulders, pouty mouth and irresistible crooked smile.

She kept all the positives to herself. Now was not the time for an ego stroke. In fact, she did not plan on stroking any part of Reed Larkin ever again.

"And the touching . . . well, come on," she said, warming to the subject the longer she talked. "Let's be honest here. We both know *that* part worked for you."

"Damn it, Gabby." His harsh whisper sent the waiter scurrying in the other direction without stopping to pick up the discarded plates.

She snorted. "I may not see when a guy loses interest, but I know when he's aroused."

"Lower your voice," Reed said in a tone that grew louder with each word.

"Why?"

"*Why?*"

The faster he unraveled, the more in control she felt. "Yeah, that's what I asked. Why?"

"For starters, we're in public." He exhaled as he tugged on his ear a second time.

"You should have thought about that before you chose the how and where for your big scene."

He waved the waiter away when the poor man ventured toward the table again. "If you'd stop talking for five seconds and let me finish a sentence, we could have a civilized conversation about this."

She noticed how Reed said "we," as if he had the first clue about what she really needed. If "he" did, then "they" would be testing her newly washed soft sheets by now instead of listing her shortcomings over surf and turf.

"You want to talk, Reed?" She sat back and folded her arms across her chest. Even tapped her foot a few times. "Go ahead."

"Give me a minute to catch up."

"Stop stalling." Her frustrated voice lifted above the soft jazz playing in the background, causing a few diners to look her way.

"I'm not—"

"Just say it."

"Fine," he shot back. "I need more excitement."

A sharp silence followed his bombshell.

"Damn it." He shook his head on a deep inhale.

"You can say that again." She pushed the words out past the numbness in her throat.

"Do you see now why I tried to do this a different way?"

"You just called me boring." She said the words nice and slow, trying to process them as she spoke.

"I did not say that."

"Sure sounded like it."

If only he knew about her real job . . . but he couldn't and that was part of the problem. He had to see her as a forensic accountant and nothing more. Everyone did.

"I'd like to point out that you develop computer programs for a living. Not exactly a career chock-full of excitement, unless, of course, you enjoy talking to things that don't talk back," she said.

"How I work really isn't the point."

"You have one?"

His broad shoulders stiffened until most of his six-one frame loomed over the other side of the table. "The issue is about meeting needs."

"Did we even get to the needs part of our relationship?" She had needs. Like the need to strangle him with his blue patterned tie.

He picked his napkin back up and folded it, unfolded it and refolded it again as he visibly regained his control. "Look, I didn't mean for the comment to come out that harsh."

"Uh-huh."

"There is nothing wrong with you."

"Gee, thanks."

"We just don't connect. I'm sorry."

For some reason his mumbled apology ignited her rage even more. Probably because it sounded so lame.

"Let's just skip to the part where we say goodbye," she said in the lightest voice she could muster over the roaring of blood in her ears.

"Really?"

"Sure."

A half smile returned to Reed's lips. "Exactly. This is not personal."

"Of course not." She just experienced an impersonal personal rejection. Right. Whatever.

"I knew you'd be reasonable about this."

"Yeah, that's me. Miss Reasonable." That fury bubbled up inside her unchecked and ready to spill over.

"We can be adult," he said in his most rational computer guy voice.

"We could, but you know what, Reed? I prefer acting like a child." She stood up and dumped the contents of her wineglass over his head.

"Gabby!" He shoved his chair back too late. The liquid hit him straight on before dripping down his face and onto his suit jacket.

"And, thanks for the wine recommendation. I'm happy I went with the house red. The color goes so much better with those little horns on your head."

"Why did you—"

"Because I didn't have a brick." Gabby smacked the glass against the table with a clink. "Thanks for the interesting evening. It's been great. Really."

Chapter 2

Reed considered being soaked with wine while thirty or so restaurant patrons looked on about as far from "great" as possible. Waiters scrambled to clear a path for Gabby while liquid dripped off his chin and down his shirt. The rest landed in a puddle on the table.

With a quick wipe of his face and a nod to the gawking crowd, he sat back down. Ignoring the chuckles and finger-pointing proved a bit harder.

He had known Gabby for weeks and never seen her get riled. She stayed calm, including in the face of heavy rush-hour traffic. He never expected to see a spark under that cool self-confidence.

Knowing what lay beneath the surface, seeing the way her butt swished from side to side beneath her slim black skirt as she walked away, sent a spark of a different kind shooting through him.

Where did all that heat come from?

And why the hell hadn't she unleashed it before now?

Petite and all of five-foot-four, Gabby possessed a sweet, round face and huge hazel eyes. She looked more like a recent college grad than a woman of twenty-eight. Vibrant and alive with a sexy little smile that lit up her face.

Well, it did up until about three minutes ago. Amazing

how the undercurrent of attraction disappeared along with her control. He had the puddle of wine in his blazer pocket to prove it.

"Well done." The sarcasm behind the comment shot through the transmitter and directly into Reed's ear.

"Shut up," Reed muttered just loud enough to be picked up by the small microphone dot planted on his tie.

Pete Thompson's voice echoed in the earphone. "Do you know anything about women?"

"That should be obvious. No." Certainly less than Reed thought he did before he sat down to eat.

"That was one hell of a crash and burn."

Reed could picture his partner sitting in the van, grousing about drawing the surveillance side of this job and wishing he were the one inside the restaurant with Gabby instead of out in the parking lot by himself.

"Thanks for your support," Reed grumbled, keeping his voice low enough to prevent attracting more attention.

"I'm here for you, buddy."

"Hate to hear what you would say if you were against me."

"How's the wine?" This time Pete asked the question over a round of chewing and laughing.

Good thing someone found this situation funny. For Reed, it sucked. No girl. No leads. The case got more screwed up every second. That was why he wanted Gabby out and safe. Why he sat in a pool of alcohol rather than on a bed between Gabby's bare legs.

Pete whistled. "I can see Gabby out front by the valet right now."

"How does she look?"

"Mad as hell. But, oh so fine. There's no way I'd push her out of bed."

Reed found the conversation less funny by the second. "Drop it."

"Of course, you wouldn't know anything about being in bed with her since you skipped the sex." Pete cleared his throat. "Why was that again?"

Because I'm an idiot. Reed could not come up with a better explanation than that.

He had sure as hell thought about sex with Gabby. About spending a few hours in her bedroom doing something other than searching. He had started leading with body parts other than his head the day after he met her.

She could hold a conversation on almost any topic and stop a man's breath with her wide smile. Her shoulder-length light brown hair she wore tucked behind her ears with a few strands brushed across her forehead. Small features but rounded everywhere a woman should be rounded. And she was smart as hell.

For some reason, her drenching him in wine did not make her any less appealing. If anything, her show of outrage made her all the hotter to him, sick bastard that he was.

"Boss lady says you blew the assignment." Pete was not chuckling now.

"When did Charlotte call in?" Reed pretended to cough into his napkin so that no one would think he was talking to his dinner plate.

"About ten minutes ago." Pete stopped crumpling food wrappers and eating long enough to explain.

"And you waited until now to warn me?"

"I was busy watching Gabby."

"You do know you're supposed to be on my side, right?"

"Then let me clue you in on your next problem. Charlotte's been watching your scene with Gabby. Saw the whole thing."

Now there was a stinking heap of bad news. "Charlotte's with you in the van?"

"Worse. She's in the restaurant with you. Sitting nearby with her own listening device. Which, lucky for you, she turned off when Gabby started talking about stroking you." Got the call to cut transmission right about the time you broke up with Hot Legs."

Gabby's legs. Yeah, those were the last two things on the planet Reed wanted to think about at the moment. He knew cutting her loose was the right choice, the only choice under the circumstances, but the decision stung. Especially now that he had witnessed Gabby's more passionate side.

He thought . . . actually, it did not matter what he thought as far as Gabby was concerned. He not only had burned the bridge, he had torched the land at both ends.

"Charlotte's headed your way," Pete said. "Should be at your table any minute."

"One question for you, genius. If the boss said cut, why are you still tuned in?" This time Reed wiped a hand across his mouth for cover.

"Wouldn't miss a front-row seat to your ass kicking by two women in the span of ten minutes for all the money in my wallet."

Charlotte Rhames's high heels clicked against the marble floor as she walked up behind Reed. Without a word, she slid her almost six-foot frame into Gabby's abandoned chair. Her pale blue eyes zeroed in on him with laserlike precision.

Looking across the table, Reed wondered which woman could kill him faster, Gabby or Charlotte. Too close to call.

"I didn't know you were here," Reed said as if that fact were not obvious.

Commanding in designer suits and expensive gold jewelry, Charlotte could have been forty years old or sixty. No one dared to ask. The woman was scary enough when not ticked off. No need to invite her anger.

"I am here to assess your job performance."

He wiped off the rest of the wine the best he could and threw the napkin on the table. "How am I doing?"

"Not well." She signaled for the waiter without breaking eye contact with Reed. "Would you care for something to drink?"

"I'm good with the beverage I'm wearing, but thanks."

Charlotte ordered white wine and waited for the server to leave before returning to the conversation. "Is there something you wish to tell me?"

Almost never. "The steak is good here."

With her usual lack of humor Charlotte didn't crack a smile. "About your surveillance of Ms. Pearson."

"That?" Reed cleared his throat. "No."

"I am sure you have an explanation for why Ms. Pearson is waiting for a taxi instead of sitting here with you."

"Gabby's out of this assignment."

Gabby also wanted him dead, but Charlotte knew that part. Charlotte knew everything about everything as far as Reed could tell.

Charlotte's slim eyebrow lifted in question. "Your job objectives on this assignment were very clear."

"True."

"You were to follow Ms. Pearson. Get close and watch her."

"I attended the initial case briefing. You don't need to repeat this."

"Then you know you were to see if our source was correct about there being a relationship between Ms. Pearson and Greg Benson. Your job was to determine the nature of their connection and report back to me."

And he had done all of those things.

"Implicit in those instructions was the requirement you await further orders from me before taking any action with regard to Ms. Pearson other than information gathering."

That was where he moved off plan.

Timing was a factor. Reed knew the sooner he took an innocent civilian out of the dangerous situation, that civilian being Gabby, the better. He did not want her standing anywhere near him if and when Benson figured out about the government's false promises and plan to take him down.

Controlling and minimizing collateral damage ranked high on Reed's list of mission objectives. Charlotte knew that. She just arranged her priorities in a different way.

"So, Reed, which one of those assigned tasks are you performing right now?"

How 'bout covering his balls before Charlotte cut them off and handed them to him. "My job was to search without Gabby knowing. I did that. There is no connection between Gabby and Benson. That being the case, my mission as to Gabby is complete."

"I decide when your mission is over."

He just knew Charlotte was going to say that. "Our intel was wrong. It's time to move on and find a way to corroborate what we have on Benson's dealings with someone who actually knows him."

Charlotte tilted her head and stared him down. "And you deduced all of that how, exactly?"

"I talked with Gabby. Saw her every single day for a month. Dated her. Searched her files and her condo. Pete researched. Nothing turned up. Her record is clean. No lines, accountant or otherwise, tie her back to Benson. She's a dead end in the investigation."

"Interesting."

At least one of them thought so. "There was no reason to keep Gabby involved anymore."

Charlotte leaned back in her chair and stared at him without blinking for what felt like fifteen minutes. Reed suddenly knew how a bug felt when a scientist slapped it on a slab of glass and squashed it under a microscope.

"You purport to know a great deal about a woman you never bothered to take to bed." Something close to a smile curled at the edge of Charlotte's lips. "I make it my business to be familiar with the, shall we say, most fundamental of happenings of those who work for me."

Though he would not have predicted his night could get worse, it did. Slid right into the abyss.

With the evening shot to hell, Reed decided to salvage a fraction of his dignity. "Last I checked my sex life was not part of office protocol."

"In your most recent briefing you stated you knew Ms. Pearson."

"So?"

"Intimately."

"There's no way I used that word."

"From your report I assumed the two of you had been intimate."

"I do have a few skills outside of the bedroom, you know."

"Tell Charlotte I'll volunteer to have sex with Hot Legs." Pete's voice echoed in Reed's eardrum, reminding Reed that more than two of them were engaged in this bizarre conversation.

"I have never known a woman to turn your head so far around that you would risk a job for her." Charlotte covered Gabby's uneaten food with a cloth napkin. "I would hate to think you are losing your edge."

"That hasn't happened."

Hell, is that what just happened?

"Sure sounded like it," Pete joked. "Twisted your head right up your—"

Reed ripped out his small earpiece and tucked it under his shirt collar. "My edge is fine, Charlotte. You know that."

Charlotte scooped up the wineglass as soon as the waiter set it on the table. "Whatever the issue, you need to figure out a way to win back Ms. Pearson's affection."

"That's never going to happen. I made damn sure to eliminate that possibility."

"By 'never' you had better mean tomorrow."

Shit. "Why?"

"Benson set up a meeting with Ms. Pearson for two days from now."

"What?"

"You have a very small window within which to reconnect with Ms. Pearson before she and our target confer." Charlotte took a long sip, drawing out the moment.

She could have skipped the added drama. The news carried enough of a shock without the fake delay tactic.

He searched his mind for the piece of information he had overlooked. Nothing came to him. "But they don't—"

"Know each other? So you keep saying." Charlotte ran a manicured finger around the rim of her glass. "Apparently you missed something or failed to investigate the matter fully."

"This isn't possible." Reed shook his head, trying to assimilate this new information with all the collected data. Nothing fit.

"I assure you it is. Maybe next time you will refrain from going solo and will, instead, stick to the assignment you are given."

"I can't promise that," he grumbled under his breath.

"You have one day to reconcile with your girlfriend."

"I'd need a year and a protective cup just to walk in the same room as Gabby right now." Reconstructive surgery and a new identity wouldn't be bad ideas either.

The Gabby who had dumped wine over his head was not going to be all that receptive to a simple apology followed by a round of make-up sex. Which was a damn shame because the latter sounded good after this evening.

"You have less than forty-eight hours. Make it happen, Reed."

"You're a woman. Well, sort of . . ." When Charlotte's frown deepened, Reed skipped over the rest of his explanation and got to the point. "It will take more than a night or two to win back Gabby."

"That is all the time you have." Charlotte's eyes sparkled with an evil gleam. "You could always try a new strategy."

"Hypnosis?"

Charlotte finished off her wine with one last sip. "I was thinking more along the lines of one of those *other* skills you have used in the past."

Worse than dumping Gabby on the brink of bedding her, now he had to win her back, get information from her that she didn't even know she had and somehow protect her at the same time. Maybe he could juggle flaming knives while he was at it.

"Gabby's going to kill me."

"And?" The monotone sound made it clear Charlotte did not see that as a negative outcome.

"I'm saying the fact out loud because I want to be on record when this mission goes to hell."

"I trust you will not let that happen before we have the information we need about Ms. Pearson and Benson."

"That's the plan."

As if he actually had one of those.

Chapter 3

Fifteen minutes later Reed stuck Charlotte with the bill and headed for the door. On the way out he returned stares from fellow diners who acted as if they had never seen a guy get his ass handed to him in public before.

He would head home and shower to erase the stench of liquor from his clothes. Amazing how fighting with angry women could make a guy yearn for his couch.

Ignoring the snickers around the hostess desk, he kept walking and slipped his earpiece back in to check with Pete. "I'm back."

"Where the hell have you been?"

"Getting that ass kicking you wanted to see." Reed felt a rush of cool air against his face as he slipped out the door and into the dark night. "We're done for the night. I'm heading home."

"Not yet you're not."

"I know we have a disaster on our hands. We'll meet tomorrow and try to fix—"

"Damn, I've been shouting for you for five minutes," Pete yelled into the microphone as if to prove his point.

"I'm getting tired of people interrupting me while I'm talking."

"Tough shit." Pete pronounced the "t" in a tone sharp

enough to send a pop through the microphone. "I was just about to walk in there and drag you out."

"You were smart to stay in a Gabby-free zone."

"Where are you right now?"

"I just came outside." Reed glanced to his left and acknowledged his partner's van with a nod.

"You have a problem."

"Tell me something I don't know. Last time I go to that restaurant." Reed looked down at the red blotches staining his chest. "Or wear this shirt."

"This goes beyond your suit."

Reed fumbled for his keys, grateful he did not have to hang around waiting for the valet. "But it was a nice suit."

"Gabby is leaning against your car."

Reed's head shot up. "Are you shitting me?"

"'Fraid not."

"My—"

"Car. Yeah."

"What does she think she's doing?" The sleek black sedan sat across the street to his right. Being three cars away and with traffic between them, all Reed could make out was an outline of a figure hovering near the front end. "Can you see her right now?"

"Oh, yeah. You're lucky she's not holding a wine bottle."

"You're telling me she did something to my car? Why didn't you stop her?" He had visions of scratches and lipstick marking his pristine paint job.

Grabbing the prime parking spot rather than waiting for the valet suddenly seemed like one more bad idea in an evening full of them.

"Can't tell."

"Look harder."

"She probably decided to kill you and is waiting around to carry out the job." Pete laughed. "Not that she's hiding. She's fuming. You should see her—"

Reed stopped listening. He was too busy jogging across the street and around the cars stacked up at the light to keep up his end of the conversation.

Shoes thudded against the pavement. Keys jangled in his fist. Car horns blared. Reed blocked out every sound and every face except Gabby's furious one.

Fuming. Pissed. Mad. Ticked off. Yeah, in the glow of the streetlight she looked all of those things. Maybe even a bit homicidal. She sat on the hood of his car and banged her high heels against his up-until-then perfectly unscuffed paint job.

He skidded to a halt next to her. Thanks to regular workouts he handled the run without trouble. Handling Gabby was going to be the bigger problem.

Problem as in the probable death of him.

"I thought you went home." Reed asked the question in the friendliest tone he could muster while his car sat in the direct firing line of Gabby's anger.

"Not yet." She scraped her heel against his fender.

He felt the screeching sound echo down to the pit of his stomach. "Yeah, I see that."

As if sensing his discomfort, she banged her heel a second time.

"Could you not do that?"

"Sit?"

He rubbed his hand over the cool metal and winced when he felt what he feared was a deep scratch. "Vandalize my vehicle."

"Do you have a better target in mind?" Her voice dripped with disgust.

He pulled back until he stood out of kicking range. "So, the idea of this meeting is to finish me off in the middle of the street?"

She stopped watching the front door of the restaurant and started scowling at him. She may have even snarled.

"What, a man can't ask a question?"

"You're making me think that finishing you off has some merit."

"Maybe we should go back inside."

"Why?"

"Because there are people in there who can act as witnesses and the ambulance is only a call away." He adjusted his earphone to make sure she could not see it.

Pete was not talking, but Reed could hear him breathing. Reed hoped his lazy partner also had 911 on speed dial.

"I'm not going anywhere with you."

That was pretty clear, but her comment did not explain everything. "You have me at a disadvantage here, Gabby."

"There's an interesting take on this evening's festivities."

"Uh-oh," Pete whispered on his end.

Reed saw the trap without Pete's help. Making the lovely lady even angrier was not a good plan. If Reed knew how to prevent that possibility, he would.

"What are you doing out here?"

"Standing."

"On my car?"

"Feeling dramatic, aren't you?"

"You're the one who threw the wine and beat up my car." He cleared his throat in an attempt to send an I-mean-business signal. "And, feel free to jump off it at any time."

She saw his I-mean-business signal and raised him a your-car-is-at-my-mercy look. "After everything that's happened tonight, you're telling me the only thing you care about is the vehicle? Typical male."

It did not take a genius-level I.Q. to know the comment was not a compliment. "Did I miss the part where you explained why you're out here?"

"I'm waiting."

That explained . . . nothing. "For me?"

He almost hoped she would say no.

"Yes." She slid off the hood, clanking her heels against the car a few more times before she hit the ground.

"Could you be careful—"

"You have my keys." Her icy tone made the back of his neck itch.

"I do?" He patted his suit pocket but felt only the wet and sticky remnants of his dinner beverage. No keys. "I don't have—"

"They're in your glove compartment."

Sounded plausible, even though opening the door meant turning his back on her for a second. "When did you stick them in there?"

"When we parked. They didn't fit in my purse." She waved a square black box in his face.

"Then why buy it?"

Her eyebrow inched up. "Excuse me?"

Words stuttered to a halt in his throat, but he forced them out anyway. "Just seems like it would be more practical to carry a bag you can stick crap in."

"Do you really want to have an argument about my accessories right now?"

"That would be tough since I have no idea what that even means." Then he saw the flat line of her lips. "And then there's the part about the lack of witnesses to my potential homicide."

"You might want to keep that in mind."

"I am. Trust me."

Pete's chuckle echoed in the earpiece. "She is so damn hot."

"Get my keys." She said the words like an order.

"You didn't have to wait out here. You could have . . ."

Reed was not sure how to end that sentence since a return

trip to the table likely would have resulted in more liquor throwing. "Forget it."

"The keys." She held out her palm. "Now."

"Sure." The horn sounded as he hit the unlock button. A few seconds later the glove compartment popped open. "Here you go."

She grabbed her keys but did not move. "I wasn't waiting for you."

"You said you were."

"I lied."

"Man. I'd run." Pete whispered, but the warning boomed through the ear speaker and straight into Reed's brain.

Somehow Reed focused on the furious woman in front of him instead of the wise words in his ear. Probably had something to do with the fact Gabby held her keys like a weapon.

"My initial thought was to break your car window and get the keys myself," she said.

So, she *had* thought about using violence. Now there was some bad news. "Lucky for me you came up with a second option."

"Not yet." She pursed her lips together as if thinking of her next move. "I want you to understand something."

That he was a dead man? Yeah. He got that part. "Which is?"

"What you gave up." She dropped her keys on the hood.

"Hey, be careful—"

When her lips covered his, he stopped talking. Stopped thinking. Stopped giving a damn about his car. She took his breath until he had nothing left. Including common sense.

"Whoa." The awe in Pete's voice matched the excitement thrumming through Reed's body.

She shoved his back against the car, letting her hands

wander over his body as her tongue slid over his. With each pass she deepened the kiss. Drew him in, clouded his vision, until he felt those palms find their target.

One hand landed on the small of his back. The other cupped the bulge behind his zipper. Caressing his erection until his skin caught fire from the double dose of her hands on his body and her mouth against his.

Her breasts pressed against his chest. The triangle between her legs opened to him. Cradled him. Inflamed him.

"This is better than porn," Pete said with more than a bit of awe in his voice.

In the distance Reed heard car horns and a few shouts of encouragement. In his head, he heard a death march.

Her lips seduced. Her fingers tempted. The heat from her body singed his suit. And the shocking kiss went on and on. Passion. Fire. She held nothing back.

His petite accountant unleashed a firestorm inside him, melting his nerve endings from the inside out as his dick rose and begged for attention. She sucked and kissed and touched and rubbed until his hands burned with the need to shove her into the backseat, strip her bare and test out all those positions he had been dreaming about sharing with her.

Then she stopped cold. Just dropped her arms and stepped back in mid-kiss.

His lips followed until he tasted only air. His brain tried to signal his hands to stop holding her, but every body part refused to listen. His chest rose and fell as he pulled in huge gasps of oxygen.

When his eyes opened again, his palms rested on her hips, and a good foot separated their bodies. "Why did you stop?"

"For the same reason you ended our dinner." An evil smile formed on her lips. "You don't excite me."

"My ass." He tried to pull her closer and prove how

lame that theory really was, but she ducked faster than he swooped.

"Oh, you have a fine ass. I don't debate that." She pried his hands off of her and stepped back and out of grabbing range. "But, that's not enough for me."

"Your body says otherwise." He stared at her hardened nipples to back up his point.

"Physical reaction. Would happen with anyone."

"Are you trying to piss me off?"

"You can't tell?" Pete asked from his view in the van.

Gabby shot Reed a look of pure pity. "Come on, Reed. Like you said, it's not personal."

"So this is about payback." The kind that would keep him up half the night.

She tapped a finger against her lips. "It's not you. It's me."

"Don't know about you but I need a cold shower," Pete mumbled.

Reed ignored the whispered comment. The only attention he wanted right now was from Gabby. "We should go somewhere and talk."

"Not interested."

"Now who's lying?"

"Thanks for getting my keys." She waved. Actually waved her fingers at him.

"You aren't the only one who knows when the opposite sex is interested, hon."

"You had your chance."

"You want to give me another." He knew that to be true.

"That's what you get for thinking."

"That's why I rarely try it."

"Good plan." Her smile grew even wider. "Now, I'm going home."

"Don't leave."

"Good night." She winked and turned around.

For the second time in one night, she staged the perfect exit. Took off with those high heels slapping against the pavement. Head held high. Back straight. A final verbal slap. Everyone rushing to move out of her way.

Reed knew he should take up the chase, but he refused to run after her. He would win her back without begging. He could get this case back on track without letting Gabby clip off his testicles and hand them to him in a paper bag.

"Damn, man. I think I'm in love." Pete sounded as winded as Reed felt.

"It's lust."

"Whatever it is, I'm in." Pete whistled. "Was that kiss as smoking as it looked?"

Hell, yeah. "It was okay."

Yeah, no big deal. Women gave him tonsil-sucking kisses all the time. Once he got the indentation of her body out of his shirt, he would be fine.

Never mind the fact he could still taste her. That her perfume lingered on his clothes, blocking out the stale smell of wine. That he would feel her climbing all over him every time he closed his eyes during the next month.

"You know something?" Pete asked in a serious voice.

"Other than the fact the night sucked?"

"That woman is going to be the death of you, man."

"Like I said before, tell me something I don't know."

Chapter 4

"He dumped you last night?" Doug Richards stopped chewing on the end of his ballpoint pen long enough to ask the question for the third time.

"He did not dump me. He broke it off." Gabby guessed her coworker's refusal to believe Reed called off the relationship held some sort of flattery, but his wording ticked her off. Thanks to Reed, she had spent most of the evening ticked off and was sick of it.

"Isn't that the same?"

Yes. "No."

"I just can't believe he dumped you."

The flattery angle was wearing thin. "It's time to talk about something else."

"Man." Doug shook his head and said something about dumping under his breath.

Gabby blamed Reed for this. He had ruined her evening. Now the mere memory of him was ruining her workday.

Doug's mumbling built back up to full-fledged talking. "It's unbelievable that guy would—"

"You've said the word five times now. One more time and I'll get violent."

"What crawled up your ass? You're the one who . . ." Doug stared, nodding. "Oh, I get it."

"What?"

"This is because the nerd dum—"

"Forget I asked." Gabby tried to slam her plastic water bottle down on her metal desktop for effect. Being empty, the thing bounced instead.

Doug's mouth hung open for one glorious quiet second before the chatter started again. "You never get pissed."

"I am human, you know."

"And you don't take breakups very well." Doug made the annoying tsk-tsk sound as he slid into the seat across from her at their double-sided desk.

"Before you use the word 'dumped' again, know I am an inch away from killing you with my stapler." Gabby could find only her tape dispenser, so she held that up as a weapon instead.

Doug snorted. "Guess that's better than trying to use your tissue box."

"Leave her alone." Sondra Alonso, Gabby's best friend and their team leader, delivered her order without looking away from the bank of television monitors in front of her.

Sondra had one of those fancy, glassed-in corner offices on their high floor overlooking Washington D.C.'s Mc-Pherson Square Park, a small patch of grass known more for political protests than picnics. The same modern and stylish office where Sondra spent, maybe, ten minutes in a day.

Being the hands-on type, Sondra preferred analyzing data to filling out paperwork, which meant hours and hours investigating data with the rest of the team. With her dark features and mixed Japanese and Puerto Rican heritage, Sondra could have been a model. For some reason, she focused on numbers instead.

"Besides"—Sondra lowered her black frame glasses and scanned the pages of financial documents on the multiple screens—"Reed may be a computer geek on paper, but he's a damn good-looking computer geek."

Now there was an understatement. Something about Reed's bright blue eyes reminded Gabby of a crisp autumn sky and sent her temperature soaring. The fact that he looked better in a suit, and even better lounging in jeans on her couch, than any man she had ever seen didn't hurt either.

Not that she still thought about him even a little.

"Good-looking or not, he's an ass," Gabby said, hoping the comment would end the subject once and for all.

"I wasn't commenting on his personality," Sondra said with a chuckle.

"Stop helping me."

Sondra flashed a smile over her shoulder before returning to the monitors. "What are friends for?"

To stop you from getting in your car and hunting down the deadbeat who dumped you. To take the spoon away when you threaten to eat two gallons of ice cream after the car-attack plans fall through and you are left with the memory of how you had planned to whisk that same deadbeat off to bed that evening. Sondra did a little of both for Gabby the night before.

Doug kicked back into his usual position: sneakers on desk and fingers linked behind head. "What does this nerd have going for him that he thought he could trash our Gabby so easy?"

Gabby noticed her state had just moved from dumped to something less attractive. "Who said anything about being trashed?"

"Uh, me. Two seconds ago."

Gabby considered pulling the fire alarm to get Doug to stop talking.

"Actually, Reed's completely clean. Not so much as a parking ticket." Sondra stopped taking notes.

"Remember how you weren't going to help me anymore?" Gabby looked around for that alarm.

"In a second." Sondra waved her friend off.

Doug snorted again. "A nerd's a nerd."

"How about we try a minute or two of silence?" Gabby asked.

Sondra being Sondra, she kept right on task. "Reed's exactly the opposite of a geek in terms of his looks and appeal."

"Give me a break," Doug mumbled under his breath.

Sondra tucked her pen behind her ear and spun her chair around to face Doug, all pretense of work gone. "I checked Reed out. Ran his financials. His history. Tracked down some clippings."

"Wait a second." The news temporarily trumped Gabby's anger at Reed and frustration with all the meddling. "You investigated Reed?"

Sondra shrugged. "Sure. I do that with all of your dates."

Something Gabby figured she should have done, but still . . . "Why?"

"It's part of my job." Sondra looked serious when she made the comment.

"I want to see the manual outlining that job requirement right now."

"Of course it's her job," Doug said, as if gathering confidential work information for personal concerns was a regular occurrence.

Actually, maybe it was. "Did I miss a memo on the use of office resources or something?"

Doug nodded. "It's more of an informal thing. I checked but don't remember thinking the guy looked like anything other than a typical loser nerd."

Reed was not the usual anything, but this was a matter of privacy. Well, it was more about being left out of the loop. Gabby hated that.

"No one thought to share the Reed Larkin file with me, the woman dating him?"

"We figured you already knew." Doug shot Gabby an apologetic half smile.

Doug's short, spiky brown hair and deep brown eyes gave him a carefree air younger than his thirty-four years. Gabby knew better. Doug could crack a joke and shoot a gun with equal precision. A stint in the navy, followed by a few missing years he refused to discuss, made Doug much more lethal than his sleepy bedroom smile suggested.

Despite those impressive good looks, Gabby never saw Doug as anything but a brother. Probably had something to do with the string of short-term relationships he enjoyed so much. Relationships in the sense of responsibility-free month-long sex romps.

Doug's stories made her more than a bit envious since her last sexual adventure occurred long enough ago to be counted in terms of years rather than months. Well, almost, but she refused to take the time to figure out if she had crossed the line from eleven months to twelve.

"Come on, Gabby," Doug joked. "What good is having all of this intelligence at our fingertips if we can't use it for personal questions and snooping on neighbors and old high school enemies and stuff?"

"The manager side of me will pretend I didn't hear that," Sondra said.

"Right. Didn't say anything about the guy who steals my newspaper or how I found out about his Internet porn addiction." Doug narrowed his eyes at Gabby. "But let's get back to the dud who dumped our Gabby. We should have dropped this Plant guy—"

"Plant?" Sondra asked.

Gabby knew where Doug was going with that remark. "His name is Reed not Plant."

"—to his knees in the restaurant parking lot for dumping Gabby."

"That would be a bit obvious, don't you think?" Sondra asked.

"Then there's the fact I wouldn't let either of you two touch Reed."

"Why?" The way Doug's eyes narrowed, Gabby knew the question was a serious one.

She made sure to deliver the answer in an equally clear manner. "Because the thought is ridiculous."

Sondra's eyes lit up with mischief. "Do you think we could actually get someone to beat up Reed?"

"Not someone. Me." Doug puffed out his chest.

"You?" Sondra asked.

Gabby tried to intercede. "Both of you stop."

"Sure, it's my responsibility as the only man on our team."

And with that, the conversation veered into crazy territory. Next they would put out a hit on Reed, a thought Gabby might have favored last night when the fury still burned white hot, but not today when it just simmered at a low rage.

Sondra pursed her lips together. "Actually, there was that guy with the FBI who had a crush on Gabby last year. Jenkins or Johnson. What was his name, Gabby?"

"I am not participating in this madness."

Sondra ignored Gabby in favor of her FBI enforcer theory. "Anyway, that guy could have taken Reed."

The FBI guy's face popped into Gabby's mind and then popped right back out again. For some reason only Reed's face refused to leave her head.

Doug frowned at Sondra. "I don't need help to beat the crap out of some guy named Fig."

"Reed," Gabby repeated without thinking.

"What kind of pansy-ass name is that anyway?" Doug asked.

"Rein in that testosterone there, caveman. All I meant was Reed might be harder to beat up than you think." Sondra's dark eyes clouded for a second. "He's got these shoulders—"

"Stop!" When they did, Gabby decided she should have tried yelling much earlier in the conversation.

"Now what's wrong with you?" Doug asked in a tone as serious as his last question.

"That's enough about Reed. Reed's shoulders—Reed's anything—are off limits."

After a beat or two of precious silence, Doug rolled his shoulders back, as if he was trying to flex his muscles. "I could take him."

"Why did I come into the office this morning?" Gabby finally asked the question out loud.

"There's nothing nerdy about this, sweetheart." Doug whipped out his leather billfold and flashed his government badge.

"You do know we have those, too, right?" Gabby reached for her identification. After a brief pat down of her low-waisted navy dress pants, she realized she had misplaced her card. Again.

She spent her days dissecting and tracking complex financial dealings looking for criminal activity. Holding on to her entry badge was a different story.

Friendship or not, Sondra would take her head off this time. There were rules. The most basic of which dealt with badges and not losing them.

They worked on a secure floor of a secure building, held secret clearances. Carried official-looking badges, or were supposed to, despite the clandestine nature of their organization.

Their company, Financial Solutions, was fronted by a real accounting office. The sixth-floor offices were used for that purpose. Workers without government clearances sat down there taking care of corporate taxes and other confidential financial work. The tenth floor, Gabby's floor, housed the *other* employees. The individuals believed to be managers working on high-profile client matters.

In reality, Gabby and everyone else on her floor engaged in forensic financial research and investigation. Through contracting arrangements with numerous government agencies, including the Drug Enforcement Agency, the Federal Bureau of Investigation and others, Financial Solutions searched for illegal financial activity.

Forget filing tax returns. Gabby and her team provided the background evidence and confirmation needed to make arrests. Doug participated in those arrests and with the hands-on aspects of the job. Gabby was not sure exactly what he did when he walked out of the building for what he called a "take down," but he carried a gun to do it.

All aspects of her job qualified as much cooler stuff than the pen and pencil work Reed believed she did every day. Gabby just wished she could rub that fact in Reed's smug face.

"Is there a problem, Ms. Pearson?" Doug asked in a mocking tone.

Only a small issue of violating federal law by losing my credentials. "Everything's fine."

Gabby tried to ignore the discussion and focus in on her search. She had flashed her stupid badge to get past the guards and through the card reader when she walked off the elevator on her floor this morning. Her silk blouse did not have a pocket. Nowhere to stick it in her camisole either.

Where the hell was the stupid thing?

Doug dropped his feet to the cement floor and opened his desk drawer. "Looking for something, sunshine?"

Damn. "No."

"You sure?" Doug asked.

"You're having trouble with repetition today." At least he had stopped saying "dumped" every two seconds, which showed some progress.

He waved her badge, hideous photo and all, in the air. "Maybe you're missing this?"

"How did you get it?"

"Picked it up."

"Give me that." Gabby leaned over and swiped at the card in Doug's fingers, but he avoided her grab.

"Nope."

"When did you take it?" She took a second swing and missed.

"You dropped it at the elevator."

"Doug, give her the badge," Sondra said.

"But making her work for it is so much more fun."

"Maybe, but she needs it to go downstairs." Sondra pointed at the blinking red light on Gabby's phone. "You have a visitor."

"Me?" She did not get guests. Office policy and the security restrictions made drop-ins tough.

Sondra leaned in and stared at one of the computer screens on the desk. "Uh-oh."

"That sounds interesting." Doug tried to get a good view of the monitor. "Who is it?"

"This visitor definitely wants you, Gabby."

"I don't have an appointment." The working lunch the next day was the only bright spot in Gabby's week. Her one chance to show her bosses she could do more than math.

"It's hard to tell without the wine over his head," Sondra said, being as dramatic as possible. "But your visitor sure looks like your favorite geek."

Gabby knocked her water bottle to the floor and shoved Doug's chair out of the way to get to the screen. "Reed's here?"

"Are you dating another geek we don't know about?" Sondra asked as she tapped on the computer keys and zoomed in on Reed's face.

"I'm not even dating this one." Gabby joined Sondra in the leaning and staring.

Yep, there he was. Reed Larkin. Black suit and teal blue tie, standing right in the reception room of the downstairs office.

"Maybe he's thirsty." Sondra pretended to scan the room. "Do we have a beverage you can throw on him?"

"He never tried to come here while we were dating. Why now?"

Doug stepped up until he hovered right behind the ladies. "Probably dropping off his dry-cleaning bill."

"Well, he can shove that right—" Gabby turned around and ran smack up against Doug's chest. "Uh, could you take a step or two back?"

"Here's your jacket." Doug held it up as if he were tempting a bull.

In a way, he was. Seeing Reed standing there in her workplace all confident and calm worked like a red cape on the anger welling inside Gabby.

"I don't have anything to say to Reed."

"Yeah, but we want to know why he's here." Sondra hit the button again and zoomed back out to watch Reed pace the reception area.

"I'll go down and take care of him for you." Doug topped off his offer with an impressive, ready-to-fight knuckle crunch.

The last thing Gabby wanted was a reception room smack down between Doug and Reed. If anyone had earned the right to do some smacking, she had.

"You stay here." Gabby delivered her command to Doug.

"She's right." Sondra nodded to back up her pronouncement. "It's better if Gabby takes care of this herself. End it once and for all on her terms."

Before Gabby could come up with an appropriate and snotty response, Doug slipped her jacket over her shoulders and shoved her toward the door. "Out you go."

Gabby broke free of Doug's grasp and did some shoulder flexing of her own. "Turn the monitor off first."

"That's never going to happen. Get moving." Doug shoved a little harder.

Gabby had to put up her hands to keep from running straight into the metal door. Doug reached around and opened it, this time guiding her through and to the elevator before she could blink.

Gabby let him because she was curious. That was it. Nothing more than simple curiosity.

She tried to shout one more warning over her shoulder to her teammates. "No eavesdropping."

"Uh-huh." Doug pulled the office door shut behind Gabby and stalked back to Sondra's seat at the computer console. "You haven't moved."

"I'm not going anywhere until I see why Reed's still sniffing around."

"So, we're watching this. Right?"

"Of course," Sondra answered, but her focus was on the monitors. "Saw you slip Gabby's badge back into her pocket. Thanks. One of these days she's going to forget that thing at the wrong time and land in a lot of trouble."

Doug took the open seat next to Sondra. "I didn't want to run downstairs and risk missing part of the *Gabby and the Geek* show."

"Oh, I don't know. Catching the live version might be worth a run."

"Only if Gabby throws food at the guy this time."

"We can hope."

Chapter 5

Reed flipped through the stack of glossy financial magazines sitting next to him on the reception room table. Photos of happy fake families on fake family outings littered the covers. Each article title sounded more boring than the one above it.

Nothing interesting to read but much to see in Gabby's building. Not the sort of activity he expected for an accounting office. A guy with an oversized neck that made him more suited to military maneuvers than answering phones sat behind a large metal bunker doubling as a reception desk. Reed knew the guy's job because there was a little sign identifying the guy's space.

More men in nondescript dark suits milled around the open area on the sixth floor. They all carried thin portfolios. One with an obvious earpiece and habit of twisting the ring on his finger stood guard at the elevator.

Yeah, plenty of muscle available to help Gabby beat the crap out of him.

As if she needed help. The flash of fury he saw in Gabby's eyes followed by the tongue tonsillectomy last night convinced him the woman could hold her own. Could probably pick up a building with one hand and sweep him under it with the other if she wanted to. Right now she probably did.

If only he were a computer guy with a simple desk job and no stress other than normal job pressures. Then he could test Gabby's turbulent waters. Figure out how they translated to the bedroom and see what happened next.

But Reed had dismissed the white-picket, two-point-two-kids type of life long ago. Not possible even if it were his thing, which it most definitely was not.

Along with the dangers and clandestine nature of his job at the top secret Division of Special Projects came the stark reality that women like Gabby belonged in another world. A safe one where lying came in the form of harmless excuses for forgotten birthdays rather than outright deception and nonsense explanations for missing weeks while he worked on a job.

Women fit into Reed's job or his bed. Never into his life. He had sex when the job required or when his body screamed for it. Simple as that. Since there were plenty of women out there to scratch his itch without asking for much other than a return scratch, Reed never found a reason to complain.

Until Gabby.

She lingered. Made him laugh. Made the thought of sex seem like something more than a physical release.

When the reality that the job objective and being with her were not related, he had bailed and saved her awesome ass. Cut the strings before he savored a real taste of Gabby. Now that the information from headquarters led in another direction, Operation Gabby was back on.

Reed stood ready to do the necessary work to get the job done and collect the information he needed on Benson, including turning Gabby into a conquest, if needed. Bedding Gabby would not be a hardship. Sleeping with her appealed to him on a very primitive level. On every level, actually. Fed a male need long buried.

But when the job was finished, he'd walk away and leave Gabby one in a long line of faceless pieces of work roadkill. Charlotte knew it. He knew it. Part of him despised the work because of it. But he had made the choice long ago, so he lived with it.

"Ms. Pearson will be down in a second." The six-foot-two, two-hundred-twenty-pound neckless guy at the receptionist desk delivered the information with all the finesse of a drill sergeant frying in the southern heat. "Wait in the chair."

Reed no longer followed orders unless they came from Charlotte, so he balked at the other man's tone. "Makes more sense for me to go to her office. Point me in the right direction and I'll get out of your way."

No Neck looked Reed up and down, frowning at whatever he saw. "You'll meet her here."

Not exactly the private setting Reed hoped for to woo Gabby back. He walked over for a man-to-man talk with the gruff receptionist.

"Look, the conversation with the lady is private," Reed said.

"Should have had it with her at home, then."

"Cut me a break here."

"Can't."

Reed decided the male code thing was overrated. "You mean won't."

"Yeah." No Neck's smile turned into a snarl. "I mean won't."

Reed looked around for a more accommodating guy, but all of the men stood staring at the floor. Looked as if a sudden case of shyness hit the room.

None of the guards fit with the office's high-end environment. The joint reeked of big money and little personality. Quite a difference from the institutional gray walls of the small office Reed shared with Pete. Theirs had one window with a five-cent view of an alley. Typical government covert shit.

In Gabby's place, artwork consisting of large blobs and

slashes of color any talented kindergartner could have painted hung on the walls. Reed guessed the works really cost a fortune. Just like the real estate in this building.

For the second time he wondered about the odd number-cruncher setup. When he said he was there to see Gabby, a nameless worker bee escorted him into this separate lobby area. Men with buzz cuts manned the place. Not a single call had come in to the reception desk in the fifteen minutes since he walked through the metal detector and into the office.

No visitors. No clients. No real activity other than the goon squad. The show of force struck Reed as overkill for a bunch of accountants, even for accountants who dealt with rich playboy scum like Greg Benson.

Reed made a mental note to recheck the place when he got back to his desk. At this rate, he figured that might be a while. Gabby wasn't exactly rushing down the stairs to greet him. Probably wanted to find a gun first.

"Reed." Gabby's husky voice shot across the lobby, echoing off the marble floors.

Instead of coming from the direction of the elevator bank as he expected, she walked through a side door marked "private." Snuck up on him. That sure as hell summed up their relationship to date.

He expected one thing. She showed him another.

Good news was that he could not see a gun or knife in her possession. If she wanted to kill him, and Reed supposed part of her did, she would have to resort to hand-to-hand combat.

He approached her, moving slow and taking in the blank expression and pale cast to her flawless skin. The angry flush that stained her cheeks the night before had disappeared. The Gabby in front of him looked very in control and downright bored by his presence.

He sighed, more in frustration over his part in this scheme than anything else. "I needed to see you."

"Lucky me."

His arms hung loose at his sides just in case a wall of liquid came flying his way. "You have every right to be mad."

"I know."

"I'm here to—"

"If you're about to say you came to collect my half for dinner last night, you can forget it. Consider the salmon collateral damage."

Her stare might be blank, but anger bubbled right underneath the surface. The more pissed off she got, the faster she talked and the fewer sentences she let him finish.

A dead man recognized these things.

Ignoring the probability of impending doom, he tried again. "My behavior last night was reprehensible."

"No arguments there."

This just got better and better. "I need to apologize."

Her eyebrow lifted all pissy and mad. "This should be interesting."

Another bad sign. "I aim to please."

"If you say so."

No yelling or swearing. Maybe that was progress. Hell, he was dumb enough to hope that was true. "As I was saying, I was way out of line last night."

"I'm not arguing with you."

She folded her arms across her chest. The move trapped her thin camisole tight against her breasts, outlining every curve.

The sexy sight threw him off task. Their relationship never passed through the bedroom door, but he knew what treasures hid under her clothes. Hell, last night she pressed so close to him that he still had the imprint of her body on his. At least that was true in his mind.

He had skimmed his fingers over the smooth tops of her breasts. Savored the swell of her soft skin under his touch. Felt the weight of her in his palms. The way she highlighted her shapely body now made him wonder if this was her version of torture.

Either that or she folded her arms to keep from strangling him. If so, he admired her self-control. If the roles were reversed, he . . . actually, he didn't know what he'd do since he generally took the role of the dumper, not the dumpee.

"There's no excuse for how I acted." There was, but she could not know about that. "I was an—"

"Idiot."

"Well, yes." He tried to imagine how this scenario could go worse. "Gabby, I know you're angry."

"Very astute of you." She dropped her hands to her sides, looking ready to bolt. "Was there anything else?"

"As you can imagine, this is a little awkward for me." Kind of like waiting to get kicked in the balls.

"Not for me."

He glanced around at the one, two, three guys waiting for Gabby's signal to pounce on his ass. No more staring at their feet. No, they were all watching him now.

"Is there somewhere we can go to talk?"

"I'm not hungry."

Did he mention food? "Uh, okay."

"Thanks to you, if I don't go into another restaurant this year, I'll be thrilled. I'll probably never order salmon again."

He massaged the back of his neck and fumbled for something intelligent to say. When that failed, he settled for lame. "I can understand where dining out could be an issue right now."

Her fists tightened until her knuckles turned white. "That's you. Mr. Understanding."

Sarcasm. Great. Next she'd stomp him with those spiky heels she had on. For some reason the image did more to ignite the heat pulsing through him than the memory of her breasts pressed against him.

For the fiftieth time he wondered why he never tried to get her into bed. She gave him the green light, but he held back. Something about chivalry. Decency. Being a good guy.

And what did that get him? A pocketful of liquor, that's what.

Screw morals. He wanted this woman naked. This time he would follow through. Solving the case stood as his number one priority. Enjoying some touching time with Gabby would be his bonus. That was how he would view it. Sure, he would leave, but they would both be satisfied when he did.

Since broaching the idea of sex bordered on suicidal, he fell back on rational conversation. "How about we finish this talk in your office?"

"No."

He was getting sick of hearing that word. "Why?"

Her expression turned from blank to incredulous. "Because I don't want you in there."

The reception dude pretended to fiddle with something on his desk, but every time Gabby spoke the guy let out a chuckle. Neither one of them left a lot of room for Reed to work his magic.

"There are people"—Reed shot his own glare at the *people* in question—"nosy people, listening in."

"You mean Clyde?"

"The guy's name is Clyde?"

"Does he look like an Ann to you?"

"More like a Butch or Meathead."

A calculating smile crossed Gabby's lips. "I dare you to say that to Clyde. Better yet, ask him if he's really the receptionist."

Clyde picked that moment to send a scowl in their direction.

"I'd prefer to keep all of my teeth, but thanks," Reed mumbled.

She shrugged. "Your choice."

"Then, teeth it is." Reed glanced around. "If not your office, is there a place around here where we can talk? Alone."

"No."

"Did you just learn that word?"

She raised her chin. "Reed, do you honestly have anything to say other than what you've already spit out?"

Well, no. He hadn't really gotten this far in his win-back-Gabby plan. Charlotte had given him a day. Pete had not stopped laughing long enough to be of any real assistance. Reed knew he was on his own with this one.

"Of course." He snuck in an are-you-kidding scoff. "If I just wanted to apologize, I could have called."

"I wouldn't have answered."

"Now there's a surprise." He rubbed his hands together. "So, about that private room?"

"Fine." This time Gabby glanced around. The flat line of her mouth suggested she was as lost in the surroundings as he was.

"Problem?"

She looked at him from head to toe. "Yeah, it's about six-two and has this annoying habit of—"

"Actually, I'm just shy of six-two."

She shook her head and mumbled something about "idiots" under her breath. "Wait here."

"Where would I go?"

But she was already off and over talking to No Neck Clyde. They engaged in a whispered argument. One Reed could not hear, which ticked him off.

"This isn't a big deal," Reed said in an effort to break up the private meeting they had going on.

"Quiet," Gabby said in a voice that was anything but.

"We could just—" Reed stopped when they hit him with a joint frown. "Right. You guys go ahead."

Reed strained to pick up bits and pieces of the conversation. No luck. He saw Gabby talking and No Neck shaking his head. That was about it.

Finally No Neck let out a frustrated exhale, one Reed recognized from his own dealings with Gabby. There was something about Gabby. She possessed a strange power to make grown men sigh.

And swear.

And lose their common sense.

After what felt like an hour but amounted to less than a minute, No Neck nodded his head in the direction of the hallway to the right of the elevator bank. He produced a key and handed it to Gabby.

The whole scene was off. For a woman who worked in the office, Gabby was strangely unsure. Her steps faltered, and she looked for directions before heading where No Neck indicated. Reed worked in a fourteen-story government office building, half of which stayed in top secret lockdown most of the day, and he knew where the conference rooms were.

Unlike Gabby, he also managed not to walk around with a security badge sticking halfway out of his pocket. Confidential client information was one thing. Security badges and armed guards were another. Something was going on at this Financial Solutions place that had nothing to do with accounting.

"You coming or not?" Gabby took off without waiting for Reed.

He caught up to her in two steps. He was determined to figure out what was happening in the office while he figured out how to get close enough to Gabby to get her to trust him with a few secrets.

"What was all that chatting with your goon receptionist about?" he asked.

"Clyde wants to kick your butt."

"I picked up on that. The feeling was mutual, by the way."

She unlocked the door without looking at Reed. "What did Clyde do to you?"

"Nothing. Nothing *for* me either."

"I guess you think he owed you something as a fellow male."

"Exactly." Reed cleared his throat, aiming for a tone more seductive than questioning. "Any reason you didn't let Clyde take a shot at me?"

"Because I'm the one who's earned that right to kick your butt."

So much for seduction. "I guess that's fair."

"We'll see if you think so after our private talk."

Chapter 6

Gabby turned the key to the unoccupied room, wondering what she would find inside the office she had never entered, on the floor where she never worked. Without Clyde's directions, she would have accidentally ushered Reed right into the ladies' room or a broom closet.

Not that Clyde accommodated her request for a quiet place to talk to Reed without griping. Nope. Clyde refused to give her the location of an unmonitored room. Muttered about protocol and mandatory restrictions on Reed's movements. Also said something about Reed being a weasel.

Gabby tended to agree with the Reed-as-rodent assessment. While she possessed all the allure of a wet dishrag this morning, Reed waltzed into her place of employment, delivered a lame apology and looked as tasty as he did before he dumped her.

Damn him. Didn't he know the kiss she laid on him was supposed to wreck his world?

She entered the room, walked over to the window and peeked around the drawn shade to watch the parade of cars in the traffic below. If Reed said one wrong word, she vowed to open the window and throw him out of it. Depending on how much he bugged her, she might not even wait to open the thing.

Turning around, she leaned back against one of the conference room chairs at the long glass table. The goal was to look at ease. No reason Reed should know that she held the black leather behind her back in a death grip.

"So, Reed. You got what you wanted."

"How do you figure that?"

"Clyde let you live."

"Yeah, well, it's still early."

"Look, this is as good as it's going to get. We're in a private room. No one is watching." At least she hoped that last part was true.

Having Sondra listen in was bad enough. The idea of putting on a live show made her queasy. Audience participation qualified as too much help, friendship or not.

"Thanks for agreeing to see me." Reed smiled, looking far too grateful and forgiven for Gabby's taste.

"I did it so Clyde would not get stuck cleaning up the marble in the lobby after he killed you."

"There's a nice image."

"You said you had something important to tell me."

His gaze traveled over her face and down across her shoulder. Then down . . . "You're wearing pants."

Not exactly the line she expected. "Is this a new way of apologizing?"

The door locked with a click behind him. Then he started to move. Each step as graceful as it was predatory. Each one bringing him closer and pushing her farther from the goal of keeping two states between them at all times.

Today's teal blue tie highlighted his black suit. Perfect cut and fit. This man knew how to dress. Worse, with his handsome face and those dreamy eyes, so sexy and sure, he knew how to make a woman forget that most of what he said amounted to pure crap.

He had dumped her, but for whatever reason, the angry shield she built up over the last fifteen hours against his memory refused to stay up. Suddenly quality alone time with Reed seemed like a *really* bad idea.

She actually missed the familiar sounds of her office. The paper shuffling, the sound of Doug throwing a rubber ball against the wall, Sondra's humming. All of it.

"Was there anything other than the clothing analysis or are you done?"

"This is one of the few times I've seen you wear pants."

"For an eloquent guy, you seem to be stuck on my pants." When he chuckled, she realized she messed up the delivery of the line. "That is not what I meant."

"Well, you weren't wrong."

He dragged his fingertips across the glass tabletop as he walked. When he stopped, his hand was level with her thigh.

"If you're into women's clothes now, I have a pair of ski boots at home you can borrow. They'd look great on you."

This time, instead of laughing, he stalked her from only inches away. His body closed in until she could smell a hint of his aftershave. Feel the heat radiate off of him.

"Whenever we met for lunch or for dinner after work, you showed up in some above-the-knee number. Slim and sexy, yet professional. A skirt that showed off your unbelievable legs."

She shifted position, taking up shelter behind the chair instead of in front of it. She hoped the leather would prevent the vibration in his deep tone from affecting her.

"Reed—"

"Silk or cotton. Pattern or monotone. See-through or not. I'd notice the skirt and immediately wonder what you wore underneath."

On the days she felt ready to show him, which were most days, the answer was nothing much. All that changed less than twenty-four hours ago. Today she wore boring cotton, the type of panty meant for comfort not playtime.

"I'm guessing you didn't drop in here today to talk about my clothing choices."

The edge of his mouth kicked up in one of those smiles

that telegraphed a green light straight to her lower half. The sort that bypassed her brain and every intelligent cell in her body.

"Your panties are worth a few minutes of discussion, don't you think?"

"No."

"I disagree."

"Are you into women's panties now?" Okay, that question sounded wrong, too. Something about being this close to him wiped out her brain function.

"I was hoping—"

"My point is that we went out for a month. During that time you never once mentioned my choice of skirts over pants."

He pushed the chair to the side and edged closer until he stood near enough for his breath to tickle her cheek. "I never gave you a compliment?"

"Never."

She stepped back and rolled the chair closer again. She wanted it in front of her. She settled for having it wedged on her right side.

Not to be outdone, he eased forward, taking bigger steps compared to her smaller ones. "I'm sure I did."

"I'd remember. Every stupid thing you said last night stayed in my memory." She cleared her throat in an attempt to keep her hormones from staging a coup of her brain cells. "About that—"

"You're always beautiful."

That soft look in his eyes was not going to work. She fell for that one before, more than once, and it never ended well.

"Not first thing in the morning."

A smile played on the edges of his lips. "Now that you mention it . . ."

"You had your chance, stud."

"A chance." His palm edged up to rest on the back of

the chair. The same chair blocking a portion of her body from his.

When his knuckles brushed against her stomach, every muscle inside her jumped. Time to put a stop to this. "Don't."

With his other hand, he trailed the backs of his fingers down the slope of her chin to rest against her exposed neck, then across her collarbone. "So prim and proper on the outside but with a deep river of feminine energy simmering underneath."

"Just muscle and bone. No river."

"Very, very sexy."

She swatted his hand away. "That's more than enough touching."

"We're talking."

"You're seducing."

"Is it working?"

"Not on me." Okay, it worked a little, but she tried to ignore the twinge of interest.

"After you took the lead last night, I thought I should try today. Only seemed fair to share the seducing duties."

She knew the moment on the car would come back to haunt her. Anger and sexual frustration balled up and rolled right over her common sense. "That was a goodbye kiss."

"I don't think so."

"Let's just say I'm not buying whatever it is you're trying to sell."

Well, most of her wasn't buying, but parts of her were willing to be rented out for an hour or two. She tried to shut those disloyal sections down.

"Seduction implies false emotion. I promise you, honey, there's nothing fake going on between us. Not on my part." The words rolled off his tongue so easily a woman could almost believe them.

"I'm not your honey."

"Not true." Those hands of his started moving again.

She stepped back before he could touch her. The dodge jammed the backs of her knees against the credenza under the window.

Trapped. Terrific.

"Did you suck the wine out of your suit jacket this morning?" she asked.

"I tend to prefer my drinks in a glass."

"It's like you are having a liquor flashback or something."

He closed one eye as if he were thinking about the statement. "What exactly is a liquor flashback?"

She had no idea. "Did you think I'd be so desperate that . . . that . . . that I'd fall for this act?"

"Not desperate."

"That I'd strip off my clothes and throw myself across the conference room table while you ravished me?"

There was a beat of silence before he answered. "A man can hope, can't he?"

"As long as he does not try to act on that feeling, yeah."

"So, I guess getting naked is out of the question."

From the strain in his voice, she knew what he wanted the answer to be. Unfortunately, she wanted the same thing. Well, the part of her that did not want to strangle him did.

"You go ahead. I can call Clyde in to watch."

"Maybe I am not making my preferences clear." A small smile formed on his lips as he tucked her hair behind her ear.

A hint of sweetness lingered behind his touch. The way he skimmed the back of his hand over her cheek made her feel cherished and . . .

Dumb as a rock.

When the light turned on in her tiny malfunctioning brain, it blasted full force. "Oh, hell."

"Are you trying to impress me with your use of profanity?" His smile broadened as if he loved the idea. "If so, you'll need to do a bit better than that."

"I wouldn't waste my time."

His hand froze right over her hair. "Am I missing something?"

"A lot."

"Care to clue me in?"

The sting of disappointment hit her with the force of a thousand bees. "You're unbelievable."

He dropped his hand. "That's definitely not a compliment."

"I mean the sick, twisted, macho kind of unbelievable."

"I should sit down for this." He pulled out the chair at his side and plunked his impressive butt right down in it. "You were saying something about me twisting you."

"It's obvious."

All trace of his smile disappeared. "Not really."

"You are one of those."

"Those being?"

"Oh, you know." She waved her hand, dismissing his attempts at being obtuse.

"Not yet."

"You are the kind of guy who wants a woman once it is clear you can't have her."

"Oh."

"Yeah, oh."

"Reasoned that out, did you?"

She sat down perpendicular to him at the head of the table. Only their knees separated them, so she shoved her chair back just far enough to be outside of touching range.

The extra distance was not necessary. He did not come closer. Instead, he stretched back and threaded his lean fingers together across his stomach. He looked far too comfortable for a man who should be on his knees begging and pleading before getting thrown out of the building on his butt.

The lying little weasel.

"I never would have guessed." She tapped her fingernails against the glass top. "Look at you just sitting there."

"You want me to stand?"

She snorted for what she figured was only the third time in her entire life. "Spare me."

"From sitting?"

"From the crap."

"Maybe I'm sitting because this seducing thing is hard work."

"Imagine how hard it would have been if you were any good at it."

A wide grin broke across Reed's lips. "You are determined to make this apology as difficult as possible."

"Do you blame me?" Gabby figured she had earned the right to torture him a little. Okay, a lot.

"Wouldn't admit it if I did." Laughter lightened his voice.

And softened something inside of her.

With her anger dissipated, her curiosity took over. "So, why don't you tell me whatever it is you *really* came to tell me?"

"I did."

"I'm serious."

"I am, too."

The wave of disappointment came rumbling right back. Leaving before engaging in another round of "Can you follow my logic" with Reed was her best course. "Okay, then. I guess we're done."

"Wait." He scrambled out of his lazy position and grabbed her arm before she could stand up. "Hear me out."

"Thought you were done."

"Only with talking."

Chapter 7

Gabby thought about tugging out of Reed's grasp and storming from the room, but, really, the whole storming thing was not her style. Once in twenty-four hours was more than enough.

"Get to the point fast, Reed."

"I'm trying, but your constant interruptions make it tough." The second she settled back into the chair, he leaned in with his elbows balanced on his knees and looked her straight in the eye. "I screwed up."

No shit. "You already said that."

"Let me finish."

She waved a hand at him. "Go ahead."

"See, before last night I figured our relationship wasn't going anywhere. There didn't seem to be much in the way of fire on your part."

How did he miss the fact she almost threw herself at him during the car ride to the restaurant before his big dump scene?

He lowered his head and stared at his hands. "As I sat there at the table, the words came out of my mouth just as I practiced them. But, once they were out, everything felt wrong."

"You should have been on my side of the table."

"I knew I was blowing it but couldn't stop and go backwards. Then you left—"

"Stormed. I stormed."

"Yes, you did."

"The busboy I ran into didn't think so."

"It was something to see."

"I could tell by the way you didn't bother to follow me." That was another sore point. Since they were discussing his sins and miscues, she decided to put them all out there.

"Didn't have to since you met me at my car. When you kissed me, I went wild. Wild as in had to have you, wanted to rip off your clothes and climb inside you in the back of the car. That sort of wild."

Well, then. "You're saying if I kissed you like that earlier, you never would have given me the big blow off?"

"I wanted you before the scene on the street."

"Instead you sat at the table and watched me go."

"To be fair, the wine weighed me down at that point."

"You're lucky I didn't pour the rest of the bottle, too."

His jaw tightened. "I'm a computer nerd as you said. Grand gestures aren't my thing. Emotions and apologies aren't exactly the norm for me either."

She used to think that was true. Now she wondered.

Gabby cut off that line of thinking the second it snuck into her brain. Only a stupid woman would fall for this explanation. She was not a stupid woman.

"Is that all?" she asked as she tried to rebuild that wall against him.

"No." His hands slid under her blazer sleeves and a short way up her bare arms, awakening every nerve ending and killing off those smart girl brain cells along the way. "Give me another chance."

To prevent disaster, she kept her answer short. "No."

"Just one more."

"No."

His fingertips slipped back down her arms to her wrists before traveling down to rest on her hips on the outside of her blazer. "It's all I'm asking for, Gabby."

"Still no."

Then he tugged, bringing her to the edge of her seat, forcing her knees into the vee between his strong thighs. "Let me prove I'm not a jerk. That I'm not that guy in the restaurant."

"You were a pretty convincing jerk."

"I can be a nonjerk, too."

That was what she was afraid of. That and her weakening resolve.

His palms coaxed her in even closer. His fingers soothed and caressed. Even through layers of fabric she could feel the heat of his hands blazing a trail over her skin and against the small of her back.

Smart women made smart choices. She repeated that refrain over and over until it echoed in her head. Reed was a dumb choice. A hot and sexy dumb choice, but a *really* dumb choice.

"Gabby?"

"I appreciate you coming here, but this isn't going to work." She shook her head, trying to break whatever spell his deep voice cast over her.

"Not if you don't relax." He whispered the words against her lips.

"It's hard when you are practically sitting on top of me."

"Because you are fighting me."

She sure was trying to. Problem was that she wanted to listen to him. To follow his lead. Really, what harm could come from one kiss? A goodbye kiss. A thanks-for-apologizing-now-get-out kiss.

A hide-your-sister-and-run-for-cover kiss.

That was what she got. When his warm lips fused against hers, all pretense of common sense and womanly smarts packed up for vacation.

This guy could kiss. Long and deep, insistent yet questioning. His hands left her sides and slid up her body. Thumbs brushed against her cheeks in soft and gentle strokes.

His mouth pressed against hers, hot and wanting. A touch of his tongue against her lips, at first light and then more frantic. Scalding heat pouring off his body and seeping through the legs of her pants. A nudge of his growing arousal against her knee.

Goodbye. Hello. Whatever this kiss was, it worked for her. But, just as she sank into his touch, let her body loosen up and her muscles grow lax, he broke it off.

He rested his forehead against hers. A good thing, too, since her neck had turned mushy from all the lip action. Without him for support, her head could have fallen right off and rolled across the tabletop.

With his palms resting against her cheeks and his head against hers, with this shocking sense of intimacy, she could almost trust him. Almost.

Then a vision of their audience jumped into her head. The thought of Sondra and Doug watching this, of the two of them wondering just how desperate a woman could get to fall for Reed's lines, snapped her back to reality.

When her brain cells began firing straight again, she tried to pull back. "Reed, this isn't—"

"The time or place." He sighed, dropping a light kiss on her nose. "Yeah, I know."

"You do?"

"I'm going to go."

"You're leaving?" How was she supposed to kick him out and restore her dignity if he left first?

He shot her one of those sexy lopsided smiles of his. "I wanted to see if you still felt something for me."

Her back stiffened. "I don't."

"I worried I had blown it so badly that there wasn't any hope."

"You did and there isn't." She liked the way her voice sounded stronger that time around.

"Your mouth says no now, but two minutes ago—"

"Leave my mouth out of this." The right words refused to fall into position. Her internal dictionary appeared to be on the fritz.

He stood up. "I would prefer not to."

"Look, this is not going to happen."

One of his eyebrows lifted. The look should have been sinister. On him it worked. "I think it already did."

"Wrong. That"—she waved her hand between their bodies—"that was a goodbye kiss."

"I thought last night was the goodbye kiss."

Right. "This was the encore but definitely a goodbye."

"Felt more like a *hell-o* to me."

"Again, I appreciate your coming here, but this—"

He bent down and planted a firm kiss on her open mouth, cutting off all of her solid common-sense arguments and forcing her eyes shut in response. No foreplay. No buildup.

When her eyes opened again, he was headed for the door. "Hey!"

"I'll see you tonight," he said.

It took two seconds before she gained enough leg strength to charge after him, but she made it to the door first. With her back against the exit, she faced him down.

"You need to listen to me, Reed."

"You need to stop talking."

Well, well, well. "I guess you are done apologizing now."

"You are the one who made all those snide comments about me being a boring old computer guy. Seems to me what you need is a spark. A man who takes the lead and does not bore you." He trailed his forefinger over her lips. "I plan to be that man."

She somehow created a macho monster. "You've got this all wrong."

He reached around her and pulled the door open, making her the most inefficient doorstop on the planet. "I'll see you tonight."

And a presumptuous macho monster at that. "Where, exactly?"

She walked down the hall after him as fast as her heels would carry her. She refused to run. Smart women did not run after jerky guys. Of course, smart women did not make out with their exes while their friends watched via closed circuit television either, but that was another story.

"Ompf." She turned the corner and ran right into Clyde.

"Something wrong, Ms. Pearson?"

"Everything."

Clyde leaned down, his face all scrunched up in a serious frown. "Mind if I say something?"

"Of course not." Everyone else seemed to, so Clyde might as well take his turn.

"There's something wrong with that guy."

She saw the guy in question exit the building with a confident swagger. "Tell me about it."

"You should watch him."

That was the problem. She could not stop watching Reed.

Chapter 8

"You see that?" Doug knocked over his chair as he jumped to his feet.

"I do have eyes." Sondra managed to stay in her seat and rewind the tape of conference room confrontation they had just witnessed.

Her job depended on her staying calm. Having her best friend trapped in a room with a guy working a hidden agenda did not make that task easy.

"Un-damn-believable." Doug whipped his pen against the metal desk. It bounced off one of the monitors with a ping and flew to the right.

"Are you upset about the kissing or—"

"That lying nerd used the kiss as cover as he pocketed Gabby's damn ID badge." Doug skipped throwing things this time and cut straight to yelling.

"Yeah, wondered if you noticed that part."

"It's my job to pick up on these things. It's hers, too." Doug tapped his finger against Gabby's image on the computer monitor. "She's sure as hell off her game."

"It would be fair to say she's focused on other issues at the moment."

"Like having some nerd's tongue down her throat."

A wave of guilt hit Sondra. She took the blame for this

mess. She had encouraged Gabby to take a chance on Reed. To open up to some fun with a man just for the sake of having fun, regardless if the enjoyment ever reached the serious stage.

On paper, Reed looked like a good candidate. Nothing in his past suggested a problem. Now there was no doubt the guy harbored secrets. The sort that could cost Gabby her job.

So much for investigative skills, Sondra thought. "I'm not sure Gabby realizes what happened during the lip lock."

Reed had impressive moves. Just what Gabby needed in the bedroom. The aggravation of an internal investigation and the fallout of a stolen ID badge were not.

"And that's another thing." Doug stomped from one side of the room to the other in a form of agitated pacing. "What's wrong with women?"

"Is that a general question or do you have a specific concern you want me to address?"

"She was crawling all over him."

And enjoying every single minute of it. "Not really."

"Sure looked like it."

Sondra ignored the comment in favor of a long sip of her tea. She tried to gather her thoughts before she jumped in her car and ran Reed Larkin down.

"He is scamming her." Doug emphasized each syllable. Even added an extra few.

"Yeah, Doug, I get it. I was in the same room and saw the same thing you did."

"I don't know why you said I couldn't go downstairs and shoot him."

"A subtle approach, yes, but not practical."

Sondra resumed typing, bringing up screen after screen of information. One monitor played the conference room tape. Photos of Reed and lines and lines of numbers and personal information about him filled two other screens.

"What are you doing now?" Doug ignored the chain of command and demanded rather than asked.

Sondra understood. Doug possessed some odd sense of protectiveness toward the women on his team. Forget the fact one female outranked him and the other needed much less help than either of them could accept.

Gabby might come from a privileged background, but she was tough. All she needed was the time to show her steel.

"I'm gathering all of the info we have on Reed Larkin."

Doug stopped pacing long enough to step in front of one of the screens and block Sondra's view. "Screw that. We know all we need to know."

"That you have lost your mind?"

Doug did not budge. "The guy's got a game going on, and he's playing it with Gabby."

Sondra tried pushing Doug to the side. When he refused to move, she shot him an exasperated sigh. "Do you mind?"

"Yes."

"Look, I need to gather all of this before Gabby gets back upstairs." When Doug scowled, she explained. "I can't exactly investigate her boyfriend behind her back while she sits here and watches."

"There is nothing else to check. He grabbed her badge. Call security."

"While I'm at it, I'll tell them to shoot to kill."

Doug jumped on the idea. "That's more like it."

Time to act like a manager rather than a friend. "Maybe we should start with something other than a planned homicide."

"Fine. We'll grab the guy and throw him in a room." Doug fidgeted and grumbled as if he were making a huge concession.

"Ah, I see. We're going with the beat-first-ask-questions-later routine."

"He is not getting away. Not after he fed Gabby that line of garbage about getting back together and being sorry."

Nothing Sondra had not heard before. Nothing new to any woman. "Sounded like typical guy bullshit to me."

She finished off her tea, feeling not one ounce better about the situation with the warmth in her belly. The leader in her doubted Reed's sincerity. The friend in her wanted to believe.

"And the stuff about her legs . . ." Doug snorted. "Gabby's going to go apeshit when we tell her about the badge."

"We are not telling her yet."

"Are you nuts?"

Sondra swiveled her chair in front of the equipment to keep Doug from punching a hole through the computer monitors. "Gabby has her first shot at doing some field-work after more than a year of begging for a chance."

"So what?"

"She's got a meeting set up with Greg Benson. It's her one, probably only, opportunity to prove she can do more than be a desk jockey."

"I've seen the office memos. I know the drill."

"My point is that during all of this, Reed showed up."

Doug leaned against the edge of the table. "And?"

"His timing is suspect, don't you think? Reed wants something from Gabby. Something that might relate to Benson."

"He wants more than one thing if you ask me."

"I think that's true."

"So I should put my fist in his nerd face."

Sondra smiled. "Eventually. Until then, we rerun everything we have on Reed, dig deeper and do it fast. Now, go get Gabby before she reaches into her pocket and figures out her badge is gone."

*   *   *

"A badge." Pete wiped ketchup off his hands and picked up Gabby's security pass. "Why is your woman carrying government identification?"

His woman. After that kiss, Reed certainly thought of Gabby as his woman. Or he did until a few minutes ago when he started questioning her real identity.

Gabby. Sandy. Lucy. Susie. He did not even know if Gabby was her real name at this point. From the visual and touching tour of her body, Reed knew Gabby was a she. Nothing else was certain.

"With all your snooping into her life, why didn't you know about this before now?" Pete turned the badge over in his hands, then dropped it on the computer desk between their two chairs.

"Good question."

"Care to answer it?" Pete rolled his hamburger wrapper in a ball, leaned around Reed and took a shot at the garbage can on the other side of the room. The wad bounced against the rim.

"Nice shot." Without thinking, Reed grabbed the miss and whipped it into the can.

"All I need is practice."

"Uh-huh."

"Let's get back to you. You've been all over Gabby's condo. How did you miss a big badge with her photo on it?"

"You're the computer genius. You've been checking her record. Why didn't *your* background check come up with a badge?"

Pete stopped chewing on the burger. "Now is not the time for blame."

"Yeah, that's what I thought."

Pete popped the last bits of his hamburger into his mouth, but the smell of fried onions lingered. "Guess we both fell asleep on this one."

"Or someone hid the information." Reed leaned on the back two legs of his small chair. "Wish I knew who and why."

"Let's see what we can find. Now that we know about the badge, we have a new place to look."

Pete fed Gabby's badge into the card reader in front of him. He entered a few passwords, bypassed a couple of screens and questions that people without his technical abilities would never be able to work around. A few flashes later, Gabby's clearance information appeared on the screen.

"Well?" Reed asked, even though he dreaded the answer.

"Whatever she's doing, she has an active clearance to do it. It's a Secret level, so she deals in confidential information but probably not stuff relating to weapon systems and the like."

"That's a relief." Reed loaded the comment with sarcasm.

"If you say so."

The front legs of Reed's chair dropped to the floor with a thud. "Where does it say who she works for?"

"It doesn't. I can get some basic information we already know, like her name and work address. The only new info is her clearance level, which is the type of thing a security officer would be privy to."

Reed glanced over at his partner. "Unless you changed jobs before I got in this morning, you are not a security officer."

"The computer does not know that."

"Enough said." The last time Reed tried to hold a partner's secrets, the partnership ended. He was not looking to go there again.

"Even with the use of my advance hacking skills, we don't know the agency that holds her clearance. She could work for the Department of Defense or Energy. Maybe even be an offshoot of Homeland Security like us. The info is not on here."

Reed rubbed his eyes. "And you call yourself a hacker."

"Actually, the police called me that, but I beat the rap. And, without me you would still be staring at the badge, trying to figure out how to shake the information out of the plastic."

"Would it kill the employer to print its name on the card?" Reed slid back in his chair and folded his arms behind his head.

"Do you forget the background investigation and multi-day polygraph we had to undergo to work here? It's tough to keep stuff confidential if you advertise it. Same goes for Gabby."

"No, but from that police comment I am wondering how you managed to pass."

Pete wiggled his eyebrows. "Really, though, there's a reason our office's very existence is classified even from fellow Homeland Security employees. No one is supposed to know about DSP."

"Hell, some days I wish I didn't."

"You are not alone."

Reed stared at the ceiling and mentally flipped through all of the information he had gathered on Gabby and her life. Nothing fit in with the idea of her handling secret government information.

"She's not one." Reed did not realize he voiced the thought until Pete answered it.

"Of us?" Pete continued to scan the system for information, but nothing new came up. "Her clearance level is lower than ours, but she is doing something other than accounting in that office, which is odd for a woman who claims to be an accountant."

"No arguments here."

"Maybe her firm does specialized government work. She could be a private contractor. Or . . ."

Reed's senses flashed to high alert as his attention moved from the ceiling to Pete. "What?"

"Maybe her meeting with Benson isn't so innocent."

Reed had already mentally investigated the idea and dismissed it. The only possibility less feasible than Gabby being a covert agent was Gabby being on the wrong side of the law.

He let his head drop back. "This operation is so fucked up."

"Yeah, hard to see how it could be worse." Pete clicked on the keys, trying a few more times to get past the security encryptions hiding Gabby's actual employer. "If it's any consolation, from what I can tell she does not deal with national security issues."

Reed sat up straight in his uncomfortable metal chair. "Of course not."

Hell, he could not be that far off his game. If Gabby worked undercover, he'd sense that . . . wouldn't he?

"As Charlotte pointed out, you might not be in a real position to know what Gabby really is up to." Pete cleared his throat. "You're not sleeping with her."

Reed had been doubled up with Pete for only about five months. It took Reed almost all of that time to start to trust his new partner. In light of how he lost his last partner, Reed figured it would be years before he established the trust he needed.

"We have a problem here, Pete?"

"Nah." Pete stretched and let out a loud yawn. "I'm just wondering what it is about this woman that has you spinning. She's not the first woman you slept with on work time. She won't be the last."

True or not, Pete's comment hit Reed right in the gut. Everything Pete said about Gabby made sense. Didn't mean Reed had to like it. Or wanted to hear it.

His mind flashed back to the kiss he shared with Gabby in her office. She started tentative and untrusting, but then, man, the way her body melted into his. Controlled on the outside. On fire underneath just like the kiss she initiated at the restaurant.

If her whole office setup had not struck him as being off. If the marine dropouts were not manning every office door. If Gabby had known anything about the floor and room they went to. If he had not seen her badge and grabbed it when he kissed her.

If, if, if.

Without all that suspicion, he would be in a different position right now. Not trapped in a room with Pete.

"Can you break the code on that thing?" Reed nodded in the general direction of the badge and computer monitor.

Pete shot him a wild grin. "I guess we're done talking about you sleeping with Gabby."

"Yeah."

"Shame."

If Pete mentioned Gabby's legs, his head was going through the screen. "She's a job."

"Sure."

The muscles across Reed's shoulders tensed again. "If you've got something to say, then say it."

Pete shrugged. "I am sitting here minding my own business."

"Gabby is part of an operation. That's all."

Pete's fingers hesitated over the keys for a second. "I hear you."

"Doesn't sound like you believe me." Which made sense since Reed barely believed it. "Actually, forget it. Get back to work."

"That means you need to get back to seducing."

Yeah. Reed just wished he knew a little more about the *real* woman he was supposed to make the moves on.

Chapter 9

Gabby's doorbell rang the second after she stepped into her condo and flicked on the living room lights. A woman should be able to come home, take off her jacket and throw her briefcase on the floor before every phone pest and doorbell-ringing solicitor on the block crawled out from wherever to bother her.

"Uuuuggggh! Where is the doorman?" She grumbled her question as she pivoted on her high heel and retraced her steps to the entrance.

With one palm resting against door, she peeked at the visitor through the peephole. Her briefcase slipped out of her fingers and smacked against the hardwood floor before she could tighten her hold.

Papers swooshed. Her wallet opened. Change spilled out. Pens bounced.

Only Reed could cause this much trouble without saying a word.

"Gabby?"

And only Reed could start a tiny buzz pulsing through her body with one word muttered through a wooden door.

"Are you hiding or not home?" His voice sounded even deeper this time.

"Go away."

"So, you're in there."

"I am not." She could hear him chuckle, but her fingers refused to curl around the knob and pull.

"For some reason I don't believe you." He followed his comment with a soft knock. "Hello?"

He promised she would see him later, and here he was, on her doorstep, demanding her attention. Where was this my-word-is-my-bond thing when she wanted to take their relationship to the next level? Now that they were through, he excelled in the stamina department.

She shoved her briefcase out of the way with her foot, sending her favorite lipstick rolling into the coat closet next to the door. Without thinking, she smoothed her palms over the wrinkles in her shirt. She tucked her hair behind her ears and plastered a plastic but thoroughly un-welcoming smile on her face before opening the door.

There Reed stood, filling up every inch of available space, looking as self-assured as he had this morning. One elbow rested on the trim around the door. He had the other hand tucked into his pants pocket.

The only signs of his full workday were his loosened tie and the slight crease on the bottom of his suit coat. She, on the other hand, possessed her usual end-of-the-day weariness, complete with dark under-eye circles and sore feet.

She hated men.

And she had plenty of reason to dislike *this* man.

"Hello, Reed."

"I thought you weren't home." He moved his shoe into the path of the door. Probably thinking he could stop her from trying to slam it shut.

"I'm not."

"Are you confused about what 'out' means?"

"Let's pretend I'm not home." She tried to ease the door shut, thinking she could gain the advantage if she surprised him.

He moved faster. One minute he lunged. The next his hand shot out of his pocket and grabbed the edge of the door.

Shame he was not as quick at *other* things.

"Nice try, but you're too late," he said.

"That's what you think."

"So, may I come in?" He sounded all cheerful and friendly.

"No."

"Maybe if I start over." He cleared his throat. "Hi."

He delivered the greeting with one of those cute lopsided smiles. The kind that reeled her in that first day in the coffee shop.

"What do you want?"

"That is not much of a welcome." He had the nerve to look hurt by her rejection.

"It is all you're going to get."

"Bad day at the office, dear?"

"No."

"Then I'll assume your lack of charm is due to me."

"That and the fact we're seeing more of each other now than when we dated."

"We are still dating."

This time she skipped the attempt to shut him out with the door and used her body to block his entrance instead. Not that she could have stopped him if she wanted to.

Not that she really wanted to either. Not when she wondered what his next big plan would be.

"If I throw another glass of wine on you, will you go away?"

"No, but I'll be wet and dripping in your hallway. You would not want that. Probably a violation of the condo rules."

He had her there. The board prohibited everything from barbeque grills on the balconies to welcoming mats in front of the doors. Leaving a soaking-wet, six-foot-something computer nerd abandoned in a public space had to be an infraction of some sort.

"Come on. Let me in. We need to talk." He glanced over her head and into the comfortable living room behind her.

The room she loved, having picked every stick of furniture and painted every wall. This was the first place she could call her own. No help from family. The condo and everything in it belonged to her. Well, to her and the bank.

"You have ten minutes." She stepped back to clear a path.

As soon as she moved, he walked right in, dropped his briefcase on the sofa table and slumped down on the leather ottoman in front of her favorite chair.

"Gee, Reed, make yourself comfortable."

"Believe it or not, 'comfortable' is not the word I'd use to describe how I'm feeling right now."

"Whose fault is that?"

"Uh, yours?"

His! It was his!

She slammed the door and did some dumping of her own. Off came her spiky torture heels. Down to the floor went his briefcase to make room for hers on the table. She kept her jacket on, but only because her shirt was a bit too thin and see-through for this confrontation.

Rather than sit, she leaned her thigh against the arm of the couch. The position gave her a side view of Reed. Partial was better than full in this case. She had a fighting chance at ignoring her attraction to him if she saw only half of his face.

"Just so we understand each other, you are not staying long." She figured she needed to emphasize the point.

"Can't stay forever, sure."

"Good—"

"I have to go to work tomorrow."

Wrong answer. "No."

His eyebrows raised in a look of innocence worthy of an Oscar. "Actually, I do. Unless you plan to write a note for my boss, but I doubt that would help."

"You will not need a permission slip from me."

"Spoken like someone who has never met my boss. She's a mean woman. And she hates me."

"Sounds like a smart lady to me."

He shot her what she assumed was his best misunderstood face, mouth turned down, eyes all sad. Looked a lot like his scamming face.

"Now that I think about it, you would probably get along with her just fine. You both misunderstand me."

"You work for a woman?" The idea made Gabby chuckle.

"Some women like me, you know."

She snorted. "They've obviously never dated you."

"I am wounded." He pressed a hand against his heart in exaggerated pain.

"Face it. Your man-woman skills need work."

"I did not hear you complaining this morning. In fact, I thought we could—"

"No."

He steepled his fingers and tapped the tips together.

"Again with the 'no' thing."

"It's a legitimate word."

"You use it a lot."

"Then you should be used to it."

"I can stick around, maybe teach you a few other words. Expand your vocabulary in more positive directions."

"You will not be staying long enough for that sort of thing."

"I'm free all evening."

She wondered why she had bothered opening the door.

"Reed, you are not spending the night. You are not even spending the hour."

"You need to be more open-minded on this issue."

"No."

"No one is going to want to play with you if all you do is say no." He shot her a broad grin. "Except me, of course."

She laughed before she could stop it.

"Did I make a joke?" Amusement lit his face.

"I should be sainted for how nice I'm being to you right now."

This time he was the one who laughed. "That's laying it on a bit thick, don't you think?"

"If the description fits."

"Sounds about as inappropriate as calling you a nun . . ." His smile fell. "Wait. That *would* be wrong, right? The vows. Celibacy. Comfortable shoes. Not really your style."

"All I'm saying is that most women would have stabbed you in the restaurant."

His mock surprise returned. "Violence?"

"I refrained."

"Never would have guessed you possessed such a mean streak."

"You almost saw it firsthand. I probably would not have needed a knife or fork either. Could have used the salt shaker. Possibly a napkin." All of those scenarios flipped through her mind during the last few hours.

"Technically, a napkin would have been strangulation not stabbing."

"Both work. Believe me."

"I do." He swung his legs around until he sat facing her. "And, about what I said before. The thing with most women liking me. Just so you know. You're the only woman I care about."

Why did schmaltzy stuff like that sound sincere coming

out of his sexy mouth? The looks. The big doe eyes. Something about him made inane flattery and flirting work.

"Can it with the lines, Reed." Before she started believing them.

"I thought women liked romantic talk."

She folded her hands across her waist and absently toyed with the buttons on her blazer. "Women like not getting dumped in public."

He groaned and let his head fall between his shoulders. "Are we back to that?"

"We never left it."

"But we should be able to get past it." He peeked up at her with one of those stunning blue eyes. "Shouldn't we?"

"The 'it' you're referring to happened less than twenty-four hours ago."

"So, this is a timing issue? You would rather I held out for a week before coming to my senses and returning to apologize for my behavior in the restaurant?"

The argument sounded stupid when he said it that way. As if she was making him wait out a period of shame before she could forgive him. Which she wasn't . . . was she?

"We can try being friends." She said it but did not mean it.

"After all this trouble I went to for you?" He threw his arms wide in a gesture as dramatic as his tone.

She glanced around her condo, looking for some sign of whatever it was he was talking about. "Did I miss something?"

"Did you . . ." He broke off and shook his head. "Women."

"Yeah, we're great. Apparently blind, too, since I do not see whatever it is you are trying to show me."

He slapped the back of one hand against the palm of his other as he ticked off a list. "My hard work. The sweat. The tears."

"The hallucinations," she said, adding the most obvious of his issues.

"Oh, it is all real."

"Then it all happened before I got home." She looked him up and down. While she enjoyed the visual tour, she did not see a cupcake or daisy anywhere. "And disappeared."

He resumed his list but avoided the clapping sound for this part. "The flowers. Dinner."

"Okay, let's try this." She held up her hand. "How many fingers am I holding up?"

His eyes narrowed. "Two. Why?"

"I'm trying to figure out if you're blind or delusional."

"Probably a bit of both." He walked over and squatted in front of his briefcase. The locks clicked open. When he stood back up, he held a small bouquet of sweet pea blossoms in his fist.

Not roses in a stuffy florist arrangement. Not something he ordered or let a professional pick out. Just a riot of distinct wildflowers.

This guy was good.

The delicate purple petals wilted in his large hand. "They are unique and beautiful. They reminded me of you."

Really good.

"Pretty," she said as she focused on the flowers.

"That's an understatement," he answered as he focused on her.

She cleared her throat. "You mentioned something about food."

"Uh, right. Hold these." He put the flowers in her palm and closed her fingers around the short stems.

The sweet smell hit her without moving her arm any closer to her nose. She inhaled, letting the powerful fragrance fill the air around her. "These really are lovely."

"Happy you like them." He rubbed his hands together. "So, you ready?"

"Definitely not."

Nothing prepared her for this side of Reed. For the flirty, ready-for-bed side she had been hoping hid under all of that computer speak.

"Come on. Walk on the wild side."

"There's no way I am saying yes to an open-ended statement like that."

"Understandable, but you'll be sorry."

"Right now I'm just confused."

"I give you"—in a grand gesture, he swept his arm and aimed his hand at the door—"pizza."

She looked at him. In the direction of the door. At him again. Nothing happened.

"Uh, Reed?"

He continued to hold out that arm and stare at the door. "Yeah?"

"Should someone with pizza be knocking about now?"

He dropped his arm to his side. "No, but wouldn't that have been great?"

Her stomach picked that moment to grumble. All of the talk about greasy fast food made her hungry. "I would settle for any delivery guy at this moment."

"Me, too."

"So, fill me in here. You did or did not order pizza?"

"I did."

"Do you see it right now?" She used her best talk-me-off-the-ledge tone.

"Smartass."

"I'm not the one who promised food and isn't delivering."

"The pizza guy's tardiness is not my fault." Reed stood in front of her and blocked her view of the door. "It's really hard to find good help these days."

One second she saw a white wall. The next she saw only miles and miles of Reed Larkin. Pizza no longer sounded like the most appetizing meal option on the evening agenda.

"How dare he mess up your moment?" She made the joke more to break the tension than to be funny. Which was good since she missed the funny mark by a mile.

"No tip for him." Reed put his hands on her hips. "But you . . ."

"You are not going to offer me money, are you?"

"If I thought it would work and not get me stabbed, maybe. Right now, though, my inclination is no." He pulled her closer until leg touched leg and only a few yards of fabric separated their naked flesh.

"Good call."

"I may be slow but I get there eventually."

That was exactly what she feared. "You could go downstairs and look for the delivery guy."

"I would rather be right here. With you." He inched even closer.

"Oh." With her fingers wrapped around the bouquet, she could not push him away. Not that she wanted to at this point.

"Instead of cash, how about a kiss?"

"You are not forgiven, you know." She whispered the statement as his head dipped toward hers.

"Uh-huh." His lips tickled that sensitive space behind her ear.

"Flowers. Cheese melted on bread. Those won't absolve you."

"Cheese. Absolve. Got it." He trailed a line of kisses across her jawline and ended with his mouth hovering directly over hers.

She squeezed the stems of her flowers so hard she thought she heard them snap. "I said *no* absolution."

"Right." He brushed his lips over hers. Once, twice. "None."

Before he could land the kiss and otherwise blow her resolve all to hell, she stepped back, flowers clenched and bare toes curled into little balls. His palms still rested on her hips, but at least some air stood between them now.

"Water." That was all she managed to get out. One illogical word.

Something about Reed made her stupid. Babbling and stupid.

"You on fire?" He sounded downright gleeful at the idea.

She rolled her eyes. "Your ego is outrageous."

"Wait until you see how bad it is after I eat."

Food. Right. She evaded one kiss, but he would try again. She hoped for onion pizza just to be safe.

"We still don't have any of that promised pizza."

"Be patient." He dropped his hands and gave her a small tap on the butt.

"Hey!"

He nodded at the drooping blossoms in her fist. "You go put those in a vase. I'll call the pizza place and see what's taking so long."

"That sounds like an order. I don't take orders."

"You are the one to blame for my behavior."

She knew he would say something to make her mad eventually. And here it was. "How do you figure that?"

"With or without food, I want you. Now that I know the feeling is mutual, we're moving ahead. No more slow. It is fast forward from here," he said, the joking tone gone from his voice.

It took a month, a breakup and a wine bath, but Reed was not hiding his interest for her now. Which meant she needed to set the ground rules. Ones that set up the bedroom and any other flat surface as no-touch zones. Forget flat. Any surface, rough, smooth—whatever—was off limits.

"We have not made up."

"So you keep saying." He whipped out his cell and started dialing.

"This is a truce for one meal only."

"I hear you."

"We eat and then you leave." She grabbed the perfect small crystal vase out from under her sink.

"You are a tough woman to please."

She arranged the light and dark purple petals to her satisfaction. "Smart. I'm a smart woman."

He winked at her. "Never thought otherwise."

Chapter 10

"This pizza is amazing." Gabby made the pronouncement right before she moaned. Again.

The woman was slowly killing him. The sounds. The way her tongue swept across her wet lips. How she licked her fingertips.

She eyed another piece of pizza but took a sip of red wine instead. Then another.

"How many have you had?" She asked him but stared at the food.

"Drinks?"

"Slices."

"Are we in a competition?"

She finally looked up. "We're sharing."

"There are sixteen pieces. You are safe eating about five more. Go ahead."

"Hmmm." She thrummed her fingers against the side of her wineglass a few times. "I shouldn't."

"Why?"

She frowned at the pizza as if it were the enemy. "I've had a lot."

"Since when did you start worrying about gaining weight?"

The tapping stopped as she pinned him with one of those men-are-so-stupid stares.

Crap. "What? What did I say?"

"It was the way you said it."

"Out loud?"

"Like a man."

"I am one, you know. I have the parts to prove it."

"Good for you."

"Wanna see them?"

"You sound like you're twelve." She took a long sip of wine. One he sensed was meant to hide a smile.

"So, is that a yes?" he asked.

"No."

"That's your twentieth 'no' tonight." The good news for him was that each one sounded less convincing than the one before.

Her resistance cracked with the flowers. So long as he did not rush his delivery and nothing unexpected occurred, he was good to go. Being in the right position, the right place, to collect information on Benson was the plan.

She tilted her head to the side as if to size him up. "I bet you never worry about how wide your hips are or if you have a double chin or stuff like that."

"Only when I'm sitting in curlers getting my toenails painted," he said in his driest tone.

"You have a favorite color?"

"Puce."

She glanced at her light pink nails. "Is that close to purple?"

"I have no idea. Pulled the word out of my ass." He threw his napkin on the table and stretched his arms over his head, inhaling the smell of warm crust and cheese.

With his fingers locked behind his head, he watched her rip the crust off an innocent slice of pizza she had been eyeing. Forget stabbing. This woman could tear him apart with her bare hands if she wanted.

He hoped to hell it never came to that.

Stomach full and at ease in Gabby's home, he sat back in her kitchen chair and assessed what he had accomplished in the last few hours: He got in the door. Still had all of his body parts. Even managed to complete his most important task—Gabby's badge now rested safely back in her jacket pocket.

Pete checked and found out she had not reported it stolen during the day. A violation of security protocol, yes, but one that benefited Reed. He slipped it back in her pocket when he went in for a kiss before dinner.

Amazing how a guy could feel so satisfied and like such a shit at the same time.

The growing erection behind his zipper came from pure need. Nothing fake there. He did not need to pretend as he had before with other women. In the past, if needed, he would work up interest he did not feel for a woman on a job. Nothing stopped him if he was in information-gathering mode.

Sure, a twinge of guilt came with the territory unless the woman under him knew the score. With Gabby he felt more than a twinge. More like an avalanche.

"You never told me who was on the phone." For some reason the lapse bugged the hell out of him. She was talking to someone when he came back in with the food. She hung up the minute he walked in.

Newsflash for Gabby: she could date later. Once he was gone.

"I didn't think you noticed." She popped a piece of dough in her mouth.

"On a good day I can pay for a pizza and hear a phone ring at the same time."

"On a bad day?"

"I drop most of the pizza on my shirt."

"Smooth." She toasted him with her glass.

"One of my many talents."

"Know a lot of women who like sloppy men, do you?"

"Be happy to show you a few of my other charms."

"I'll pass."

She possessed the self-confidence of a woman fully in control of her surroundings. From her relaxed stance to her easy banter to the sparkle in her eyes, she believed she had gained the advantage.

Which was exactly what he wanted her to think.

"All you have to do is ask. Come on, Gabby. Ask just once."

"Wait, what is that word you hate? Oh, that's right." She leaned toward him, flashing a smug smile. "No."

He met her halfway across the table. Watched her eyes widen at his approach. "Can you say 'yes,' Gabby? Try it for me. Y-y-yes."

"I would, but 'no' rolls right off my tongue so easily."

He vowed right then to make her scream "yes" immediately after she shouted his name in bed.

She broke what was left of the charged moment by sitting back in her chair. Red liquid swirled in her glass in time with the jazz playing on the radio.

"The call?" he asked.

"A couple friends. They plan to stop by later."

Interesting. In the month they dated, she never introduced him to any of her social circle. He knew from her file that she put work before most everything else in her life, so the oversight never struck him as odd.

"Are you sure you didn't seek out reinforcements? As in, maybe you weren't sure you could control yourself around me."

She tried to snort, but it sounded more like a grumble. "Hardly."

Even more interesting.

"So, you are saying these friends of yours just happen to be coming by on the night I said I would be over."

"Your point?" she asked even though her smile suggested she knew the point.

"Seems convenient."

"Don't flatter yourself."

"Someone has to."

"These are friends who happen to be coworkers. They need to fill me in on a project before tomorrow morning."

He processed the new information. "Accountants have homework?"

"Professionals work from home sometimes, yeah. Don't you?"

"I have trouble keeping work and home separate now and then." Reed wondered how he got the words out without stuttering.

Like it or not, the two overlapped more and more lately. He wanted to blame his ex-partner, Allen Frank. Allen's decisions and mistakes had shaped the rest of the department. Nearly ruined Reed's career. Changed its trajectory if nothing else.

"You strike me as a workaholic." She closed the pizza box and pushed it to the side.

"Just dedicated." He decided to bring the conversation back in the direction he wanted it to go. "What time is the cavalry coming?"

She glanced up at the clock on the wall. "In less than an hour."

"Have any ideas on what we can do until then?" He had a few. All involved getting her out of that suit jacket. Some even related to the work he was there to do. Most did not.

"You could go home," she suggested.

"And miss the opportunity to impress your friends?"

More like to engage in a bit of subtle interrogation. Reed knew if these folks really were coworkers, then they carried badges and performed whatever type of work Gabby did. They could connect with Greg Benson. Reed could not let the opportunity for a little investigation to pass.

"Chances are they won't like you," she said as she picked up her plate and glass and walked to the kitchen.

"You insist on thinking I am unlikable."

"That's certainly been my experience."

"See, now, that wounds me." He grabbed up the rest of their dinner remains and followed her. "And after I brought all these nice gifts."

"You're not going to cry, are you?"

"I try to be romantic, put my emotions out there, and you shoot me down." He sounded as dejected as possible, but all he got from her was a laugh. "A man cannot win with you, you know."

"A man *can* put up his money."

He held a glass under the faucet, letting the warm water run over his fingers. "Meaning?"

"Let's bet."

Not what he expected but she had his attention. "The wager being?"

"If they immediately like you as you think they will—"

"Did I say 'immediately'?"

"—you can stay for a few hours. If you lose, you go home and stop the seduction routine for good." She dangled a towel in front of him.

"Those are not fair terms." But she was getting closer to a deal he could manipulate.

"Win or lose, the pizza stays. It was a gift."

He gasped in fake outrage. "Come on, woman. The pizza? That's asking too much."

"Take it or leave it."

"What about my terms?" He leaned his back against the sink.

"They do not matter."

"They do to me."

She waved him off. "Irrelevant."

"That's where I have to disagree with you. We need to modify the proposed terms."

"No." She turned around and settled against the counter next to him. Her mannerisms mimicked his from the folded arms to the crossed ankles.

"You should at least wait until I tell you what they are before you say no."

"This saves time."

He waited until she relaxed before pushing his point. "So, under the modified terms, I get a half hour to win over your guests—"

"When did we—"

"Shhh." He pressed a finger against her lips and held it there while he spelled out his idea of a bargain. "If I win, I stay the night. If you win, I leave you alone for the rest of *this* evening."

"Talk about bad terms," she mumbled under his finger.

"Not for me."

"When did we start worrying about you?"

"And you say I'm the one who lacks charm."

"Charmless." She pushed his hand away. "You are utterly without charm."

The sharp intake of breath when he touched her told a different story. Gabby wanted him as much as he wanted her. Through all the lying, that much was true.

"If that is true, this should be an easy one for you. What's to lose?" he asked.

"My sanity. Your dignity." She held both palms out flat in front of her as if weighing the two.

"You have the advantage, so it's more like this." He moved her hands so that one was level with her shoulder and the other with her stomach.

"How do you figure?"

The demonstration ended with the light touch of his fingers against the soft flesh of her palms. "You know these people. I don't. I'm betting they have heard about our misunderstanding at dinner last night."

"Oh, I understood you just fine last night."

"About how you stomped off."

"I had every right to—"

He groaned, drowning out the rest of her sentence. "Stab me. Yes, I know. That is your side of the story."

She dropped her hands. "You do not get a side."

He knew arguing the point would only dig his hole deeper. Best to let her win this one.

"So, Gabby, bet or no?"

She nodded, slow at first, then faster. "You are on, stud."

Before she could escape, he spun around and trapped her against the counter and between his arms. "Let's say we seal the deal with a kiss."

"Reed." The deep vibration in her voice screamed out a mix of invitation and agreement.

No denial. No pushing away. Just a slow wipe of her wet tongue over her bottom lip. A slight opening of her mouth.

He clenched the cold stone of her countertop in his fists. Concentrating on the beat of the music filling the room, on the rise and fall of her breasts with each breath, he eased his grip. Tried to gentle the thing inside him that clawed and begged for him to take her. Gabby deserved caresses not a pawing.

Before he could move from seduction to foreplay, she ducked under his arm. In two steps, she was back at the table and a safe distance away from him and all of his plans.

"Deal." No vibration this time. Only a wide smile of supreme satisfaction.

Gabby could dodge and weave when the mood struck her. He admired that in a female. Also liked the way she refused to back down.

Hated the fact his lower half hummed with anticipation when satisfaction loomed so far out of reach.

"Now who's smooth?" he asked.

"We have a deal. No touching required."

Gone was the faint blush on her cheeks, the dreamy look in her dark eyes. Reed knew in that second he'd been had.

Round One to Gabby.

He headed for the hallway instead of chasing her around the kitchen like a dork. A guy had to have some pride when it came to a woman hell-bent on shredding his dignity.

"Since I have some time, I'm going to use your bathroom."

"If the plan is to work on your supposed charm while you're in there, don't bother. You will not have enough time." She shouted her thoughts at his retreating back.

"I would prefer not to meet your friends while standing in a big puddle."

"There's a nice image. Of course, I'd probably win if you did."

He stopped at the kitchen doorway. "Not necessarily."

She flashed him one of her sunny smiles, the kind that telegraphed sweetness. The kind he now thought of as a fraud.

"You sound sure of yourself," she said.

"Always."

Chapter 11

Doug and Sondra were on the way to her condo.
Reed refused to leave.

Times like these Gabby wished she owned protective
gear. Actually, forget the helmet and shield. She needed to
know what cleaned blood out of beige carpet.

When Doug and Reed met—even worse, when Sondra
and Reed met—there would be fireworks. Not the sexy,
happy kind. More like the someone-call-the-police kind.

Gabby took part of the blame for that since she basically challenged Reed to stick around and meet her co-
horts. Not her wisest move. She had made a series of
not-so-wise moves lately.

She wanted to see her friends interact with Reed. But
still, this was no way to spend a quiet weekday at home.

"Why are you frowning?" Reed asked.

Gabby gazed into the mirror over the fireplace and
watched Reed enter her cozy family room. He folded his
tie and put it in his briefcase. Unbuttoned one, then two,
now a third—

"The bigger question is why are you disrobing?"

"I am more charming if I'm not being strangled by my
clothes."

She turned around and faced him, drinking in a good

long look. Her bathroom water must have possessed magical powers because after only a few minutes of splashing around in her sink, he appeared fully refreshed and ready to go.

Those blue eyes sparkled with mischief. Gone was the uptight computer nerd façade. Shirt now hung open at the top. Sleeves rolled up. Jacket thrown somewhere. Face washed. Hair rumpled just enough to be cute.

She had the sudden urge to throw the bet.

So, she stayed right where she was, grabbing on to the fireplace mantel as if the world were about to blow apart.

"Do these friends of yours know I'm here?" he asked.

"I didn't tell them."

She doubted she needed to announce she had company. If her guess was right, Reed was the main reason for the impromptu intervention by Sondra and Doug.

When Gabby had returned to the office after her morning run-in-turned-kiss with Reed, her friends acted strange. That was pretty much the norm for Doug. But, even for him, the level of strange seemed high. Plus he avoided eye contact. Not his style at all.

Sondra left the room to work in her office. The glorified closet she used as an office. Closed the door to work in private. Until that moment, Gabby did not know Sondra's office even had a locking door.

Reed's kiss. The office monitors. Now a visit at home. Yeah, Sondra and Doug had something planned for her. Something involving a lecture on men and their motives, no doubt. Something that promised to be annoying and condescending.

Gabby knew she should be flattered by her friends' protective streak. She had the exact opposite reaction. This need everyone had to shelter her had started with a childhood tragedy and followed her into adulthood. Being petite and looking younger than her real age no longer satisfied her as excuses for holding on to past fears.

Their concern suffocated her. Made her feel as if she lacked control over her life and her decisions. Like she was some scared little kid.

The whole reason she insisted on taking the Benson assignment was to prove she could manage to do more than the "safe" thing all the time. Instead of sitting in a room analyzing data, she yearned to go out and retrieve it. To take a risk like Doug did. To not always play life so safe. She had done enough of that and needed to put that life behind her.

"Are they going to want some dinner?" Reed asked. "If so, that may cut into my charm time. I will want credit for any delay caused by food."

"Your terms. Too late to change now. You are stuck with them."

"I do not remember signing anything." He slumped down in her favorite chair and picked up the mystery novel sitting on the table next to it.

"Give me that." She snatched the book out of his hands.

"We are never going to Las Vegas together."

The idea of taking a trip with Reed threw her off balance. "Why?"

"Gambling makes you grouchy."

"People touching my stuff makes me testy." Having Reed act so at home and comfortable in her life was the real problem.

"It is a paperback not diamonds."

"I didn't want you to lose my page."

He grinned. "Fifty-one."

"What?"

He nodded at her hands. "Check it."

She flipped through the pages until she found a bent-back page. Fifty-one.

"Fancy trick. Care to tell me how you did that without opening the book."

"Just one more of my many talents."

The doorbell rang. Again, no announcement from the doorman. Gabby wondered exactly what she paid that steep monthly condo fee for each month.

"Any chance answering the door is one of those skills of yours, Mr. Charm?"

"Since you asked so nicely." He stood and bowed, pretending to tip a hat to her.

"I'm happy to issue orders if you prefer."

"You are a bit too willing on that score."

No kidding. "Nothing makes me happier than to push grown men around."

"We are going to work on your manners once we get rid of your friends."

"You forget that you'll be leaving with them." For some reason the thought of Reed leaving, of not pursuing her, made her a little sad.

"You act as if I am going to lose our little bet."

"Well, you're not going to win."

One of his eyebrows lifted in question. "Want to make another bet on that issue? Raise the stakes?"

"You should try to survive this bet before you try another one."

He tweaked her nose. "So little faith."

Before she could smack his hand away, he walked to the door. If he did not stop touching her soon, she would . . . well, she had no idea what she would do. Probably wrestle him into the bedroom and let him *really* use those hands.

The faint rumble of conversation died off in the hallway the minute Reed opened the door. Gabby peered into the quiet from behind Reed. The stunned look on Sondra's face matched Doug's furious one. Neither of them moved.

"What is this about?" Doug asked the question with his usual subtle grace.

"I'm not sure where you're from, but here on Earth it is

normal to say hello when someone opens a door to greet you." Reed started to shut the door.

Doug caught the edge just before it slammed into his face. With his cheeks puffing in and out, he looked ready to explode.

"Reed, let them in."

"Why?" Reed answered Gabby but kept his attention on Doug.

"They're my friends." Gabby tugged on the back of Reed's shirt to get his attention. "I told you my friends were coming over."

"We'll talk about your choice of male friends later."

"Who the hell is this guy?" Doug shouted his question this time.

Reed picked that moment to morph from easygoing to battle ready. Stiff spine. Flexed muscles. Jaw clenched hard enough to break.

"The same guy who decides if you can come in or not. I am leaning toward no, in case you're wondering."

Gabby had seen the signs often enough to know an overblown male moment hovered on the horizon. To avoid the inevitable, she stepped in front of Reed. "Actually, I own the house so I decide."

A noise resembling a growl echoed in her ear.

"Stop it," she mumbled to Reed before turning back to her friends. "Come in."

Since Doug and Sondra qualified as coworkers as well as friends, Gabby decided to refrain from getting upset about their impromptu visit. Until she knew which role they were playing and measured their level of interference, she vowed to stay calm.

"We didn't think you had company." With a manila folder tucked under her arm, Sondra telegraphed an all-business manner.

"Apparently," Reed muttered.

The way the three of them crowded around her in the small foyer made Gabby wonder if the plan was to protect her or smother her. "Everyone take a seat."

Gabby pointed in the general direction of the fireplace. No one seemed to notice or try to jump in it, which she took as a sign of how little attention they all really were paying to her.

Her three guests circled the available seats. After a few rounds of an odd game of musical chairs, Sondra sat on the couch, and the men stood on either end of it. Gabby decided to follow their boy-girl example and sit next to Sondra.

"Isn't it time for you to go?" Doug demanded more than asked Reed the question.

"No."

Gabby thought about throwing both men out. Let them find some other woman to drag around by her hair.

"This is private." Doug directed his comment to Reed.

"So was the conversation before you arrived, but I'm not complaining." Reed yawned.

Gabby tired of the verbal volleys. "I can honestly say you are both bugging me."

"All I did was open the door," Reed said.

Doug turned his anger on her. "You want me to get rid of this nerd for you?"

"Nerd?" Reed asked.

Sondra tried to diffuse the testosterone leak with rational thinking. "Let's all calm down."

Doug rubbed his hands together. "Just say the word and he's gone."

"The word is 'no.' " Reed broke from the glaring contest he had going with Doug to grin at Gabby. "You're right. It does roll right off the tongue after you say it a few times."

Since it was clear rational thought would not work with these two, Gabby jumped up and stood in Doug's path. A few more steps and he would have been all over Reed.

Not that Reed seemed to care. He continued to stand

there with his hands linked behind his back. The man was either simple in the head or cold as ice.

Gabby refused to use her family room as the testing site for that experiment. "Doug, that's enough."

"Yeah, Doug. That's enough." Reed chose to repeat Gabby's warning in a singsongy voice.

"Reed, you're not helping," she said.

"Sorry." There was not a lick of contrition in his voice.

Sondra cleared her throat. The sound was soft, but it caught everyone's attention. "I'm Sondra. The leashed animal here is Doug."

"Reed Larkin." Reed extended a hand to Sondra in a gallant greeting. "Gabby's boyfriend."

"Like hell," Doug muttered.

Sondra cleared her throat a second time. "I understood the two of you broke up."

"Ahhh. That explains the rabid-dog act by Doug here." Reed held on to Sondra's hand a fraction longer than was necessary as he shot Gabby a sideways glance. "You told them your side of the dinner story, didn't you?"

"I told the truth."

"What color wine goes best with the suit you have on today?" Doug looked around the condo as if hunting down a bottle.

"No one is throwing beverages around my new couch." Gabby turned on Doug and pointed to the couch in question. "You sit."

He glared at her before looking over her shoulder to Sondra. Whatever he saw had him taking the open seat next to her.

"Now get him to roll over," Reed said.

When Doug started to get up again, Gabby resorted to a second round of finger-pointing. "I said, sit."

Lucky for Reed, he hovered right out of elbow range, or he'd have hers in his gut. She'd kick both of their sorry male butts if they did not start behaving.

"And you." She turned and sent Reed her most withering look. "Stop tormenting Doug."

Doug snorted. "As if a computer nerd could get to me."

"At least I was invited."

The blood in Gabby's temples started to pound. "Reed, I just warned you—"

"That wasn't tormenting. If I had told him to fetch or stay or pee on a hydrant, then you would have an argument."

"Why are you here, Reed?" Sondra's steady reasonable voice provided a nice break to all the arguing.

Reed balanced against the arm of the chair and motioned for Gabby to take a seat. She was so grateful not to play the role of human shield that she accepted the silent offer.

"I owed Gabby an apology. I said some stupid things. Frankly, I acted like an ass the last time we were together."

"Now that's hard to imagine," Doug said in a voice loaded with sarcasm.

Reed rested an arm across the back of Gabby's chair. A second later his hand landed on her shoulder. She thought about scooting over, but Reed curled his fingers around her shoulder and held her steady.

"You were saying?" Sondra's smile encouraged conversation over fighting.

Gabby knew the calmer and quieter her friend became, the more incensed she was on the inside. The tension thrumming through the room vibrated off of Sondra as well as Doug. The thickness would choke her unless the testosterone overload knocked her out first.

"We probably do not need to go into all of this right now." After all, the "private" in private life should mean something.

"Sure we do," Doug said. "Let the nerd explain."

Reed gave her shoulder a squeeze. "I messed up. I admit it. Not that it undoes the damage to Gabby or her feelings, but I brought some stuff for her."

Doug and Sondra snuck a peek at each other. If Gabby had not been so intent on finding something else to focus on besides the feel of Reed's firm thigh next to her arm, she would have missed it.

Intervention, hell. This qualified as an inquisition.

"Like what?" Doug asked in a monotone voice.

"Dinner and flowers."

"Can I see?" Sondra asked with her fake smile back in full force.

Reed smiled. "You have a weak spot for pizza?"

With a delicate shrug of her shoulders and a small hair flip, Sondra turned up the charm to match Reed's flirtation. "The flowers. I love flowers. You know how women are."

Gabby considered vomiting.

Not that a good case of nausea would end the chatter. Reed and Sondra would miss it since they had moved to the kitchen. The talk of flowers turned to food and, inevitably, to the cold pizza leftovers. Reed clanked the dishes around while Sondra stayed glued to his side.

Gabby turned around to confront Doug and ran forehead-first into his shoulder. "Owwww."

"Careful," Doug said as he tried to steady her.

"And you." She grabbed Doug by his elbow and pulled him around until his back was to Reed. "What the hell is going on?"

"Being friendly."

"If friendly means homicidal."

Doug's mouth dropped open. "I resent that."

"You are acting like a nut on steroids and you know it."

"And here I thought that drug incident had been expunged from my file."

Gabby shoved the heel of her hand against Doug's shoulder. "This is not funny."

Doug sobered. "Neither is your *boyfriend.*"

"He's not."

Doug dropped his voice to a harsh whisper. "Funny or your boyfriend?"

"Either. Talk."

"About what?"

This time she grabbed the front of Doug's shirt. "Do not make me hurt you."

"I outweigh you by about a hundred pounds."

"Won't stop me."

"Maybe you can get your *boyfriend* to pick up a roll of tape and help out." Doug made an expression that consisted of half a smile and half a snarl.

Not the most attractive look Gabby had ever seen. Not the most comforting one either.

"Pain. Yours. Ten minutes. I mean it." She dug her fingernails into Doug's skin to let him know she meant business.

"Damn it, woman. That hurts." He hissed the comment under his breath as he broke her hold on his shirt.

"That is why I did it."

"I do not get you." Doug rubbed his chest. "This guy dumped you. Now you are playing house with him."

"You make him sound like a doll."

"Hardly."

She understood Doug wanted to help. She just hated his tactics. "Look, Doug. Reed came to apologize. That's it."

Doug stared at the floor, not saying a word for a few seconds. In the resulting quiet, she heard the low rumble of conversation in the kitchen. Reed's voice mixed with Sondra's giggling.

Giggling! Sondra ran an office. She spent years undercover in the CIA. Giggling was not Sondra's style.

Gabby's last hold on calm snapped. "What aren't you telling me?"

Doug lifted his gaze. All traces of emotion had left his face. No concern. Not even anger. Only unreadable eyes and a blank stare. The change was stark enough to make Gabby nervous.

"Get rid of the nerd and I'll explain."

Chapter 12

Reed left Gabby's house about twenty minutes later. She figured getting him out would be harder, but Reed went as soon as he wrangled a promise from her to call him later. More than likely he calculated the odds and decided their visitors put a permanent stall on his seduction plans for the evening.

But not forever. Reed made that much clear. He whispered in her ear at the door. Something about winning the bet and collecting later.

The spot on her neck still tingled from the feel of his warm breath. Not so much as a kiss passed between them.

She blamed Sondra and Doug for that loss.

Gabby rested her back against the door and stared at them. "That was an interesting show. A little heavy on the caged-beast act by you, Doug, but still worth the ticket price of admission."

"What about the scene nerd boy caused?" Doug twisted a pen between his fingers as he paced from her couch to the kitchen and back.

"His name is Reed."

Only she had the right to hate Reed. Doug needed to at least pretend to be civil.

"Like I care."

She tried again. "What's with the caveman routine?"

"Did you want me to kiss him hello?"

Frustration rumbled around in her chest. "Yeah, Doug. Those are the only options you have when you meet another guy, behaving like an asshole or necking."

"I could have congratulated him on doing such a good job of dumping you."

She refused to revisit that argument. Since Doug had sidestepped a straight answer, Gabby turned to Sondra. "And you."

"What did I do?" Sondra asked the question as she poured herself a glass of red wine.

"Other than make me queasy with all the dumb giggling? Hell, I'll probably hear that sound in my sleep."

"I never giggle." The bottle clanked against the granite countertop as Sondra set it back down a bit too hard.

"I admit it was a new thing for you, but it was most definitely a giggle. And a nauseating one." Gabby dropped into the stuffed couch cushions.

"Don't forget scary. The sound was downright freaky," Doug said, adding his two cents between long steps.

"What is so odd about a laugh? Perfectly normal."

"For a seventh grader. Thanks to you I had a junior high flashback."

In Gabby's mind that was a bad, bad thing. Styleless hair. Ugly clothes. No self-esteem. Mix in a death threat and a kidnapping courtesy of her parents' work and you had the worst time of her life.

"A woman should be able to find something someone says funny without being called names," Sondra mumbled into her wine as she took a sip.

With all glass objects out of breaking danger, Gabby took one last stab at remaining calm. Screaming like a possessed monkey would not resolve her friends' concerns.

"I appreciate that you are both looking out for me. That you cared enough to come over and check on me."

"We came because we were—"

Doug finished Sondra's thought. "Stunned. Sickened. Scouting out places to hide the nerd's body after I kill him."

Sondra cleared her throat. "I was going to say concerned."

"There was no need," Gabby said. "I am fine."

"Except that your nerd radar is off," Doug said.

"You do not need to protect me." Gabby slid her hands under her thighs to keep from strangling either one of them.

"It is more involved than that," Sondra said.

"Look, I know Reed made a mistake."

Sondra's eyes popped open. "You're defending him now?"

"Not his behavior." Gabby insisted there was a difference. If not, that meant she was excusing him, and she was not quite ready to let that happen.

Doug took his turn. "Are you even sure his name is Reed?"

"What the heck does that mean?" The question came out as a shriek. Gabby chalked up the sound to the pressure of a long day and the adrenaline pumping through her over her meeting tomorrow.

"Gabby, where's your badge?" Sondra sat down on the couch and rested her elbows on her knees.

"I thought we were talking about Reed."

"Humor Sondra." Doug sat down on a bar stool.

Gabby saw him eye her purse. "Do not even think of touching that."

"A woman's purse is a scary place. Wondering what all you have in there."

"Not my badge." Gabby reached into her blazer pocket

and pulled out the plastic square. She held it up for them to see. "That's here. See?"

"I'll be damned."

"With your mouth, Doug, I bet you're right," Gabby joked, but neither Sondra nor Doug laughed.

"How is that possible?" Doug asked without directing the question at anyone in particular.

The seriousness sobered Gabby. "Okay, I give up. What's going on?"

"Let me see it." Sondra took the badge, turned it over in her hands and investigated it from every angle. "When did you find the badge?"

"You assume I lost it." Which she had—many times—but not since Doug had found it this morning.

"Did you?" Sondra asked.

"Not after Doug handed it back earlier. Been with me ever since." This time. Other times she wondered if the thing had legs because it never seemed to be where she put it.

Doug and Sondra glanced at each other. Neither said a word, but their body language said plenty. There was a huge problem here somewhere. One they refused to share.

"Stop doing the conspiratorial staring thing," Gabby warned.

"I do not stare," Doug insisted while staring at a piece of cold pizza.

"You both do. It is making me downright nuts."

No one said anything. For a few seconds, the only sound in the room came from the jazz CD and the squeaking of the bar stool under Doug's butt.

"You're right." Sondra passed the badge back and forth between her hands.

"I am?"

"She is?" Doug asked.

Sondra nodded. "Absolutely."

Gabby knew to hold off on the celebration. "Happy you think so. About what?"

"We were overreacting," Sondra said.

Doug reached out to grab the ID but stopped short with his hand frozen in midair. "What?"

That was Gabby's question. Sondra never capitulated. Never admitted fault. The contrite act rang as untrue as the girlie giggling.

"Gabby's a grownup." Sondra's stare bore through Doug.

Gabby tried to count the seconds between Sondra's blinks, but since she did not move her eyelids at all, there was nothing to count. And Doug missed all of it. He was too busy tapping the badge against the side of the plate in front of him to pick up on Sondra's nonverbal message.

"We need to respect her dating decisions and not barge in to her condo and threaten her boyfriend," Sondra continued.

"Ex." Gabby liked the speech. Sure, the delivery lacked a certain ring of truth—any truth, actually—but the sentiment sounded nice.

Doug's jaw clenched even tighter.

"But she needs to know—"

"No, Doug. Gabby's right. We need to *drop this.*" Any wider and Sondra's eyes would have taken over her entire head.

Know what?

A thousand "why" questions bounced around inside Gabby's mind. As in why no one was telling her what the "this" was. Why Sondra's behavior took a sharp turn into friendly land all of a sudden. Why Doug's mouth grew thinner and thinner with each word Sondra spoke.

Why her friends stood in her family room, looked her right in the eye and lied their stinking heads off.

Gabby decided to test the new hands-off policy. "So we agree my sex life is off limits."

"You're sleeping with the nerd now?" Doug hit the plate hard enough to send it spinning on the counter.

Just as Gabby thought. Sondra and Doug had a secret that excluded her.

"Butting out includes keeping your nose out of my bedroom," Gabby said to tweak Doug.

"You cannot sleep with that guy." Doug's order ended with a deep scowl in Sondra's direction. "She can't."

"Oh, I bet I can."

"It is not our business, Doug." Sondra gritted the words out between clenched teeth.

With the tension zapping between Doug and Sondra, Gabby could not resist poking one more time. "I'm thinking the sex would be good. Reed has this thing he does with—"

"Stop." Doug actually looked as if he was in pain there for a second.

"Why shouldn't I enjoy a round or two . . . or more with Reed?"

Doug's mouth dropped open. When it closed again, he engaged in a good bit of swearing before he gave his explanation. "Because he's an ass."

"Sondra liked him." Gabby knew where Doug stood. She wanted to see Sondra's reaction. "Didn't you?"

For a second Sondra turned as green as Doug. "Your life is your business."

Gabby took the nonanswer as a negative on Reed. A monumental turnaround since Sondra had been a huge supporter for weeks of the idea of Gabby enjoying a fling with Reed. Something about the need for an outlet.

"We will not interfere," Sondra said.

That cinched it. No way Sondra meant that.

Gabby added one more assignment to her list. In addition to all of her other work, she had to figure out Sondra and Doug's angle.

All while weighing the pros and cons of sleeping with Reed.

Chapter 13

Reed knocked on Gabby's door, muffins and coffee in hand, early the next morning. The woman loved food. He hoped to capitalize on that weakness.

Staying awake would not be a problem. He had started pumping caffeine right after he left her house the evening before and had not stopped since. Sleep ranked low on his priority list.

He knew the reason for the visit from Sondra and Doug. Him. Not just *him* the bad boyfriend, but *him* the guy lying to Gabby.

Reed might have been able to write off Doug's reaction as unwelcome jealousy if it had not been so extreme. But Sondra. Cool control radiated off that woman. She charmed and flirted. All the while, she planned and calculated. Reed knew the type. Hell, he was the type.

No question Gabby's coworkers could do some damage to his plans. To decrease the possibility, he had roused Pete out of bed around midnight and put him to work gathering more information, starting with full names and bios.

Turned out the files for Doug and Sondra were even cleaner than Gabby's. The sort of "clean" that pointed to past black op undercover careers. Damn spies were everywhere these days.

Gabby's past did not match those of her coworkers. She appeared to be more of a pawn than a player. The question of the day centered on how much, if anything, Doug and Sondra had put together and passed to Gabby while they all were alone.

The flowers and apology bought some goodwill. Reed worried Doug and Sondra stalled the forward progress. Planted a doubt here. Reminded her of the restaurant incident there. Ruined his shot at getting in the door now.

With Greg Benson pretending to run a legitimate business and Gabby stuck in the firing line, Reed could not afford to lose access. Being cut off from Gabby was not an option. She was wading into a heap of danger and potential criminal activity which made Reed her shadow. At least for now and until he knew what role, if any, she played in Benson's business.

He knocked again, knowing Gabby still wandered around inside. No way she got by him. Not with him looming in the hallway, Pete staked out at her car and an undercover dressed up as her doorman. Unless Gabby grew wings and flew out the window, she was in there. Probably plotting his death while she was at it.

After another set of taps, the door flew open with enough force to bounce against the inside wall. Flushed and out of breath, Gabby stood in a white fluffy robe that covered all of her most interesting parts except a peek of skin above her breasts.

From this vantage point he saw the rise and fall of her chest. When she shifted her weight, the slit in the material flashed him another shot from bare knees to painted toenails.

It took some effort, but Reed forced his gaze back up her body to her face. Huge mistake. Her body screamed an invitation, but the frown on her lips warned him to stay back.

"What are you doing here?" Anger flashed in her eyes as she brushed a damp strand of hair out of her eyes.

Bad. Very bad.

He thought about dropping the pastries and running. Instead, he fell back on the act from last night. Until he knew the damage, he would continue with the same play.

"You never called."

She blinked several times. "What?"

"You said you would get in touch with me after your friends left." He peeked into the condo behind her. "I'm assuming they did leave."

"Oh. Right." Her white-knuckled grip loosened on the edge of the door. "Sorry."

"It's fine. Not flattering, but fine."

Her mouth broke into a sheepish smile. "All the pizza went to my brain. Better there than my hips, I guess."

No way was he touching that comment. "Speaking of dough, I'm here with breakfast."

"Breakfast?"

He shook the paper bag in front of her. "You've probably heard of it. It's the meal most frequently eaten in the morning."

She looked down at the cup holder tray in his other hand. Her eyes turned all soft and dreamy. "Is that coffee?"

Relief washed through him. Whatever had her frowning when she opened the door lost out to hunger and an apparent caffeine addiction.

"One for you. One for me." And one in the car that he downed on the drive over.

"You should know that I'm not a low-fat banana loaf type of gal."

"Is that female code for something?"

"I'm just warning you before you talk up this meal and get me all excited only to reveal calorie-free crap."

Excited. Yeah, now they were getting somewhere.

"Fair enough," he said.

"Now, what's in the bag?" Her hand slid down the door.

Blocking the entrance gave way to eyeing the bag in his hand.

"Nothing healthy. I promise."

"Let me see."

"You'll have to let me in first."

Uncertainty lingered at the corners of her eyes. "Okay, but only for a minute."

"You said that last night, then let me stay."

"You caught me in a weak moment."

"I didn't realize you had any of those." He stepped around her, scanning the room as he walked into the kitchen and fetched two plates. No work papers. No sign of anything new or potentially damaging.

When he glanced up again, he noticed she had not moved. She still stood with her hand on the knob and the door wide open.

Looked like his lady needed a nudge in the right direction. "Expecting someone else?"

"Huh?"

"See, it's customary to eat breakfast inside the condo instead of out in the hallway."

A rosy glow lit up her cheeks as she slammed the door a bit too hard. "It's just that I cannot be late today."

He glanced at his watch. "Unless you have to drive to Ohio instead of just downtown, I'm thinking you have time. It's barely six-thirty."

Meaning he had been up for more than twenty-four consecutive hours. Also meant Gabby had two more hours before she checked in at work. Plenty of time for whatever. Lots of whatever.

"I planned to go in early this morning," she said.

"Are you going to wear that outfit when you do?"

She grabbed the lapels of her robe and pulled them together. "Of course not."

The action hid the hint of bare skin. One of these days he would learn to keep his big mouth shut.

"Early or not, Gabby, you have to eat."

"I've skipped breakfast before." She walked into the kitchen and reached around him to pick through the danish and muffin choices.

"I find that hard to believe since you are a woman who loves her food."

She stopped searching and stared him down. "Meaning?"

If humans possessed the power to melt each other into gigantic puddles of liquid with one look, he figured he would fit in a glass right about now.

"You. Like. Food."

"Is something wrong with that?" She tossed a blueberry muffin in the air like a baseball.

"No."

"You have a problem with women who eat?"

"If we're fighting, you need to warn me so I can put down my coffee. I am not really in the mood to wear another beverage."

"Uh-huh."

"Don't really want to get hit with a flying pastry either."

Her jaw unclenched a bit. "Fine. No fighting."

"You still look ready to pounce to me."

"That's my hungry face." She unwrapped the blueberry muffin and plopped a big chunk in her mouth.

To prevent a detour into a conversation he could never win, he changed the subject. "What's so special about work today?"

She grabbed one of the coffees. "Big meeting."

Yeah, he knew that much. Even knew with whom, but

he needed to hear her say it. "Bunch of accountants getting together and practicing their multiplication tables?"

"We did that last week." She slid onto the bar stool next to him, facing the back tiled wall of her kitchen.

"Subtraction?"

"We've moved on to long division." She crossed her legs. The robe parted before she could catch it. Fabric dipped, falling to either side of her bare thighs.

The urge to stare, to spin her around and drink in every inch of her naked skin, proved a pretty big temptation. So did her hunger. He sat there dreaming up ways to get her flat on her back on the counter. She concentrated on freeing a muffin from its wrapper.

So much for seduction.

He tried another angle. "When you talked about your work in the past, I got the impression you didn't meet with clients."

"I don't."

The caffeine burned as he gulped down the last third of the cup. "Are you getting a promotion or something?"

"When?"

"At this meeting."

"No, but I am hoping eventually." She ripped off another piece of muffin and chased it down with a coffee shot.

He was running out of angles. "It's not tax season."

"More like flu season since it's October." She did not say "duh," but Reed heard it in there.

"Are you trying to make this the most difficult conversation ever or is it my imagination? It is fine if you are, but I'm running out of small talk. The weather and the price of corn are all I have left."

She froze. "Corn?"

"My favorite vegetable."

"More like a starch." Eating the muffin gave way to her

picking at it. "You know I do forensic accounting work, right?"

The transition came out of nowhere, but he followed. "I'm guessing that does not mean you dissect numbers with tiny scalpels. Although that would explain your stabbing obsession."

He knew she conducted business evaluations for corporate sales and purchases. Conducted some end of the year audits. Since the "forensic" part generally meant courtroom evidence, he knew her research helped out in divorce and business lawsuits as well.

"I review and investigate corporate documents."

"To figure out how much the companies are worth for audits and such, right?"

"Uh, yeah." She dove back into the muffin.

Between the lack of eye contact and the way she mangled the top off the poor defenseless pastry, he knew he was getting close to her uncomfortable territory. Which was exactly his plan.

"Did I say something wrong?" he asked.

Her head popped up. "No."

"You sure? Because the muffin is about to call 911."

She looked down at the pile of crumbs in front of her and wrinkled up her nose. "I prefer the tops."

"Shredded in a million pieces?"

She brushed the evidence off her hands. "I think I'm just nervous. Meeting face-to-face is different from focusing on documents."

"Only because numbers do not talk back." He slid off the stool and stood behind her.

The sweet smell of her floral shampoo hit him first. He associated the fresh scent with her. He chose the flowers to match her unique fragrance.

"Not usually." Her voice sputtered out. "What are you doing back there?"

"Square dancing." He rested his palms on her shoulders.

"I need to see your face when you throw out lines like that; otherwise I can't tell if you are serious or not." She peeked at him over her shoulder. "By the way, please tell me you are kidding."

"I'll practice another time." He leaned forward until his cheek rubbed against hers. "How about a massage instead?"

"Really?"

With her mouth this close, temptation roared through him again. "It will help you relax. Trust me."

"Oh, you do not have to convince me. Go ahead."

Almost seemed too easy. "Guess I could have skipped the flowers."

"Those were mandatory. So is the massage now that you've promised one." She pointed to her back. "Get to work."

"You really need to stop playing hard to get."

"You're still talking." She lowered her head, exposing her slim, pale neck, and snapped her fingers at him. "More hands. Less chatter."

"The words every man longs to hear. Probably could have done without the bossiness, though." He began the massage with slow, even strokes.

"Worked, didn't it?"

"I'm easy."

"Those sound more like the words men like to hear." The end of her comment dragged out as he kneaded her shoulders through the thick robe that dwarfed her slim frame.

With every sweep of his fingertips, every press of his thumbs against her back, her muscles loosened. Her hands fell palms up on the counter. Tension flowed out of her, causing her neck to dip lower in relaxation.

Dissatisfied with the barrier keeping him from her skin, he took the one step that could force her out of her slumber. And get his ass kicked the whole way to Cleveland. Sliding the bulky cotton over her shoulders to her arms, he bared her creamy skin to his gaze.

No shirt. No bra. Only Gabby's unblemished skin greeted him.

He half expected her to grab for the robe, slap him, start yelling or all of those. Gabby being Gabby, she did the unexpected and snuggled closer. She might have purred, too.

Since the part of him that suffered the greatest lack of control in her presence now nestled against her backside, he no longer trusted any of his senses. Too many blood cells rushed out of his brain for it to be functioning at top speed.

Her body rocked back and forth in a sway. With every push of his hands against her flesh, the small of her back eased closer to his lower half.

"You are a genius." Her husky voice rumbled right behind a groan.

The sound jump-started something inside of him. Turned his focus from work to play. "That is not my mind you're enjoying."

"Who are you kidding? I passed mere enjoyment two minutes ago. Remind me to listen from now on when you start talking about those talents of yours."

The slur to her speech and those sexy growls filling the room let him know she was as far gone as he was. She tilted her head to the side, giving him an open view into the dark shadow of the swell between her breasts.

The battle between his head and his dick began in earnest. A few more moans from Gabby and his dick would take the lead. Would rule all of his actions. Would take his body exactly where he wanted it to go. Deep inside her.

"In fact, go ahead and tell me. What are some of those other talents?"

His hands stilled. "Did you—"

"I'm waiting." Her voice had deepened to a sexy purr.

"Is this one of those tests where if I'm dumb enough to answer, you smash a plate over my head?"

"Dishes are expensive."

"So . . . ?"

She tapped the back of his hand. "Keep working."

"That's very practical of you."

"Must be all of that accountant training."

His hands continued to rub over her shoulders and down her smooth back. "Could be."

"So, tell me about these other talents of yours."

He could almost hear a door opening to let opportunity walk on in. "I would prefer to show you, but we'd need more time."

She peeked up at him over her shoulder. "How much?"

The change in her demeanor from angry to interested should have surprised him, but he expected it. They had danced around each other and this subject for weeks. Playing the role of boring computer nerd, he never rushed his moves or tried to leave her breathless. Now that Charlotte insisted bailing out of the assignment was no longer an option, the next step was inevitable.

"I'll want to go slow because slow is good," he said, emphasizing the double meaning.

"Ummmm."

"Savor every minute." At his words, her skin heated under his hands.

"Sounds good."

"Touch everywhere."

"Do you have somewhere better to be now?" An eagerness played across her mouth, lingered in her eyes and filled the air between them.

"Hell, no."

Time. A bed. Desire. A condom in his back pocket. Looking down at her, seeing the trust in her face and pleasure in her smile, he knew everything they needed was right there in the condo. Including a very willing woman and a man stretched to the limits of his decency.

"Me either," she whispered.

He said the first thing that came into his head. "You're overdressed."

"You don't like the robe?"

"I would like it better off." On the floor, on a hanger, he did not care so long as everything underneath belonged to him.

Her palms folded over his until they covered the back of his hands. "I hate being cold."

"You won't be."

"Good." With a gentle nudge she guided his fingers, skimming the tips down her bare skin to the darkened shadows at the opening of her robe.

A breath hitched in his throat when she shifted his palms to the high slopes at the top of her breasts. Steered his fingers to stroke her soft skin, then cupped his palms to feel the weight of her.

"Gabby . . ." He said her name without thinking.

"Undress me."

Chapter 14

Raw need pushed away all of Gabby's doubts about Reed's newfound drive for intimacy and her friends' odd behavior. Even the pressure of her big meeting settled into a locked part of her brain as sensations slammed into her from every direction.

His hands circled and caressed her breasts. The gentle contact contrasted with the insistent press of his erection against her lower back.

"Are you sure?" His mouth lingered over her cheekbone before trailing into her hair to nuzzle there.

"Please, just—"

"I need to hear you say it."

The pounding of her heart turned to a crashing boom by the time it reached her ears. "Reed . . ."

"The word, Gabby."

She knew what he wanted. She wanted it, too. "Yes."

"Damn, baby. I can't hold back another second." With every breath he took, a small puff of air tickled against her neck.

Every word he had uttered since the scene at the restaurant showed a new boldness. One that made her rational side run for the hills.

He intended to fight for her. Nerd or not, the idea registered high on the sexy scale. Being desired, pursued even, gave her a sense of renewed energy.

Seeing his gaze blaze along the same path where his fingers skimmed her flesh made her confidence soar. She had always believed in her ability to succeed, even when others refused to see her as a competent adult. But this surge went beyond simple self-assurance. This was about feminine power at its most fundamental and basic level.

And she did not intend to waste a drop of it.

She balanced her knees against the bar. With her back supported in his arms, she shifted her hips forward, opening her body to his intense stare. By the way his heart rate changed under her ear from fast to racing, she knew she had hooked his attention.

Now to reel him in. To match his strong pass with one of her own of the less-is-more variety.

One tug on the knot at her waist and the tie loosened. The robe fell open, sending the material sliding off her lap to hang down on either side of her bare thighs.

"Damn, woman."

All that remained were the scraps of robe balancing on her upper arms and trapped beneath her. "Better?"

"If your goal is to kill me."

She brushed her palms over her bare stomach. "I think that's good in this case."

"Fucking great."

She knew how he felt without his harsh whisper of appreciation. The sudden hesitation in his breathing and the heaviness of his arms around her told her all she needed to know.

The slow rub of his thumbs over and around her nipples set off a chain reaction inside of her. To ease the building heat between her thighs, she opened her legs and let the room's cool air rush against her skin. When that failed to bring her relief, she balanced her toes on the bar stool's lower railing and opened even wider.

Reed's gaze zeroed in on the crevice between her thighs. His hands followed, wandering down over her stomach. Then lower.

A shout rumbled in her throat, but she clamped down on it in a desperate attempt to keep the sensations coming. Wet and warm, she wanted more of him and tipped her hips forward in silent invitation. When his fingertips continued to dance over the short hair covering her mound without venturing on, she gave up the last pretense of being subtle and prolonging the moment.

"Reed."

"What, baby?"

"Do it now."

A fine tremor shook his body as he placed gentle kisses along the line of her eyebrow. "Tell me exactly what you need."

How could he not know? "Everything."

"Say every word. Guide me."

A fire raged just under the surface of her skin. The touching inflamed her further, making her want to push back against him and beg for satisfaction. Instead, with one hand on his forearm and the other pressing against his wrist, she forced his palm lower.

"Hands. Use your . . . hands."

His tongue circled her outer ear as his fingers soothed over her lifting pelvis. "Show me where?"

"On me. All over." On every part of her that ached for him.

"Like this?" He dragged a finger along her jawline.

She shook her head and pressed his other wrist even tighter against her lower body.

"This?" With one hand trapped against her mound, he outlined her tight nipple with the other.

"Inside."

The word came out of her on a harsh gasp. One he swallowed with a deep kiss that went on until she could taste only him. Lips. Tongue. Heat. Craving.

When she surfaced again, the tip of his thumb edged inside her. At his touch, her breathing grew shallow and uneven. But it was not enough. Not nearly enough.

She pressed her head deeper into the space between his shoulder and chin. "More."

"Show me how."

Possessed by desire, she abandoned her inhibitions and demanded what her body needed. Grabbing his fingers, she showed him exactly how she wanted to be touched. How hard and how fast.

She dragged his fingers across her wetness. Slid his fingers against her clit. Ground her body against his palm. Anything to stop the churning inside her.

The circling and stroking set off a frenzy down deep in her stomach. Made her inner muscles pulse with life. Shook her lower body with a tremor of excitement.

She wrapped her fingers around his forearm, hoping to ride his caresses straight to the satisfaction she burned for, but without her guiding touch, he stopped. Without the pressure from her, his fingers lay still against her wetness.

The smell of her excitement reached her senses. She knew he could feel her, smell her. "Now, Reed. Now."

"You need relief, baby?" His gruff tone grated against her sensitive nerves.

"Yes." Her head shifted from side to side on his shoulder as frustration crashed into her.

"How does this feel?" His thumb swept inside her again. Deeper this time. Not just a small push and pull. No, he treated her to the slow, steady plunge she craved.

Then two fingers pressed in and out while his thumb flicked across her clit. Even when she clawed at his arm to get him to pick up the pace, the thrust and retreat re-mained steady.

His hot mouth on her breast and fingers inside her proved a heady mix. The friction of his lips against her skin and his fingers slick from her wetness broke her control.

Tension turned to sweet torture. She threw her head back to give him greater access, careful not to launch them both right off the stool and onto the floor.

She chanted his name as she closed her thighs and trapped his hand there. The move did not tighten the coil-ing inside her as she hoped. The explosion she needed hov-ered just out of reach.

As if sensing her need, Reed increased his pace. Her lower half clenched and constricted in response. Fingers inside her and his palm against her. The combination broke her control. An internal spiraling snapped her back straight and sent her hips pumping back and forth.

She cried out. Said something about his genius. Then let the orgasm rip right through her on a breathless moan.

When she opened her eyes a few minutes later, a stark white ceiling greeted her. Reed's rough breathing echoed in her ears, helping her to calm her own.

As she lay cocooned against his chest with her head bal-anced on his shoulder, she glanced down the line of her naked body. The sprawl lacked a certain level of decorum and left her naked body vulnerable to his touch and view.

Fingertips rubbed against the wetness on her inner thighs and every so often snuck inside her. Despite the booming shout of her orgasm, her muscles reacted to his intimate touch with a pulsing bordering on pain. As if being so primed, so satisfied, turned her flesh hypersensitive.

This beat her usual breakfast yogurt by a longshot.

A bit too unsteady for another round, she tried to drag him into a conversation. "These stools are sturdier than I thought."

He rocked her from side to side as if testing her words. "It survived round one."

So much for trying to drag him into anything other than sex. When they fooled around before, it never reached this level. Never felt this intimate and grounded before.

"You make it sound as if there's going to be another round."

"Damn, woman, I hope so."

She laughed at his disgruntled tone.

"I'm dying here." He mumbled something under his breath about his turn.

The lazy satisfaction clouding her brain cleared for a second. "You didn't—"

"No."

She looked up into his stunning green eyes and saw a dark storm. Took in the flat line of his lips and the hint of perspiration dotting his forehead. And silently added *unselfish lover* to his list of attributes.

"Sorry." She said the word but could not muster even an ounce of remorse for what just happened in what was usually the most tame and unused room in her house.

"I'm not."

"I got all caught up—"

"That was the idea." His lips found hers in a kiss that did more to reignite than soothe.

"But you—"

He sighed against her forehead. "Got screwed."

"Actually, I was thinking sort of the opposite."

"That's me. Give. Give. Give." He delivered the line in his best woe-is-me tone.

"I hear it's better to give than receive."

"Really? I seem to remember being a big fan of the receiving part."

She skimmed her fingers under his chin. "You poor thing."

"Happy you noticed."

"Hard not to with all of the muttering you're doing." She sat up then, letting her robe dip behind her.

The idea was to turn around and engage in a little giving of her own, but Reed's mouth stopped her. He peeled down the last bit of the robe. The move uncovered the rest of her skin in a slow striptease meant for his eyes only. And lips.

His mouth followed the material down her now-exposed back, inch by slow inch, in a trail of kisses. "Every part of you is beautiful."

"Keep this up and you'll be giving again," she said as his mouth found the shallow small of her back.

"I'd give all day if you'd let me."

"How about all night instead?" The surprising words slipped out before she could censor them.

He froze. "Repeat that."

She debated keeping up the fight and making him pay, but that game seemed ridiculous to her now. So, she abandoned the idea as soon as it moved into her brain.

"Come over tonight. After work." She never meant the words as much as she did in that second.

"I'll want more than pizza."

"Did I mention food?"

He spun the bar stool around, dragging his fingertips over her naked skin as she turned to face him. "Tell me this isn't just about collecting on that damn bet."

"You did not win that bet."

His gaze traveled down her body, lingering on each and every area he had caressed. A renewed blast of sexual heat flared behind his eyes.

"Sure feels like I won."

She wrapped her arms around his neck. "Funny, but I was thinking the same thing."

"And Doug did not kill me. That's something."

"That's a miracle."

"I am thinking about getting a rabies shot in case I come in contact with him again."

"You will, but that's enough about Doug." She wound Reed's tie around her hand and tugged him closer. From his broad shoulders to his trim waist, he filled every inch of the space between her thighs.

"No arguments here."

"Tell me what I can do to make you a happy man."

"You just did with your nighttime suggestion."

"I meant something more immediate."

"I like the way you think." She nibbled his chin. "And do not make me beg this time."

His fingers immediately went to her heat. Caressed the folds. Brought her sensitized body back to life.

"Bedroom." She whispered the command against his neck between kisses.

"We'll never make it."

She heard the rip of his zipper. Felt the press of his erection against her. "You mean here?"

"Next time we'll try the bed or the floor or wherever the hell you want. Not now." His fingers left her only long enough to reach into his back pocket and pull out a condom.

"Where did you get that?"

"It's been a long fucking month of not fucking." The packet ripped open and he slid it on.

"Not for lack of trying."

"Or a lack of wanting." He placed his hands under her knees and bent them back toward her chest.

The position left her open to whatever he wanted. Also threw off her balance. She grabbed onto the edge of the stool to keep from falling. When the grip failed to keep her steady, she held on to him instead.

His fingers dipped into her one last time. "Yes?"

Absolutely. "If you don't, I'll—"

A groan rumbled around in his throat right before his mouth descended. She was so wrapped up in the feel of his lips against hers that the press of his erection took her by surprise as he began to enter her. Slow and easy, he pushed inside. No stopping. No time to adjust. Just one long stroke until he lodged deep within her.

The weight of him. The pressure of his body against hers. The heavy fullness. The scrape of his clothing against the bare skin of her thighs. The sensations hit her from every angle and kept coming with every stroke of his body inside hers.

Gone was the computer nerd. This Reed shook with passion. This Reed could not get enough of her. This Reed was done waiting.

His hands roamed over her face to her breasts and back again. His mouth never left hers so that when she lost her breath, he gave her his. From the long sweeps of his tongue to the deep plunge of his body into hers, he lost composure.

His usual control gave way to his search for a release. He did not try to hide his need for her. And she loved every minute of it.

This time when he sank down, she wrapped her legs around his waist. With her ankles hooked behind his back, she held him tight against her.

"Deeper," she begged, despite her earlier vow not to.

"Baby, let me—" His sentence broke off on a gasp when her insides clamped down on him. "Damn, I want you."

She believed him. His emotions and words matched. Gulping air, sweating, muscles stretched to snapping. His desire was real and unhidden.

He threaded his fingers through hers and lifted her arms high over her head. With his chest pressed against hers, he eased her back until her head and hands fell against the counter behind her.

"Come for me." He followed the sensual demand by grinding his hips against her.

A shiver raced through her from head to toe. When the tension in her legs eased for a second, he took advantage by retreating, then plunging inside her again.

She did not fight the way he pumped his body against hers with increasing speed. Soon the building turned to a tightness that demanded release. In and out, her back pressing against the counter and the stool thudding against the floor, they moved.

Soft moans and mumbled words of encouragement filled the room. Lips pressed against lips as the heat burned between them. One last dip of his tongue, one final push deep inside her, and her world exploded a second time.

Rough breathing turned into a soft shout against his shoulder as an orgasm thrummed through. This time she did not speed to the finish line all alone.

His hands shook in hers, and a tiny tremble moved through his shoulders. A few seconds later, his body jerked. His shoulders stiffened until she felt every ounce of his two hundred pounds balance with her on the chair. Two more thrusts and he let out a shout that echoed through the small room.

Once the last shake of his orgasm subsided, he fell heavily against her. At first harsh breathing beat in the crook of her neck; then he snuggled.

She hated to break the moment, but what little breath she had in reserves after their lovemaking was being squished out of her. "You're heavy."

"Exhausted is more like it."

She drew her hand through his soft hair. "At least you can breathe."

The weight on her chest eased as he regained his footing without breaking contact. Their bodies still touched from stomach to thigh. Their hands remained locked together.

With his body still lodged deep inside hers, he lifted his head and shot her a sweet smile.

"Hi." The area around his eyes softened. The flash of fire she saw before was banked now.

This guy knew how to make up.

Knew how to make love, too.

She freed one hand to trail her fingers over his lips. "I can hardly wait to see what you can do in a bed."

"Since we're tight on time, I will settle for showing you how I perform in the shower."

"You better not mean singing."

"Happy to say I can't carry a tune."

"Then let's get to it."

Chapter 15

Gabby's body still hummed with satisfaction four hours later. Being in a fancy restaurant complete with pink tablecloths and all sorts of extra forks and spoons in front of her reminded her of Reed's break-up scene. Somehow, that fact did not kill off her sexual buzz.

Eating lunch at eleven almost did.

The man across from her picked the time, the place and the private room. The whole setup struck Gabby as a bit over-the-top. But, so was her business date, so she played along.

Greg Benson was exactly what her work file promised him to be. He had magazine looks and champagne taste. From his manicured nails to his white blond hair with the longish bangs flopped down on his forehead, everything about him screamed sophisticated modern male.

The guy met all of the objective attractiveness qualifications. The hostess almost tripped and fell on her face while trying to stare and usher him to the table at the same time.

For Gabby, the rich, pretty-boy type held all the appeal of wet shoes. She preferred her men strong and dark . . . and bringing her breakfast.

Which brought her to the real problem with Greg Benson: he was no Reed Larkin. Both excelled in the looks and taste department, but the similarities ended there.

She assumed Reed did well in financial terms, but he never flaunted his wealth. She did not have to guess about Greg. He reeked of money. By her calculations, his watch cost more than her college education.

Too perfect. Too coiffed. Too styled.

Too much.

"This is a delicate situation," Greg said as he sipped on his second gin and tonic in fifteen minutes.

Including too much alcohol.

The lunch was quite different from her ordinary one which amounted to bites of a turkey sandwich between arguments with Doug at twelve-thirty. And nowhere near as satisfying as spending time with Reed. Their intimacy only increased her desire to know more about him, to invest in him. To join *him* for lunch instead of her current work date.

For weeks the potential career opportunities associated with this meeting and working on Benson's case had been her sole focus. Then Reed stumbled into her favorite coffee bar and blew her well-ordered plans all to hell.

Screaming in restaurants. Sex on the kitchen counter. Not her usual life but one she could learn to enjoy.

"I understand what's at stake for you in this investigation." She did. Now she wanted to get it started and move forward.

"Whatever you need, you tell me. I am not hiding anything."

Uh-huh. Said the man hiding in a private party room meant for ten so no one would see him out in public.

"Thank you. Your cooperation will make the entire process much easier." Not that she believed for one second that Greg would cough up all the documents she needed without threats and a great deal of prodding. "It is important that the investigation be fair and thorough."

"That has not been my experience thus far."

Thus. He had used the word "thrice" right after they sat down. Now thus. Only a guy with groupies hanging all over him and law enforcement on his tail could pull out those word gems and still expect people not to laugh.

"You don't think I'm fair?" she asked.

"You are not the one to whom I was referring."

"Then I assume you are talking about the individual sent to work with you before I came on board."

"Your predecessor seethed with disdain for me and for my life," Greg said while engaging in some seething of his own. "He refused to share a meal with me. I'm sure you can see where that would be a concern for me from the start."

"Maybe he simply preferred not to eat lunch so soon after digesting breakfast." Or hated being forced to eat it in a room dark enough to require a flashlight.

She had not seen another person in the restaurant except when the waitress dropped off her salad and his drinks. Made Gabby wonder if the restaurant was even open yet.

"Please excuse the clandestine tactics. I was trying to avoid a crowd. Privacy is one of those things people dismiss until they lose it," he explained.

"Since the last guy quit, then took a job at a fast food place just to get away from you, I'll keep my complaining to a minimum. Never looked that good in a paper hat."

Greg downed the rest of his drink behind what probably qualified as a smile. On others, it would at best be considered a smirk. "The current burger flipper—not that I believe that, by the way—decided on my guilt without ever seeing a document."

"Then it is time for someone with an open mind and the proper credentials to review your information."

"You?"

"Me."

He cocked his head to the side and shot her an unreadable glance. "I am assuming you know about Mark Benson."

"Ah, him." She wondered when he would get around to this topic.

"My father."

Since she actually read the newspaper and owned a television, she knew. The whole world knew. "It's fair to say he has spent quite a bit of time in the press lately."

The elder Benson's name was connected to fake financial deals, under-the-table payments to lawmakers and the little matter of money-for-guns to some very bad people. She figured Greg knew the list of crimes, so she did not point them out.

"You would never know from the recent level of media coverage, but my father had a life before the criminal charges."

As if being charged was the key to the Benson family misfortune. "I'm sure."

"In the past, the presence of our name in the press related to his charity work."

Good grief. "Uh-huh."

The serious topic contrasted with Greg's carefree model appearance. He dressed in the current style of slim pants and blazer that highlighted his trim physique. Those blue eyes of his, almost turquoise, suggested a mix of innocence and intelligence beyond his thirty-seven years.

On some level she could understand how Greg won over most members of her sex as well as the media. But being handsome and wealthy did not help him stay out of trouble. If anything, it threw him right in the middle of it.

And since she had picked at the only parts of her salad she intended to eat, it was time to circle back around to that topic. "You've enjoyed some not-so-positive press yourself."

The ice cubes rattled in his glass. "That happens when your father is convicted of tax evasion, fraud and conspiracy."

"People think you are involved."

He raised his glass to her in a phantom toast. "Which is why we are having this lovely lunch."

"Were you?"

"I am not sitting in a federal prison, am I?"

The perfect nonanswer from a man claiming innocence while all those around him pointed fingers in his direction. "Neither is your father since he decided to flee the country instead of serve his sentence."

Greg frowned until sharp lines appeared across his otherwise flawless forehead. "Is that a judgment?"

"Just a comment."

"I have heard those sorts of *comments* before and have never appreciated them."

Interesting to know she could offend him. She filed that information away for later.

"I was merely pointing out the obvious. My job is to review the financial paperwork and information you're turning over to the government. To see if you're abiding by the agreement you made with the prosecution and divulging everything."

"You have made up your mind about my family's guilt."

"That is not true."

In her mind, Greg's obvious sin consisted of being the son of a discredited lobbyist who bilked clients and bribed members of Congress. Greg could be a poor little rich boy or fast-talking playboy or both. After poring through his financial information and all of the documents relating to the lobbying firm he ran separately from his father, she'd be able to speak to his guilt or innocence.

She understood what was at stake for him. His move in opening up his personal life would not restore his influence or get back his father's mansion in Georgetown and palatial estate in the Virginia horse country, but the proactive steps could prevent Greg from spending a good portion of his future in a small cell.

"Do you know why I insisted on this meeting? On taking you to lunch over your objection?" He stared into his glass.

Because he was a control freak and a paranoid one at that. "I have a theory."

"Care to share it?"

Not really. She knew his game. She also knew why she sat there across from him when all she wanted to do was crawl back into bed with Reed.

She dealt in confidential information every single day, but only with papers and numbers from the safety zone of her office space. She never dug in. She never got the chance to do the groundwork. She helped to convict people like Greg's father, but the punch of adrenaline that came with working behind the scenes was not enough to keep her satisfied.

"You set up our first meeting here because you like to assess people outside of an office environment," she said, quoting almost verbatim the facts from his file. "You want to see them in something other than business mode in order to determine if you can trust them."

He nodded in a semibow from his sitting position. "You have done your homework."

"Of course." Not that studying Greg proved all that taxing. As far as she could tell, he lacked depth. "Getting him" was sort of easy. Breaking him might be another story.

"Impressive."

"Does that mean you're ready to move forward or are you going to insist on interviewing another expert over brunch first?"

His smile, full of perfect white teeth, seemed genuine for the first time. "Do I sense defensiveness?"

A whole bucket full. "Can you blame me?"

"No," he said. "A smart woman knows when to be on her guard."

Gabby decided right then to make that her new motto.

Chapter 16

After earning the Greg Benson *Seal of Approval* and engaging in another round of mindless chitchat, Gabby left the restaurant. Greg had pushed back three glasses of gin before noon. Seeing that, she moved down the street for a celebration starring coffee instead of liquor.

A cup of whipped cream topping a dash of caffeine called her name. She did not fight the siren.

She settled at a table in the corner. The steady buzz of customers from the morning had died down. Two other customers waited for drinks but left as soon as they grabbed their paper cups from the barista.

When a shadow fell across her table a few minutes later, Gabby looked up expecting to see Doug.

"You?" Her guest took her by surprise.

Not Doug.

"Mind if I sit?" Reed asked.

Seeing him hovering there in his usual dark suit and blue tie threw her off stride. She scrambled to make sense of him being in her usual surroundings.

"Why are you here?"

"You keep saying 'you.' Does that mean you've forgotten my name?"

"It's Tom, right?"

"Close enough." Reed shot her the same grin he used that morning while promoting the idea of clothing-optional breakfast. "We need to work on your welcome skills."

"Have a seat." She pointed the straw at the empty chair, sending beads of cream in a line across the table. "I'm surprised to see you."

"I get around." He leaned down and treated her to a short, sweet kiss.

"I'll remember that. You doing anything in particular while you are hanging around?"

He rubbed a hand over the slight rubble on his chin. "Watching you. Any objections?"

"Not so far." She licked the whip from the end of her straw before it fell to the table and she forever lost the chance to swallow it.

"Nice trick."

"I like to keep my tongue flexible."

He threaded his fingers together and looked at her over the top of his locked fists. "Is that a pass? By the way, I'm hoping for a positive response to that question."

"We are in a coffee shop."

"So?"

"Never thought of you as the PDA type."

"I don't know what PDA is, but feel free to show me." He wiggled his eyebrows in an exaggerated motion.

"Unless I dreamed this morning, I think I already participated in a demonstration."

"That was private. I was thinking more of a public round."

Not her usual thing, but with him nothing seemed off limits. "We'd get arrested."

"Even better."

Except that. "You have a thing for a woman with a criminal record?"

"Focus on the positives."

"Like learning how to make a license plate?"

"You still are not getting the fun we could have." His hand slid over to cover hers. "A backseat. Handcuffs . . ."

Instead of looking at him, she glanced around the near-empty room to make sure they were not broadcasting their intimate details to perfect strangers. All she saw were shelves of coffee bags and cups and one lone barista.

She cleared her throat, hoping to get her mind off of Reed's suggestive comment and inviting touch. "You were explaining why you were here."

"You are obsessed with this topic."

"Won't be once I get a real answer to my question."

"Maybe I could not stay away from you."

A happy zing whipped through her. "Awww, aren't you sweet?"

"I have my moments."

He certainly did. "I'm sure even computer nerds have to go into the office now and then."

He shook his head. "We should talk about this nerd title. Can't we find another way to describe me?"

"If the pocket protector fits . . ." She licked another dollop of whipped cream off the straw, making as much of a show of the move as possible.

From the pickup in his breathing and shifting of his legs under the table, she knew the trick worked.

"Problem?" she asked in her huskiest voice.

"You are ten seconds away from a public display of potentially criminal activity."

The zing picked up speed as it hit her stomach and headed south. "I guess that would be a PDPCA. Interesting."

"That's what I was thinking."

"But I want to finish my drink."

"We can find other ways to get you that high you crave without the caffeine."

She adored this side of him. Turned out breaking up was the best thing for their relationship. "You are changing the subject. Again. That is about the fourth time by my count."

"My topic is more interesting."

He was right about that. "You mean dangerous."

"Is that bad?" He cradled her hand in both of his.

"By definition, I think it is."

"Where is your sense of excitement?"

"At home with the condoms, the bed and the closed door." Which was where she wanted to be.

"That sounds like a challenge," he said as he caressed her palm with his fingertips.

"Later."

He exhaled in the exaggerated way males did right before they gave in and let a woman win an argument. "Women."

"You are stalling. That's a habit of yours."

"Fine." Another put-upon male sigh followed. "My hours are flexible. Getting away was not hard."

"So you decided to brave the traffic and walk around until you happened to see me on the street?"

"I knew you were worried about your work lunch, so I thought I should stop by for moral support."

Sounded like the most unstupid thing she had heard in a long time. "How did you know where to find me?"

"You told me." He lifted her hand to kiss her palm. "Then there's the fact you are within two blocks of your office at the place most likely to find a caffeine addict. The same place I met you."

"See, now. Was that so hard to say? Why make me prod and poke?"

"I like the way you prod."

"Well, whatever the reason, I am happy you tracked me down." To prove it, she leaned over and kissed him, lingering just long enough to hear the tiny growl start in the back of his throat.

The sexy noise was more addictive to her than coffee. After their lovemaking this morning, the sting of their recent breakup faded into the background. Not all the way, but enough for her to give him a second chance. A fact she never spoke out loud to Reed, but she figured he took the hint when she got naked.

Doug and Sondra still did not know. Riding into the office that morning, she worried about what to say. Avoiding the subject turned out to be easy since they were both stuck in a meeting on another case until the time she left.

"Is this a celebration?" he asked. "Damn, I hope so, because I'd like to see you put that straw to productive use."

She threaded her fingers through his. "We might be able to negotiate that."

"You were smiling when I came in, so I assume the meeting went well."

Her need to tell someone of her achievement overtook her. "It did."

"You were worried for nothing."

"Terrified is more like it."

"Why?"

She shrugged. "It's an important job. Doing this one well could mean additional assignments of this nature in the future."

"I don't know what that means."

Which was why she phrased the comment that way. Her future goal focused on less desk work and more fieldwork. Possibly some courtroom work. All of that amounted to more information she could not share with Reed. Not yet.

"Basically, this case is a step to bigger cases."

His eyebrow inched up. "You mean clients."

"No." She pulled her hand away from his and wrapped her fingers around her cup. "Remember how I said I reviewed companies to determine how much they were worth?"

"Yeah."

"Well, that is not really my area of expertise. Most of the time my work is about investigating not valuing. I track information."

"For . . . ?"

She stayed as vague as possible. "Sometimes law enforcement reviews it. Police, prosecutors, that sort of thing. So, I need to be neutral."

"And all of that relates to Greg Benson somehow."

Her cup crackled in her hands. "What?"

"Benson. Criminal. Your lunch date."

People talked about getting hit with a wave of dizziness upon hearing surprising news. Never happened before. Now it had. "How do you know?"

"I saw you with him."

"In the restaurant?"

"In the very small, very dark room in the restaurant. Just the two of you. Door closed." Anger laced through Reed's voice.

She recognized the emotion since it flowed through her with abandon. "You followed me."

"Absolutely," he said without a drop of remorse.

She slammed her cup down hard enough to pop the plastic top right off. "You are not even denying it."

"Why should I?" The what's-your-problem look on his face matched his comment.

"This is my work."

"Benson."

"Not him as much as his finances."

"He is a crook." The more wound up she got, the calmer Reed grew.

She thought about throwing a second beverage in his direction to get a rise out of him. "His father is the felon. Greg has not been accused of wrongdoing."

Reed's eyes widened in a look of disbelief. "*Greg*? You call the guy Greg?"

"That is his name."

"What happened to being neutral?"

"I am."

"What you are is done with this assignment." Reed had the nerve to point at her when he said that.

"What did you just say?"

"Stay away from Benson."

"Excuse me?" When the barista looked at them, Gabby knew she had moved from talking to yelling.

Reed did not suffer from the same problem. He leaned in and pitched his voice low. "I'm serious."

"So was I when I said 'excuse me' which, in case you did not know, really means go to hell."

"Say whatever you want, just keep away from Benson."

She noticed the small stress lines at the corners of Reed's mouth. Despite her fury at his interference, a part of her wanted to be flattered by his change in mood.

"Are you jealous?" She asked, hoping that explained the change.

"Hell, no."

So much for trying to put a positive spin on his actions.

"Then you are being a complete jerk."

Reed did not back down even an inch. "Name calling is not going to change my mind, Gabby."

"Are you sure, because I have a whole list we could go through."

"I'm not trying to bully you—"

"Sure sounds like it. It is not as if you are negotiating or having a conversation. You're ordering."

Reed had managed to touch on the one male characteristic guaranteed to drive her nuts. Being supportive was one thing. Suffocating her was another.

"Gabby, Gabby, Gabby." He tipped his head back and stared at the ceiling. When he looked at her again, some of the fire had left his gaze. "Do you understand what hanging out with a guy like Benson could do to your work reputation?"

"I do not have a choice. He's my job."

Reed's eyes narrowed until all she saw were the dark centers. "So you *are* working for him."

"No."

"But you said—"

"No, you inferred."

"You implied—"

"You blew everything out of proportion and starting making accusations."

Somehow their voices growing louder deflated the fight. Probably because Reed ended by laughing.

"You are exaggerating a bit, don't you think?" he asked.

"No." Okay, a little.

"I am so happy to hear that you've regained your ability to use the word 'no' in every sentence."

"If you ever want to hear me say anything else, you will stop ordering me around, Reed. It is not endearing."

"Enlighten me." He sat back and looked at her as if he expected an explanation.

Not that she owed him one. Not by her calculations. Not when she was ten seconds away from hitting him.

Despite her resolve, she started talking. "My job is to conduct a financial investigation."

"On Benson."

"Again, of his finances."

"Isn't that what I said right before your head started spinning and the vomit flew out of your mouth?"

She refused to laugh at the joke, even though she had to bite down on her bottom lip to prevent it. "What was that thing you said about exaggerating?"

"You know I'm right about this."

"No, no, no." She shot him what she hoped was a smug

smile. She had never really tried smug, so she was not sure. "Thought you might understand it if I repeated the word a few times."

"Let's try it this way." Reed grabbed her cup and moved it out of firing range. "If you are not working for Benson, then who are you working for?"

Now there was a subject she could not discuss. "That is not important."

"I disagree."

"Tough."

"What?"

"Tough."

"Tell me you didn't just say 'tough.' "

"Actually, I said it twice." Smug started feeling pretty good.

"You have got to be kidding."

" 'Fraid not. Guess this is going to be a disappointing day for you."

"But it started so well."

Chapter 17

"Look—"

Reed groaned to drown out whatever argument Gabby planned to deliver. "No conversation starting with 'look' ends well."

"Will you just listen?"

"Will you stay away from Benson?" Reed asked, mimicking her shrill tone.

"No."

He folded his arms across his chest and stared her down. "Then I'm not listening."

"Oh, that's mature."

"So is rolling your eyes at me like that."

A group of giggling girls picked that moment to walk into the coffee shop. Never mind the fact they should be in school, they were too busy talking on cell phones and otherwise praising the teenaged attributes of a boy named Philip while ripping apart some poor thing named Samantha.

One girl's squeal nearly shattered his eardrum. "Kind of loud, aren't they?"

"Yeah, old man."

"I may be old but the parts still work."

"Amen to that." She frowned over at the group before turning her attention back to him. "Tell me something."

"As if I have a choice."

"Did you take a class in being impossible or does it just come naturally?"

"I do not remember hearing any complaints when I brought you food."

"I'm not an idiot. Pizza, muffins—those are sacred. No right-thinking woman would kick out a man bringing treats."

Good to know. Reed stored that piece of information away for later. "And the guy who brought you those delicacies knows what he's talking about when it comes to Greg Benson."

The rumble from her exhale drowned out the teenagers' bickering. "You are not going to let this subject go."

"Nope." Sooner or later she'd break down and answer a question. Reed just hoped he remained sane long enough to see it.

"I'm a CPA, have two advanced degrees and—"

He held up both hands in surrender. "I do not need a recitation of your resumé."

"My point is that I don't need a baby-sitter."

"I was trying to help."

"You were meddling." She made a grab for her coffee, but he held it away from her.

"First, keep your hands off all liquids unless I'm wearing a rubber suit." He deposited the cup on the table behind him. "Second, I will never be wearing a rubber suit."

"Is that the entire list?"

"There's more."

"I figured."

"And, third, tell me the reason behind your ballistic reaction."

She turned the frown on him rather than on the young coffee patrons. "What reaction?"

"It would probably be more appropriate to ask which over-the-top reaction just to be specific, but you are on the right track."

"Keep in mind I can order a new coffee and throw that one at you."

"Thanks for the warning." He scooted his chair back a few inches just in case.

"You won't get another."

"I was talking about your refusal to listen to common sense and stop hanging out with a guy who is under investigation and has a felon father on the run."

"Are we talking about you or Greg?"

"Benson." Reed's teeth snapped together. "Being seen with that guy is a bad move."

"I'm working, not playing, with Greg."

When Reed heard the word "play," his mind zoomed back to their morning lovemaking. Then he heard her say the other man's name for what felt like the hundredth time, and a red haze passed in front of his eyes.

"Stop calling him Greg."

"That's. His. Name." She eyed her abandoned coffee cup. "And since when do you get to order me around?"

"Ease off on the indignation. I came to see if the meeting you were so worried about went well. Seemed to be a pretty romantic thing to me."

"Uh-huh."

Apparently only to him. Showed, once again, how little he knew about women.

Pete and Charlotte would love this story. Which was exactly why neither one of them would ever hear about it.

Reed tried to make his point. "In response to my gallant gesture—"

"Are you kidding with this?"

"—I'm getting an I-Am-Woman-Hear-Me-Roar speech."

She pressed her lips together and made a soft clicking sound. He could see her reach some conclusion. One she was not rushing to share.

"Something to say, Gabby?"

"When you put the argument like that . . ."

"Sounds reasonable, doesn't it?"

The gaggle of kids gathered at the table next to them. When one started singing, Reed wished he had a muzzle strapped to his ankle instead of his gun.

"You win," she conceded. "But talking about private issues in a room full of screaming kids is not my idea of being rational."

More kids came in. The second group won the prize for loud and obnoxious behavior. "Want to go somewhere else?"

"I wish I could, but I need to get back to work."

"I would suggest we sneak back into that room at your office, but I'm pretty sure Clyde would not let me live through a second visit." And Reed did not want Gabby to enter her building and clam up. "Let's walk."

"But I know this song."

The off-key singing disguised whatever the kid next to them was bellowing. "That's a song?"

She winced. "At one time it was."

She stood up and slipped her briefcase strap over her shoulder. With a hand against her lower back, Reed ushered her out of the building and into the cool sunny day.

They dodged the tourists mingling on the D.C. streets. Car horns honked, and a bus came to a screeching halt across the street. With all the noise, he had to wait almost a full block before trying to get an answer.

"Spill it."

She rolled her eyes for about the fortieth time since they had met. "That's subtle."

"Why the violent reaction to my giving a shit about your work?"

The hand on her lower back kept her close and satisfied his need to touch her. If this were any other time, any other circumstance, he would guide her right back home to bed.

"You know how to kill a moment. It is a beautiful day." She tipped her head back and let the sun's rays beam down on her.

"I guess." As a conversation topic, the weather ranked low on his list.

"We should enjoy it."

And he refused to believe it ranked high on hers. "Now who's stalling?"

"That's not fair."

"But it is true."

Her mouth fell open, but she quickly closed it again.

"Okay, yeah. It is," she conceded.

"That's what I thought."

One of the many things he admired about Gabby was her refusal to engage in game playing. When she wanted him, she sent up a signal flare. When he ticked her off, she let him know it. None of the usual guess-what-I'm-feeling bullshit women put men through. Not with her.

Except when it came to her work and the topic of Benson.

"I am not trying to be difficult or even mysterious. It's just that this is a complex situation," she said.

If she thought her life was tough, she should try gathering intel while balancing a bunch of lies and fighting off the need for sex. "You are making this harder than it needs to be. Just tell me why—"

"I was kidnapped." She blurted out the remark, then peeked up at him.

He saw the shy glance just before he tripped right over a

line in the sidewalk. The stumble stopped their walk and had him grabbing her arm in a viselike grip to keep from falling on his face.

"What did you say?"

"You heard me."

He dragged her out of the path of oncoming crowds and into the small park across from her office building. "I'm sure as shit hoping I misunderstood."

"It was years ago. I was a kid. It shouldn't matter."

"Not . . . Gabby, tell me what happened."

"After a bunch of threats and one missed try, a group made good on the promise to take me."

He eased up on his hold before he bruised her sensitive skin. "You can't be serious."

"It is not the sort of thing I'd joke about. Trust me."

"When did this happen? Were you hurt?" Questions piled up in his head and begged for answers. It took every ounce of control to stay calm and not pressure her. Not after it took so long to get her to trust him enough to talk.

"I was fourteen. There was a big thing with cops and a ransom." She stared at the center of his chest, then finished the rest in a softer voice. "Guns and the media."

"Jesus." The thought of her being in danger made everything inside him heat until it spilled over in a boiling rage. "Were you injured or . . ."

"Before it was over, two officers were hit in a shoot-out and the kidnappers were killed."

Reed tipped her chin up so that he could see the emotions lingering behind those wide eyes. "But what happened to you?"

"Did you miss the part where the bad guys died?"

"I'm serious, Gabby."

"I had a few bruises and got knocked around. Other than threats and taunting, the worst part was being terrified I would die. They scared me but never really touched me."

"Are you sure?"

"Yes, Reed." Her fingers brushed over his. "I was gone for about two days and spent most of that time tied up and alone while the guys who took me went back and forth with the FBI on the phone."

"Makes me grateful for FBI procedure."

"Yeah, apparently the negotiating is what trips up most kidnappers."

Reed saw an open bench and sat down with her. He tried to relax the muscles in his arms and the hard clench to his jaw. She was okay. He kept repeating that fact in his head until it seeped into his brain and took hold.

"Are you sure the FBI tracked down everyone involved?"

"Positive." She rested her hands on his chest and looped his tie through her fingers. "The real problem is that the incident impacted everything that came after."

She talked about her kidnapping as if it held all the inconvenience of a bee sting. The same kidnapping that was specifically left out of his file on her. The thing contained not one scrap of pertinent history. A fact he planned to explore as soon as he heard the entire story from her.

The microphone he planted on her blazer that morning had made eavesdropping on her meeting with Benson possible. With the device retrieved and safe in his pocket, he had what he needed on that one. He would assess all of that later. Decide who knew what, and when, and why no one had clued him in.

That was work.

This was personal.

"You were scared, Gabby. That's natural after what you went through."

This time she fiddled with the buttons on his shirt. "I

had bouts of sleeplessness. Got sick. Didn't want to go out."

The need to hold her grabbed at him. He satisfied himself with running his fingers through her hair. "Baby."

"It was a tough ride, but I got over that part. The real problem came with how everyone treated me from there forward." His button held her blank stare. "Like this little porcelain doll that would break at the slightest touch."

"Your family was worried about you."

"They suffocated me. I could not do anything. I wasn't allowed to make any decisions, or go to the mall or do any of the normal stuff kids do. Every aspect of my life was controlled by my parents to the point where I lost the ability to think for myself."

With each word, every description of her suffocating life, she grew more distant. As if talking about her life pushed her deeper into the memory.

"I'm sure they felt normal parental guilt. That they somehow let it happen."

"It was worse than that. The kidnappers took me because of my parents' scientific research. I never blamed them, but they could never accept that piece."

He made a mental note to investigate her parents. "The idea of what could have happened, about what you went through and how it shaped your life is—"

"Horrible."

"Yeah."

"But that is just it." The haze cleared as she stared straight into his eyes. "In some ways, the trauma of the aftermath was worse. My anxiety touched off my parents. They hovered. They set unrealistic boundaries and handed down strict punishments."

"They overreacted."

"I just wanted to be normal."

He ached for her and all she had suffered. "That sort of thing takes time."

"Other kids whispered. Neighbors pointed. My friends scattered. No one wanted to play with the kid who got snatched. Nothing was mine anymore."

He had worked with enough victims during his life to know how the pain could rush back at odd times and mentally cripple them. "Unfortunately, there isn't a handbook for how to deal with a situation like yours. The other kids, well, I'm sure they followed their parents' lead."

"I know all that. I really do." She shifted until she almost sat on his lap. "I worked through everything. Had a great therapist who helped me heal and try to see my parents' point of view."

"Sounds healthy." He was desperate to touch her but still hesitated. Now that she was talking, he did not want to discourage her.

"I refuse to be defined by something that happened a lifetime ago. But . . ."

"What?"

"No one else understands that. It's as if this air of vulnerability follows me or something. Sure, I'm small, but I'm also strong and secure."

"Tell anyone who doubts your abilities to come talk to me."

A smile broke across her lips.

Despite the need to hear her story, to get her to finish, he gave in and kissed her then. He wanted to hold her and shelter her, but he knew she needed space. So, he settled for a brief touch of his mouth against hers.

"Even after all these years, people treat me as if I need to be protected and coddled. Most people don't know, but it still happens."

"Is that always a bad thing?"

She kept talking as if she had not heard his question.

"My parents wanted me to settle down in a nice, safe college somewhere and teach. When I didn't, they took positions out of the country rather than see me in danger."

"That's an odd solution."

"It was their passive-aggressive way of punishing me for my disobedience. That sort of thing worked when I was younger. I could not make them understand my position. I need more action. More excitement."

He heard his words echo back in hers. "Then you might rethink the teaching thing. Have you tried dealing with college kids lately? They're vicious."

"Maybe, but I needed more. My parents spent their lives in labs working on top-secret government programs. Despite the fact their expertise put me in danger, they craved the excitement. Still do. Even now they're off doing research in Northern Africa."

More information not contained in her file. Nothing about her background check matched with what she said now. He knew which version was correct. The one he heard now. He could see it in the sadness around her eyes. Hear it in the firm resolve in her voice.

"They're not crowding you now," he said.

"They don't have a choice. I'm a grownup. I make my own decisions." Then she slid her hand along his thigh, reached down and curled her fingers through his. "But it's not just them. You saw Doug. His protective streak is out of control. Sondra is the same way; she's just more subtle."

"It's natural. They're your friends. They care about you. Well, Sondra does. Who knows what the hell goes through Doug's head."

"And then there's you."

He saw the hit coming but pretended otherwise. "Me?"

"How you acted when I mentioned Greg. The sudden bossiness. Telling me what I could and couldn't do."

Reed waited until a group of businessmen had passed

before he pressed his point. Between the traffic noise and the chatter from the other people in the park, Reed wondered if they should have stayed in the coffee shop.

"Call him Benson. Please."

She slapped his thigh. "Like that, for instance. Why do you care what I call my client?"

"When you say his name I want to kill him." And that was not an exaggeration.

"You're proving my point."

"This isn't protectiveness."

"What is it, then?" Warmth moved back into her eyes.

"I don't know." He wrapped one arm around her shoulders and cradled her hand in his other hand. He could not give them privacy, but he could try to keep their distractions to a minimum.

"Typical male answer."

"From a typical male."

"There is nothing ordinary about you."

"And I'm not slow either." He had played this scene all wrong. He knew that now. "I get it. Me checking up on you felt like a statement on how competent I think you are. It wasn't. I know you can take care of yourself."

"I don't need protecting."

But she did. Just not for the reasons she thought. "Is it so wrong that I want to take care of you? Your size. Your past. None of that matters to me."

"Really?"

Really. Many people would wallow in their victimhood. Most would look for the easy way out. Not Gabby. She demanded respect. Earned it.

The new insight into her personality made him want her more. Made him even more of an ass for tricking her.

"I don't like bossy," she said.

"That's going to be a problem." He slid his hand behind her neck and pulled her a bit closer.

"For you, maybe."

He leaned down and took that kiss he had been dying for. Not a small peck. No. This was a long, drawn-out affair. Wet mouths. Tongue. He gave it all despite the choking exhaust from the passing bus. Even the public display did not matter.

When he finally lifted his head, he saw her glowing face. "I have a deal for you."

"Another one?"

"Double or nothing."

She curled her fingers around the top of his tie and pulled him snug against her. "Shoot."

"You let me in."

"I have."

He laughed. "Understand that being concerned isn't the same as being overprotective. In return I'll tone down the controlling part of my personality."

She shot him a sexy little smile that said yes. "You'll still bring me food?"

"Absolutely."

"Still check in to make sure I'm having a good day?"

He would be watching every move she made, but she did not need to know that. "Only if you promise not to yell."

"I can't make that promise." She kissed him before he could contest her answer.

"And you think men are difficult?"

"Will you let up on the job I have with Greg?"

"No fucking way. Not going to happen, babe. You deal with Benson, you deal with me." On that issue Reed could be totally honest.

"We'll argue about that later."

He winked at her. "Count on it."

Chapter 18

"I was not aware I had scheduled a meeting with you today." Charlotte did not even blink when she opened her office door and found Reed waiting.

"You didn't," he said.

"Well, then, if you will excuse me. I have a great deal of work to do today." With her omnipresent coffee mug in one hand and the other tucked into the pocket of her light gray dress pants, she slipped into her oversized leather chair.

Behind her huge cherry desk, she began sorting through her phone message slips. There had to be a hundred of them, and the light on her phone blinked, suggesting she had voice mails, too.

She clicked on a few computer keys, paged through her in box and adjusted the blinds on the window behind her desk. Basically did everything she could to pretend Reed was not sitting there.

But that would change.

He was prepared to wait her out all day if necessary. Sit there in the drab office with drab beige walls and drab beige carpet and wait. Knowing Charlotte, that could be a wishful estimate. She did everything in her own time and in her own way.

"Was there something else?" She asked the question without looking up from her paperwork.

"Yes."

She finally glanced in his direction. "I am busy here, Reed."

"Not too busy for this." He dumped a slim folder in front of her.

"What are you giving me?"

"The file I got on Gabby for this assignment. The one your office provided."

"Why are—"

"This"—he dumped a second, thicker file on top of the other one, the same one of which he had multiple copies, including one tucked into a drawer in his bedroom at home—"this one is the real dossier on Gabby. The one I should have gotten. The information Pete should have found. The background you should have provided."

"I see."

"That's all you've got to say?"

Charlotte leaned back in her chair and eyed him with a look that resembled respect. Reed knew that was an optical illusion of some sort.

"From the look of the files," Charlotte said, "I am assuming there is something else you would like me to know."

Loads, but he stuck to the most obvious. "I've been screwed."

She shot him her best schoolteacher frown. "There is no need to be crude."

"Fuck that. I want to know why."

Charlotte's mouth pulled into a tighter frown. "That sounded suspiciously like an order."

"Call it whatever you want."

"You should remember where you are." Charlotte laced her fingers together on top of the folder. "You obviously are upset about something."

He had passed "upset" about an hour earlier. "Picking up on that, are you?"

"Rather than shout and force me into a position where I must call security and have you removed from the premises, simply explain what has you so upset this afternoon."

Her. The job. Everything. "Being lied to."

Charlotte did not flinch. "You will have to be more specific."

"See, that's where I get confused." Rather than lose his cool, he mimicked her calm demeanor. She wanted icy, he'd give her icy. "Why not tell the truth? You gave me the assignment."

"That is my job, yes."

"You tasked me with certain objectives." He ticked them off on his fingers. "Investigate Gabby. Figure out her connection to Benson, if any. Get to the bottom of those contacts with her. Discover if she's helping him hide assets."

"Speaking of which, I wonder why you are here and not with Ms. Pearson at this moment."

Keeping an outward show of composure while the acid in his stomach boiled and bubbled was not easy. He did it because he had no other option. "I'm not taking one more step until I get some answers. I want the truth, Charlotte. Tell me what the hell is going on."

"You do not expect me to dignify this outburst, do you?"

"Yeah, I do."

His file lacked all of the details his partner, the supposed computer genius, should have found in his initial research. That combined with the false mission objectives had Reed squirming inside.

Not that he intended to let Charlotte see those doubts and concerns. If she sensed weakness, he would never get to the truth.

"This organization functions under set guiding principles," she said. "As you know, there often is information to which you are not privy. The chain of command cannot function in any other manner."

Reed lifted his chin in the general direction of the files he threw at her. "I know a setup when I walk into one."

"I have a file of my own." She pulled out a drawer on the credenza next to her chair.

"Will that one fill me in on what my *real* assignment is?"

"You tell me." She opened the flap to reveal a five-by-seven photo of Reed. "This one is yours. As you know, you are on probation for your involvement in—"

"Enough."

The woman fought dirty. He knew that fact, but being the target took his disgust to a whole new level.

"The investigation turned up some abnormalities and improprieties in your behavior," Charlotte said.

"You don't need to relive this moment. I was the one in the back of the room getting hammered for shit I never did."

"That is your position." She turned a few pages and began to read. "DSP has a different one."

He refused to defend his work one more time. His former partner broke the law. The guilt by association tactic had gone on long enough. Charlotte continually used it as the excuse for giving him crap assignments and demeaning jobs.

All of those thoughts passed through his head until they came shooting out of his mouth in one defensive comment. "Allen took the money and buried evidence, not me."

When Charlotte smiled, Reed knew he had stepped right where she wanted him to step. "You were his partner. You were with him every day. It is difficult to believe you did not know, at least to some extent, what was happening."

"I didn't."

"You were implicated."

"By a snitch looking for a good deal." And that piece bugged him the most. He gave the job everything and did not get respect in return.

"That may be true, but—"

Reed did not hear anything else she said. He could not think about Allen's betrayal without fighting off a wave of violence.

"You knew about Allen's activities," she said.

"Only at the very end."

"You did not report him. That poor decision made you culpable."

"I was trying to get him to turn himself in."

"Which is the reason you were placed on probation. You were involved. Some in the organization wanted you prosecuted or at least let go. I am the one who insisted DSP give you another chance."

Reed noticed she had somehow turned the conversation into a discussion on his integrity. Time to shift it back. "What the hell does any of this have to do with Gabby?"

"She is your interim assignment. A job where you have the opportunity to prove yourself."

"How am I supposed to do that with faulty information? Hell, Charlotte, you didn't even tell me she worked for the government and held a clearance."

"She works for Financial Solutions. Her company contracts with the government to provide particularized financial research. You work for the Division of Special Projects—"

"I've seen my paycheck. I know where I work." He grabbed the file he had collected on Gabby and shook it in Charlotte's face. "It's all of this other information that stumps me. Why have me investigate Gabby's relationship with Benson when you knew what it was? When Gabby was working for us the entire time?"

"You are shouting again."

"I'm two seconds away from doing something more extreme."

Charlotte's calm faltered as she dug her nails into deep grooves on the arms of her chair. "Do not threaten me, Reed. I vouched for you when superiors in the department questioned your loyalty. You would be wise to remember that fact."

As far as Reed was concerned, loyalty was the trait that got him up to his ass in trouble. After more than six years with Allen Frank as a partner, Reed viewed him as a brother. Allen's actions had blindsided Reed and left him reeling.

Being an only child of a single mother, Reed had a limited family view. His mom tried, but her rewards were a life of poverty, an outrageous work schedule and an early grave. The upbringing left Reed with an independent streak that suited him to his current employment.

"Tell me the truth, Charlotte. You owe me that much. Otherwise, I'll walk out and not look back."

He never issued empty threats. This one, he meant. For the first time in his life, leaving sounded better than staying.

"Where would you go?" She asked as if he would never have any option but working for her.

"Anywhere that's not here."

"You need this job to survive." Charlotte's smirk failed to live up to her usual style. She sensed the seriousness of his statement and they both knew it.

"I need food to survive."

"This work is part of who you are. You have nothing else."

The truth of her words hit him like a slap in the face, but he refused to show it. "This job, the bullshit, the lying, the crap, the degrading assignments, I can do without all of it."

His strong words wiped the smirk right off Charlotte's face. "What do you want?"

"The truth."

After a brief hesitation, she reached into her drawer and took out another folder. "As you know, in an effort to lure Greg Benson out on the gun-running charges and track down his father's current whereabouts, we struck what he believes to be a deal. He thinks his game is working and that he can convince us of his innocence on the more significant charges and earn a bye on the lower ones he admits to committing."

"You're setting him up. I know that part. What I'm asking is where Gabby fits in."

"You have a file. Well, this is my file on your Ms. Pearson."

He did not reach for it when it landed in front of him, but he sure as hell wanted to. His fingers itched to grab it and page through until he knew exactly what was happening.

But he needed to take a stand. "Tell me what's in it."

Charlotte raised her eyebrows. "I believe you can read."

"I'm tired of the games. Just tell me."

Her fingernails dug deeper into the expensive leather. "We needed a novice to work with Benson. He is the jaded sort and flatly refused to cooperate with our previously assigned agent."

Charlotte eased up on the leather long enough to reach for her coffee. After a few sips and a delay that set Reed's teeth slamming together from back to front, she continued. "Your Ms. Pearson wanted an assignment with more, shall we say, excitement."

No red flags so far. "And?"

"Her enthusiasm matched our needs. The fact she is attractive and diminutive in a way that tends to cause men to open up to her was a significant bonus."

In other words, Gabby was disposable. Roadkill. "You're using her."

"Ms. Pearson asked for this placement."

"She wasn't told the truth about Benson or her role."

"No one forced her."

"You're saying she knows about Benson? About our organization? About what's happening in this case?"

"She knows only what she needs to know."

"Which is?"

"That she is on a special assignment with Homeland Security."

"Damn it, Charlotte. You are lying to her."

"Ms. Pearson does not need an in-depth briefing about the Division of Special Projects or your part in it, especially since both items are classified."

That was what he had become to his employer. An item. "What is my part in this little play of yours?"

"To protect Ms. Pearson."

The one thing Gabby did not want from him. "The part where you had me tail her and investigate her was all nonsense."

"Correct. Your true assignment was always to protect Ms. Pearson."

"You just forgot to tell me that."

"Again, you are on probation. I needed to look at your skills and ability to follow orders to determine when, and if, the conditions for your continued employment had been met. Ms. Pearson provided the perfect test for you."

"You used both of us." The words tasted like crap in his mouth.

Charlotte relaxed back in her chair. "Ms. Pearson did

her job. Your inability to follow simple instructions is, however, a concern."

He refused to apologize for figuring out that his assignment was a bogus one. "I want to tell Gabby the truth."

"Absolutely not."

"She deserves to know." Needed to know. Once she did, they could put the lies behind them.

"Ms. Pearson has a job to do. She can do it with the information she now has available to her." Charlotte waited for a moment of stinging silence before going on. "And before you decide to ignore your mandate, remember that you almost destroyed the entire operation the last time you ventured off script and broke up with her."

"The fake script."

"In leaving Ms. Pearson you could have left her without protection from Benson."

"That never would have—"

"You were able to overcome that deficiency."

"I'm an overachiever."

"That is debatable." Charlotte tapped her fingers on his file. "Do not cause a new problem. We needed Ms. Pearson then and continue to need her now."

"You need her to remain clueless." The words snapped out of him.

"Uninformed of the finer aspects. Benson will be able to sense otherwise. Further, he has taken a liking to her. She did her job well."

Whenever he heard Gabby's name in combination with Benson's, pure fury raced through him. This was no exception. "There's no damn way I am letting Gabby stay involved with that guy."

"You are missing one important piece here, Reed."

"Only one?" He opened his hands wide. "Enlighten me."

She dropped the mug on the desk with a thud. "Last I checked I am still your boss."

The only question was whether he would leave before she fired him. "What else am I missing?"

"You." She made a note in his file. "Your propensity to go off on your own is becoming a significant problem. Several of us here at DPS are concerned."

His abilities and intuition were what made him a good agent. He had the medals and commendations to prove it. Leading with his gut and deviating from protocol when needed made his career, saved lives and completed missions.

If being loyal to a fellow agent who lost his way was the death knell for his career, Reed would accept that. This intermediary space where he received partial information while someone baby-sat him would never work.

"What about Pete?" That was the big question on Reed's mind.

The change in conversation took Charlotte off guard. Her blank look faltered for a second before she responded. "He is doing his job."

A typical cryptic Charlotte response that said nothing. What she did not say was more telling than the information she did provide.

"You're big on me turning in partners. Fine. Take a look at Pete. He's the research expert."

"Your point?"

"He was supposed to find out all of this information on Gabby and give it to me. He didn't." Reed's instincts told him Pete was in this hide-the-facts scam of Charlotte.

"I will take care of Pete."

Sure she would, Reed thought. Right after he grew a tail out of his ass.

"Good, because I'm done watching out for partners." He pointed at his file. "You might want to put that down in your notes. From here on out, I work alone."

Chapter 19

"Hey. I thought you were bringing—" Gabby barely got the door open and the first half of her greeting out before Reed was all over her. Hands swept through her hair. His mouth came down on hers, forcing the air out of her lungs and into his mouth.

He stalked her, using his body to back hers up until she stood pinned between the wall and two hundred pounds of hot, hungry male. She refused to question his new way of saying hello. Not after waiting all those weeks for him to make a move.

Now that he was, and he could kiss in a way that made a woman forget her last name, she planned to enjoy every second. And she would do just that once she could think again.

The intensity of the touching and kissing knocked her off balance. Literally. Just as her knees gave out, his lower body locked against hers and held her upright.

There was no mistaking the erection poking her or the need pouring off of him. No nerd issues here.

When his mouth traveled to her neck, she gasped in a breath. "Wow."

"Ummmm."

"Are you okay?"

His head snapped up. "Did I hurt you?"

"No!"

"Are you sure?" His hands moved over her.

He might have meant to check for injuries, but her body received a different message: get ready.

"It's just that—"

"What?" The impatience in his voice highlighted both his concern and his desperation to get her naked.

"You don't usually do this."

He shook his head in confusion. "What?"

"Ravish me." And that was exactly what the greeting felt like.

The confusion cleared from his face. In came the male satisfaction. "Then I've been an idiot."

If he was capable of this much emotion and could unleash it in such a thrilling way, she was all for it. She had waited for some sort of sign from him. Now that she had it, she did not plan to waste it.

"I'm not complaining. Exactly the opposite, actually."

"Good." He started to kiss that sensitive spot under her ear that drove her wild with desire.

"I'm just thinking we should close the door."

He looked around and stared at the entrance to her condo as if he had never seen it before. "Door?"

"You know, so the entire floor doesn't see me strip down and crawl all over you."

"Oh, right." After a hard slam, he came right back to her. "You said something about crawling."

For him she would. That was the sad part. In just a few weeks he had turned her well-ordered and job-driven life into chaos.

"I liked where you were going when you came in. Why don't we go back to that and see where it takes us."

Instead of answering, he tunneled his fingers up and under her stark white T-shirt as he mumbled sweet comments about her hotness. The minute he unhooked her bra and settled his hands against the soft skin of her breasts, they both sighed.

"I want to be inside of you."

The rough edge to his voice set her insides spinning. "I thought you were bringing dinner."

"We'll eat later." He pressed his open mouth over her nipple and sucked on it through the thin cotton. "Much later."

"Damn, Reed. If I had known . . ."

"Yeah?" His grunt vibrated through her shirt, causing her nipple to pucker even harder.

"I would have been meeting you here for lunch every single day."

"Let's make up for lost time now." He walked her backward toward the bedroom.

"A mattress?"

"Too ordinary for you?"

"Seems tame after the kitchen and the shower."

Whatever else she wanted to say got lost in an explosive kiss. The kind that wiped all of the multisyllable words out of her vocabulary.

He kissed and guided, steering her in the direction he wanted to go. The bed. After a few steps, he lifted her off her feet, letting her dangle in front of him and fitting his arousal between her legs.

If there was anything sexier in the world than having a hot guy lose all control, she did not know what it could be. Tremors of desire ran through him. She could feel his muscles strain under his shirt and his fingers tremble where they caressed her backside.

"You are fucking amazing." He whispered the comment against her neck.

"Remind me to invite you to dinner more often." She slipped her shoes off and let them fall to the carpeted floor.

"I'm hoping for more invitations. Lots of them."

The sensual assault did not let up once they hit the bedroom. When he finally lowered her to the floor, he did not wait for her to gain her composure before reaching for her jeans' zipper and tugging.

The soft lighting in the room and pale blue and white colors combined to create a soothing atmosphere. The warm tones and overstuffed pillows contrasted with the red-hot excitement pounding through her.

"From now on, skip the clothes when you come to the door." He sat on the bed and pulled her between his open thighs.

"Naked?" The naughty idea appealed to her.

"Saves time."

Not that the clothing slowed him down one bit. With one steady pull, her jeans dropped to the floor. The lacy black bikini bottoms she picked out just for him followed right behind. He barely gave the sexy lingerie a glance as he threw them over his shoulder.

His attention centered on what he uncovered. "You shaved."

"Waxed."

"Totally clean. There's nothing left here."

"Do you like it?"

He smoothed his fingertips over the bare skin of her pelvis area. "Hell, yeah."

The look of awe on his face filled her with a mixture of giddiness and power. When he followed his appreciation with a deep kiss on the exposed area, her body heated to scorching.

"So smooth."

"Reed . . ."

His tongue dipped down and slipped across her clit. When his forefinger sank deep inside her, the combination of his hot mouth and the friction of his caress kicked off a battle inside her. The way he took the lead and reached out excited her as much as his touch.

But she wanted more.

Him. Naked on her bed. She had dreamed about it for weeks. Now she could live it.

She threaded her palms through his hair and used gentle pressure to pull his mouth away from her center. "Let me."

He lifted his head. "What?"

She did not know what she adored more, the heat pouring off his skin or the way desire clouded his vision. "I want to undress you."

"Really?"

"No."

He fell back on the bed with his arms out to the side. "Have at it, woman."

She had to laugh at his eager tone. "You continue to be the least subtle person I know."

And the sexiest.

"I'm running low on patience, too." He closed both eyes and rested the backs of his hands on her pillow.

Lying there, fully clothed except for his shoes, and with a giant hard-on, Reed made quite a picture. One she would carry with her until the next time she dreamed about him.

"Since you've assumed the position, I'll move a bit faster."

A small smile crossed his lips. "About time you came to that conclusion."

"Oh, I plan to come. To make you come."

One of his eyes popped open. "Could you be any hotter?"

She decided right then to skip the foreplay and move

right to the main event. No caresses and getting him ready. No skimming her hands up his legs as she watched him grow bigger and more excited.

She wanted all of that.

Later.

With her legs straddling his and her bare body pressing hard against his clothed thighs, she cupped his bulge in her hands. His weight filled her palms.

"You're ready for me," she whispered against him.

His head fell back, exposing his long neck. "Damn, woman."

She leaned forward, letting her chest fall against his and her mouth linger over his jaw. "You ready to come?"

"In about two seconds."

"I'm betting you can last a bit longer than that."

"Not at this rate." He captured her mouth in a kiss then. "I don't have any control when it comes to you."

Desperate to touch him, her hands moved to his zipper. She slid it down and rearranged his considerable length to keep from catching him in the teeth. The screeching sound ended with his harsh moan as she cradled his erection, skin on skin.

"Harder," he said.

His gaze locked on her hand. As she skimmed with her palm, he fought to keep his eyes open. He hovered on the edge. She could see it in the strain across his shoulders. Feel it in his racing heartbeat.

She wanted the hovering to give way to flight. She dipped her head, watching his hands fist on either side of the pillow when she took him in her mouth.

"Oh, damn . . ." His head fell back, choking off the rest of his sentence.

"Do you like this?" She licked her tongue up his length to the tip, circled him in a wet sweep, then traveled back down again. With every pass of her tongue his hips lifted higher off the bed.

The fidgeting and groaning seemed to be his way of begging her to push his body farther into her mouth. She did not fight his silent request. Instead, she pulled him deep into her hot mouth. Sucking and licking until his forearms tensed and his shoulders lifted off the bed.

"Now, baby. Now."

She could taste him on her lips. Smell his earthy scent. Feel his legs clamp down in a search for release. Everything about him drugged her into a heavy state of sexual intoxication.

She bent down and met him halfway in a breath-stealing kiss. Lips. Mouth. Tongue.

No more waiting. She reached out her arm and blindly slapped against the mattress. After a few tries, she smacked her knuckles against the nightstand. She stopped kissing long enough to pull out the drawer and grab a condom. Her hands ripped at his tie and shirt while he rolled it on.

Then his hands started wandering over her again. His fingers found her wetness. "You're ready for me."

"Always," she whispered.

Before she could take another breath, he lifted her hips and slid her body down on the tip of his erection. Opening and swollen, she yearned for him to fill her. When she lifted her chest and sat back on her knees, gravity pulled her down. His hands on her hips did the rest.

"Ride. Me." He forced the words out through rough gasps.

"Are you sure?"

"Baby, do it."

With his control at the edge, she took over. She pinned his arms back against the bed and let her freed breasts bounce in front of his face. Every time he tried to lift his shoulders off the bed and capture a nipple, she sat back, taking him deeper inside.

The gentle tug-of-war turned harder. Faster. She took over, setting the tempo her body needed to pass from full to pleasure.

When he finally collapsed against the bed in defeat, she set the speed. Plunge after plunge she lifted her body off his and then sank down again. His head twisted, and his fists clenched and unclenched under her hands. The more he moved, the faster she bucked on top of him.

His legs shifted until the fabric of his pants tickled the backs of her thighs. "You're killing me."

She clamped her thighs tight against his outer legs and clenched her inner muscles. "Better?"

"Holy—"

"Or this?" She lifted until they almost separated, and then pushed down again. This time nice and slow, inch by inch, until his body shook with need.

This time her plan backfired. Instead of testing the limits of his control, she lost her own. No longer able to hold back the heat pulsing and building inside her, she let go.

With one final plunge, she clenched her lower body until the coiled spring inside her broke. On instinct, her body jerked and her hips shifted forward. Sunbursts exploded behind her eyes as she gave in to a shout of relief.

Tremors shook her body as Reed started some bucking of his own. She fell against his damp chest, but the sensations continued to spark. His cock flexed and moved inside of her, making her blood pound in her lower half.

His turn.

She slipped her hands between his back and the mattress. With her palms on his bare backside, she pulled him deeper inside her. The move sent a shudder racing right under his skin.

"Gabby!" His shout rang in her ears as his orgasm rumbled through him.

Gabby's last thought was that she had found something she craved more than food.

Chapter 20

The scent of their lovemaking filled the bedroom and lingered on the comforter beneath them.

As Reed inhaled the sweet smell of her arousal, then opened his eyes and glanced down the length of their entwined bodies, he noticed something else. "I'm still wearing my pants."

She lifted her head off of his chest and followed his gaze. "And your shirt."

"And tie." He loosened it as he spoke.

"And just about everything else."

"We've established that I'm still fully dressed." He would have thought the material would catch fire and burn off during their lovemaking.

She brushed her fingers across the stubble on his chin. "So you are."

"And you still have your shirt on." He dragged his hand up her back and under her shirt until he found the loose band. "And your bra."

"You were in a bit of a hurry."

"Call me determined."

She dropped back down to rest against him. "You certainly were energized."

Driven was more like it. Between Charlotte's actions

and all that talk about Gabby, all he wanted to do was get out of the office and back to her. By the time he reached her front door, his control had snapped, and pure need took over.

"I'm not myself around you." He spent a lot of time lying to people, but that part was true.

"When you change your mind about introducing sex into a relationship, you don't do it half-assed."

Little did she know there was no change involved. He wanted her from the minute he saw her. After a few initial sessions of heavy petting, he knew taking her to bed would be fantastic. The only thing that stopped him for any period of time was the half ounce of decency that still ran through him.

That had evaporated the day before. He could no sooner stop touching her than he could walk away from her and leave her vulnerable to Charlotte's plans and Benson's moves.

"I was a man on a mission."

She sat up and leaned over him with an elbow pressed against his stomach. "Then mission accomplished, big boy. That was amazing."

There it was again. Instead of hiding her enjoyment and playing coy, she put herself on the line. Told him the truth.

Something he did not do. Could not do.

Every instinct and measure of common sense screamed for him to tell her the truth. Screw protocol, his job and clearance level restrictions. She deserved to know the truth about the danger associated with her current assignment.

The real reason he dropped into her life.

Well, the initial reason.

He stuck around for more than the job satisfaction. He did not fully understand it, but he knew something else lingered there. For whatever reason, he was not ready to leave her.

Not yet. Soon, yes. Not now.

But he wanted to know she was safe first. "Have you ever thought about doing something different?"

"Using the bed was pretty different for us."

"Not that. I meant work." He soothed his palm up and down her bare arm.

He could feel her smile against his chest. "Not that again. I'm telling you, I'm safe with Greg."

"I've asked you not to call him that."

"And I've told you that's his name."

Reed closed his eyes and struggled to find the right words. After a lifetime of living on the edge, he knew what this sort of career could do to a person. If she was not careful, her need for an adrenaline high would change her. Steal a bit of her soul and smash her defenses until lying and subterfuge seemed normal.

Her past, living with everyone else's expectations and fears, made her think she needed to prove something. He knew the reality. She just needed to live her life. Whatever she thought she needed and hoped to gain from her job would elude her.

He had been there, lived that life. His goals now boiled down to surviving. He wanted Gabby to experience more.

Hell, if he could go back and undo some of his decisions, he would. The boring life he abandoned sounded damn good right now. So did the idea of settling down with Gabby night after night. But he had veered from that road long ago. He had laughed off the idea of a comfortable life when he was younger.

That opportunity could never happen, not now and not for him, but he could save her. Gabby hated when people tried to save her. Everyone rushed in to baby her, even though she was perfectly capable of finding her own way. Her drive to prove them all wrong shaped her life. She didn't see it, but he did. Turning her around and away from danger became his new goal.

He brought her hand to his lips and kissed her knuckles one at a time. "Ever think of walking away?"

"From?"

"Your job, the pressure, the research. You know, going off somewhere."

"Like where?"

For him the destination did not matter. The change did. "Anywhere."

"Why, Reed, are you having a midlife crisis?"

"I'm a bit young for that."

"Age is a state of mind."

"So is excitement." He tickled the back of her hand with his tongue. "Just seems to me you've spent a lot of time trying to overcome something that happened to you years ago."

"Exactly, and I'm ready to move on." She kissed him on the cheek as if to congratulate him for understanding her. "Getting this assignment helps me do that."

"Walking into danger won't give you what you want."

"I look at it the other way. Sitting behind a desk doesn't give me what I need."

"You sound sure." Reed felt equally convinced she was wrong on this.

"I am."

Her desire for a way in appeared as strong as his desire for a way out. The frustration over the job and Allen's situation exhausted him. Reed refused to admit he was in the middle of some sort of life crisis. He preferred to view it as coming to his senses.

"Any chance you ordered food?" she asked as she slipped the tie from around his neck and wrapped it around his wrist.

"No. Thought I'd try this visit without food."

"That's a shame."

Rather than try to lure her back into a serious conversation, he gave in to the moment. He would find a way to convince her. In the meantime, he'd revel in the comfort he felt with her.

"If I didn't know better, I would say you want me for my take-out abilities."

"Well, sure, that's part of it."

He flipped her onto her back and leaned over her. Before she could shift away, he slipped the knotted tie over her wrist. "What's the other part?"

"Not telling."

He dragged her arm up the bed and fastened the tie to the bedpost. "I'm betting it's my bedroom skills."

"Those aren't half bad, stud."

"Gee, thanks."

She lifted her other arm to the top of the bed. "If it's any consolation, you were pretty impressive in the kitchen, too."

"I guess that would explain all of your screaming in there the other morning."

"And the shower . . ."

The memory touched off his desire for another round. "Wait until you see what I can do with the couch."

"Maybe we should save that for tomorrow." Her stare bore through him as if she was trying to send a silent message.

Shame he was too stupid to figure it out. "I do have other plans for *this* evening. I'll just need another tie."

She pointed to the chair on the other side of the room and the robe belt sitting there. "There."

"Now you're talking."

"But, a woman can only handle so much sex without refueling."

"Here I am tying you down, ready to make you do my bidding, and you're stuck on food." He nibbled on her neck. "You have a one-track mind."

"Here's a subject change for you." She tilted her head to give him easier access.

"Sounds ominous, and by that I mean damn scary."

"Not at all. I was just thinking that tomorrow, instead of trying my couch maybe we could try yours."

He continued to kiss her but knew she had more to say. "When?"

"We could always meet at your place for lunch tomorrow and try out some of the rooms there."

Not her most subtle hint. She made the suggestion as if she had been saving it for the right moment.

He balanced on his elbow and stared down at her. "Why, Ms. Pearson, are you asking to see my sketches?"

"Are you an artist?"

"Not even a little."

"But it is strange, don't you think?"

He went back to kissing. Her neck proved just too delicious to ignore. "Be more specific."

"You've been inside me, but I have not seen the inside of your house. Seems like sort of a basic thing."

"Let's talk about the inside you part."

This time she pressed her head into the pillow to evade his neck kisses. "I'm serious."

"So am I." As far as he was concerned, being inside her was a damn near sacred subject.

"Is there something I shouldn't see in your condo?"

"Your place is nicer. No underwear on the floor." He glanced over at the black puddle of lace by his shoes. "Well, not usually."

Her free hand dropped from his arm. "Forget it."

The way she looked away and stared out the window made him smile. "You are welcome to my house, and especially in my bed, any time at all."

Her huge eyes filled with surprise. "You're sure?"

"Yes."

"Because I'm not the sort of woman who always has to get her way."

He rolled his eyes. "Yeah, you are."

"Not always just usually."

"How 'bout a nooner tomorrow?"

She used that free fist to punch him in the shoulder, but her smile came back with full force. "That's not very romantic."

He wiggled his eyebrows. "You say that now, but wait until you see what I have planned for lunch at my house."

"I hope it includes food."

"Always. I'm not stupid."

Chapter 21

Gabby tried to concentrate on the stacks of e-mails and bank documents spread out on the conference room table in front of her. Sondra's intense staring made the task difficult. She had spent the last hour ignoring Benson's personal and business finances in favor of paper shuffling and sending exaggerated sighs in Gabby's direction.

"Problem?" Gabby asked when she could not take one more second of the dramatics.

"No."

"Good, why don't we—"

"Unless that smile plastered on your face is permanent."

So, Reed was the issue. Sondra's attitude changed the day she met him. She had not been civil since.

Gabby knew the problem without asking. And she definitely did not intend on asking. If Sondra had something to say, then she needed to spit it out.

"When did you become anti-smile?" Gabby asked.

"When I figured out the guy who put that sappy look on your face is the same guy who broke your heart and dumped you a few days ago." Sondra tapped her pen against the arm of the conference room chair.

"He did not break my heart." Gabby preferred to leave her heart and every other body part out of the conversation. "You certainly changed your position on Reed all of a sudden. You're the one who told me to make a move."

"Sure, but I—"

"If I remember correctly, you said I should jump on him." The best advice she had received in years, Gabby thought.

The tapping stopped. "I didn't—"

"I think the phrase you used was 'let him work his nerd magic on you' or something like that."

Sondra lifted her chin in what Gabby assumed was a look of defiance. "I don't recall making those statements."

"You did."

"Possibly."

"You sound like Doug." Gabby made the comment, then mentally ducked.

"What does that mean?"

Gabby waited for the pen to come flying in her direction.

"The two of you have something to say about Reed, something that's bothering you, but you are not sharing. Oh, I'll figure it out. It would just be easier if you filled me in." Gabby hesitated for effect. "Since you are my best friend and all."

"The guilt strategy doesn't suit you."

Never had. Gabby depended too much on honest, straightforward talk to get bogged down in all the games. "It was worth a shot."

"If you say so."

Gabby moved the papers to the side and grabbed for her own pen. "Are you going to tell me what has you so upset?"

"I'm not upset."

"You look it."

"I'm worried."

"Use whatever word you want, but tell me what the problem is."

Sondra hesitated before talking. "I think you should take things slower with Reed. That's all. I'm worried about you."

Gabby felt the air rush out of her indignation. "I appreciate that. I really do."

"Reed dumped you a few days ago. I don't know why he's back—"

"Because he made a mistake and realized it."

"—and neither do you."

A tiny thread of dread moved through Gabby. "You think something sinister is going on? You've seen his file. Heck, you compiled the thing."

"And read it."

"Then you know he runs a computer company. He's never done anything wrong or illegal as far as I can tell."

"That's what the paperwork says."

"So, what's the problem with giving him another chance and seeing where this goes?"

Sondra stared at her for a second; then her shoulders fell as fast as the corners of her mouth. "Oh, hell."

Uh-oh. "What?"

"Doug's right. You *are* sleeping with him." Sondra sounded less than thrilled at the realization.

This from the same woman who pushed the idea of Reed as a potential bedmate from the minute Gabby mentioned him.

For a second Gabby considered denying the entire thing, but why bother? She was a grownup. A woman with needs. Nothing to be ashamed of.

"I am. So what?"

"Damn it." Sondra buried her head in her hands and mumbled something Gabby could not hear.

"What is wrong with you? You're the one who kept lecturing me about sex being natural and healthy, and how I should enjoy myself. Blow off steam."

"And you listened to me? What do I know about men?"

"More than I do."

Sondra shook her head again. "This is worse than I thought."

Gabby pushed Sondra's hands away from her face and forced her to look up. "What are you talking about?"

"You love the guy." Sondra's dark mood matched her dark hair and dark eyes.

"I do not."

Did she?

"This isn't about a sexual release. I can see it in the way your face grows all pink and shiny when you say his name." And Sondra looked repulsed by the idea. Even screwed up her lips as if she tasted something bad.

"That does not happen."

"You actually care for him. Really care."

"You think that I . . . that we . . ."

Sondra's shoulders seemed to shrink. "I'm right, aren't I?"

"Of course not." The words shot out of Gabby's mouth on instinct, but she stood by them.

She did not love Reed. She could not love a guy she had only known for about a month. That would not make sense. Not be responsible or mature or . . .

Damn, she did love him.

Or she was starting to.

Wanting to be with him. Craving the sound of his voice. Missing his smile and joking when she did not see him all day.

How the hell had that happened?

Panic flashed through her. Love? The plan was to have a little fun but not get involved. Her life did not have room for more than that right now. Not when her career balanced on the edge of a new direction. An exciting one she had been planning on since her first day at Financial Solutions.

Her work was her life. It meant everything. Was all she ever thought about.

The wrongness of her career thoughts hit her. All of those things about her life and her priorities were true, or they had been until Reed came along. He fulfilled her need for a thrill. Made the special assignments seem unnecessary.

"Gabby, we need to talk about this."

She needed to think, but not with Sondra. Not now. She had to talk with Reed first. Get a sense of what he wanted from her and why.

"I can't," Gabby mumbled more to herself than to Sondra.

"We could go to lunch—"

"I have plans."

"With Benson?"

"Reed. I'm meeting him."

"Cancel." Sondra snapped out the response.

Skipping on Reed was out of the question. Gabby knew she had to see him now. Had to get to the bottom of this . . . whatever "this" was between them.

She glanced up at the clock. "Too late. I need to get to his house."

Sondra froze while holding her pen straight up in the air. "His house?"

"Yeah."

"Right now?"

Love was not Gabby's only concern all of a sudden. "Yeah, why?"

"You can't."

"I'm pretty sure I can." Gabby saw the wide-eyed panic on Sondra's face. Sondra never panicked. Never faltered. She was rock-solid. Except for right now. "No more crap. What is it?"

Sondra nibbled on her bottom lip. "We have a new problem."

Gabby could tell they had walked into problem territory from the paleness of Sondra's face. "Tell me."

Sondra bit down hard on her lip this time but stayed quiet.

"I can tell this is really bad." Gabby just didn't know what "this" was.

"Doug's there."

Gabby shook her head a few times, but the explanation stayed the same. "At Reed's house?"

"Yes."

Doug went to see Reed. That could not be a good thing. Somehow Gabby refrained from lunging across the table and shaking her good friend and boss. "For God's sake, why?"

"Well—"

"And this had better not be one of those things where Doug thinks he's protecting my virtue. If so, I will kill him. You have been warned."

"We need to get there." Sondra was up and moving. She grabbed her blazer and cell phone and headed for the door.

Sondra did not run scared over Doug's antics. This went way past simple nosiness and concern.

"Tell me why Doug is at Reed's house."

"We have to get over there first."

"Why the rush?"

"It's the only way to keep them from killing each other."

Bad. Very, very bad.

Chapter 22

That something was wrong hit Reed the minute before he crossed the threshold of his small two-bedroom house. The "before" instead of the "after" gave him a slight advantage.

So long as his unwanted visitor was not lingering on the other side of the front door, Reed could enter without a sound and possibly get the jump on whoever was hiding there. He tested the knob. Locked and no signs of foul play.

He slid the key in and pushed the door open as slowly as he could. Glancing around the family room, he saw everything looked the same as when he left this morning after stopping by from Gabby's house to shower, shave and change.

Sneakers and gym bag in the corner. Yesterday's suit draped over the sectional. All cabinet doors and windows closed. Nothing stolen or broken. Despite that, something felt wrong. Almost smelled off.

He slipped the gun from his shoulder holster, pleased he had taken the time to strap it on before he left for work. Listening for sounds, any noise at all, he crouched behind the couch and tried to get his bearings.

Bright sunlight shone through the windows, eliminating

any shadows and potential hiding places. He could see every inch of his family room from this location. That left the coat closet behind him as the only place to hide in the room. The way he wedged the front doorknob against the closet's guaranteed he would hear it if anyone came out of there.

The counter blocked his view of most of his kitchen. Stainless steel with all of the newest appliances, and all he used the place for was to make coffee. Seemed like a waste but it also meant plenty of reflective surfaces to detect an intruder. Any movement and he would have about two seconds to put a plug in the chest of anyone who came up shooting.

That left the bedrooms and bath. His bet was on the bedroom. His bedroom.

For a second he wondered if Gabby had come by early to surprise him. A sexy idea but he discounted it. He knew her scent. That soft rush of flowers that greeted him when he pressed his mouth against her neck.

If she were here, he would know it. Would smell her. Sense her. This was someone else.

His instincts screamed for him to rush in and take down whoever lurked in the bedroom. Question was what the person wanted. Possibilities ran through his head.

The scene struck him as being beneath Benson. That guy would never get his fingernails dirty with a simple home invasion. Not when he could bilk millions and run to Bimini.

The other possibility centered on someone from Reed's past. That left a lot of suspects since his work history consisted of a stint in the FBI, then over to Homeland, then finally to DSP with several investigations and arrests in between.

He crept toward the hall to the bedrooms, careful not to

step on any of the floorboards he knew from experience would creak under his weight. Glancing around the door frame, he spied his blue comforter, white walls, dark guy furniture but nothing out of place.

Except his dresser drawer, the one where he kept the extra copy of Gabby's file in a fireproof safe. It stood open probably no more than the width of a pinkie finger. That was all Reed needed to clue him in.

From his vantage point, Reed knew there were only two places the visitor could be. One was his closet, which stood open out of habit. The other was—

He slammed against the open door as hard as he could, crashing into whatever hid on the other side.

"Fuck me!" A clink like the sound of metal hitting the wood floor came after the shout.

Before the perpetrator could regain possession of whatever he dropped, Reed slammed into the door again. The move gave the guy another smack with the doorknob and knocked him into the far wall.

"Damn it, nerd, knock it off."

Reed knew that angry voice. Had sparred with the guy just the other day. "Doug?"

"No shit, asshole, move back so I can get out of here."

Reed eased up until Doug reached down for whatever he dropped.

Reed pointed the gun at Doug's head. "I'd stop right there if I were you."

Doug froze halfway to the floor. "What the hell are you doing with a gun?"

"Seriously considering shooting you." Or at least scaring him for a few minutes.

Doug scoffed. "Lower your weapon."

Reed put his foot on Doug's gun and dragged it out of reach. "Not going to happen."

"You're out of line."

"This is my damn house." Reed tightened his grip on his gun to prove it.

Doug's hands shot into the air. "I'm not a threat."

"Kind of feels like you are. Most people knock. Very few break in and search the place carrying a weapon."

"Speaking of that, put yours down and we'll talk this out."

"No." Reed kicked the door shut, trapping them both in his bedroom but giving Doug a bit of breathing room.

"About time."

"Be happy I didn't hit you again." And Reed had seriously considered it. "Get up."

"I am unarmed."

"As if I give a shit."

Doug exhaled. "I'm a government agent. You shoot me, you go to prison."

There it was. The admission. The only question was which government agency. "And I'm the Queen Mary."

"Your sexuality aside—"

Reed waved the gun in Doug's face. "Do not tempt me."

"I am going to kick your—"

Reed nudged Doug's cheek with the muzzle. "How this works is that I can shoot someone who breaks into my house with a weapon to burglarize the place."

"I didn't steal shit."

"Because I stopped you by holding this big gun to your head." He shoved it against Doug's temple again as a reminder of who was in charge.

"You clocked me with the doorknob." The red mark right below Doug's temple swelled and turned purple as they stood there.

"That's going to hurt like a son of a bitch." The thought pleased Reed.

"Already does," Doug muttered under his breath, along with a sentence consisting mostly of profanity.

"Tell me which government agency you work for."

Doug hesitated. "None."

"You said it earlier."

"I lied to get you to back off."

"Lie a lot, do you?" Reed asked.

"I'll say yes since you're the one with the gun."

"You had one until I took it from you."

"I dropped it."

"Uh-huh. You get confused in the middle of doing a tax return and come over here and burglarize my house instead?" Reed picked up Doug's gun and released the clip.

"Fancy move for a computer nerd." Doug settled his hands on his hips and threw his head back with a groan. "About that, you sneak around like a guy who's had some sort of training, and then there's that safe in your drawer."

"You have a point?"

"You are too slick and well-trained to be a home vigilante."

"Wait until you see what a good a shot I am."

Doug laced his hands behind his head and shot Reed a fierce scowl. "You're either a cop or someone being chased by the cops. Which one is it?"

"Interesting deductions from an accountant." Reed opened the door and motioned for Doug to take the lead into the family room.

"How 'bout you stop pointing that thing at me."

"When you have the gun, you can make the rules. Right now, I am the one in charge." Reed yanked on the other man's arm to get him moving.

No way he trusted Doug to act like a good boy and follow all of the rules. For that reason, Reed wanted the man seated and right where the gun could reach him.

Reed marched his prisoner into the family room and shoved him onto a chair. "Give me one reason I shouldn't drop you right now."

"I'm stronger."

"Not than my bullet."

Doug stretched out his arms and settled back into the cushions. "You are not going to shoot me."

"Keep your hands behind your head."

Doug obeyed, even as he looked around the room, likely for something to use as a weapon against the gun aimed at his head. "It would upset Gabby if you touched me."

"She would get over it."

"We have a relationship."

Reed felt the sting of jealousy hit him with Doug's words. "I'm betting you are pretty damn forgettable."

"You ready to tell me why a computer nerd carries a gun?"

Reed sat on the arm of the couch and loosened his tie. If Doug decided to make a move, Reed planned to be ready and not hamstrung by a suit. "Home invasion is a problem in this part of town."

"You live four blocks away from the Potomac and right next to George Washington University. Not exactly a high crime area of D.C."

"You'd think, but look what I found crawling around my bedroom when I came home today."

"About that, do you ever work?"

"When I need to."

There was an unwelcome reminder. In another half hour Doug would not be his only guest. Explaining this to Gabby would be impossible.

"Yeah, well, I thought you would be *needing* to today. Guess not."

What Reed needed was a plausible explanation, but nothing came to him. "I should just shoot you."

"Better yet, let me do it." Gabby ignored Reed and the gun and the men waging a war of testosterone right in front of her and walked up to Doug. Her knees touched her coworker's as she stared down.

"You're early." Reed figured he would get that in before everything went to hell.

"Give me one reason I shouldn't smack you." Gabby's flushed face and tight fists suggested that she could perform the job with her bare hands any second.

For a second, Reed thought things were looking up. "I'll volunteer for the job."

Doug took the defensive and started pointing at Reed. "He's the one with the gun."

"It is his house."

"And put your hands back on your head," Reed added before he lost complete control of the situation.

"Is that necessary, Reed?"

From the sound of Sondra's voice, Reed knew the truth—all control was lost. He glanced over at Gabby. "Damn, woman, did you bring the whole office with you?"

"I came to help you," Gabby explained.

"With Doug?"

"Yeah."

Her lack of faith in his skills riled his masculine gene.

"I practically killed the guy with a doorknob. Didn't need a weapon or help."

"It was a lucky shot," Doug insisted.

"Is Clyde lurking around here, too? That guy I consider a threat." A big, mean threat.

Gabby turned to Reed. "Look—"

"Oh, here we go." Reed lowered the gun, knowing whatever chance he had at straightening this situation out without compromising the mission had left the building long ago.

"What?" Gabby asked.

"I think I prefer it when you say no all the time."

Because when Gabby used "look" in that haughty tone, Reed knew he was a dead man.

"Take the gun from him, Gabby," Doug said.

"No."

Reed knew he should have shot Doug when he had the chance. "Damn right, no."

Gabby unleashed her anger on her coworker. "Reed has every right to be upset. What you did was unforgivable."

"Yeah, Doug." Reed slumped down on the couch with his elbows on his knees and the gun pointed toward the floor.

"What did I do?" Doug asked.

"Broke into his house. Came over here acting all protective, as if you have any say in who I sleep with."

Doug started to rise off the chair until Reed raised the gun.

"You're sleeping with him?" Doug asked. "I thought we talked you out of that."

Reed tugged on the bottom of Gabby's blazer since it was right at eye level. "We're voting on that sort of thing now?"

"No."

"Wish someone had told me. I would have prepared a speech. Lobbied for sex. Maybe done a slide presentation."

Gabby looked at Reed as if he had crossed into idiot territory. "Shut up."

"Better yet, everyone calm down." Sondra sounded composed but looked ready to jump out of her skin. Her olive complexion showed signs of stress, and her long hair lacked its usual polished appearance. "Reed, why do you have a gun?"

"Isn't the bigger question why Dougie Boy was creeping around my house?"

"I did not creep. Did not steal anything. And sure as hell did not get hurt by some nerd using a doorknob."

"You were not invited either. That's a big point you seem to forget."

Gabby sat next to Reed and ignored everyone else in the room. "Since when do you have a gun?"

Reed knew the mood was about to change. Despite how they ended up here, he was about to become the bad guy. "Always."

"Why?"

Doug shifted over to make room for Sondra next to him on the arm of the chair. "And don't try to feed her that lie about this being a dangerous neighborhood. You are not a computer nerd. Nerds do not have weapons."

About time someone noticed the nerd title did not fit. Shame it had to be Doug since Reed hated to credit that guy with anything. "We all agree I need a new nickname. That's something."

"Actually, you're not a computer anything." Despite the slightly ruffled hair, Sondra appeared every inch of the in-control boss Reed guessed her to be. Straight back, no-nonsense talk. Backbone of steel.

"Jerk is more like it," Doug muttered under his breath but just loud enough for the others to hear.

"What are you guys talking about?" Gabby asked.

"Nothing," Reed said.

"His lying to you," Doug said at the same time.

Gabby glanced from Doug's blank face to Sondra's sympathetic one before turning her attention back to him. "Reed?"

"It's complicated." Reed figured that covered all of it.

"While you're explaining things, why not also tell us why you stole Gabby's badge a few days ago." Doug leaned forward and shot Reed a triumphant smile.

"What?" This time Gabby's question sounded more like a shriek than a word.

Shit. When everything went to hell, e-v-e-r-y-t-h-i-n-g went to hell.

"Yeah, nerd, we saw that. The tape is missing, but Sondra and I witnessed the entire thing. Even caught a few images as evidence. You didn't find those before you figured out how to erase the evidence, did you?"

"Doug, you are enjoying this far too much." Sondra cleared her throat in what Reed assumed was her signal to Doug to shut up. "Reed, why not—"

"My badge?" Gabby would pick that minute to catch up with the conversation.

Reed knew exactly when the pieces started falling into place. From ten inches away he could feel the heat of her anger radiate off of her.

"Nerd took your badge when he felt you up in the conference room."

"Doug, stop." Sondra's warning came too late.

"You took my badge?"

"I thought we decided the nerd tag was wrong." Reed shifted his gun to the hand away from Gabby. Not that he would ever hurt her, but he worried she might engage in some violence of her own any second.

"Answer me." She snapped out the command.

Yeah, she deserved that much. More actually, but at least he could fill in some of the gaps. "Gabby, there's something you need to know."

"Apparently."

"I am not exactly who you think I am." Reed snuck a peek in Sondra's direction to make sure she had not found a gun of her own. "I'm not a computer guy."

Gabby stood up in a move that felt like slow motion. "Who are you?"

"Your bodyguard."

Chapter 23

It was not every day a woman figured out the man she loved was nothing more than a lying, scum-sucking son of a bitch.

The realization hit Gabby and then kept on smacking her around until her bruised heart cried for mercy. There in front of her friends, in the middle of Reed's house, she wished the floor would open up and swallow her.

Better yet, it should open up, then chomp down on Reed. Chew him up into tiny bite-sized pieces and spit him out again.

And after she confided in him. After she explained her history and insecurities, went on and on about her lifelong fight against being treated like a child, and he did just that.

Bodyguard. Protection. Yeah, if Reed wanted to piss her off, that was the way to go.

The weasel picked that point to speak up. "Gabby, are you okay?"

Peachy. "Just regretting I rushed over here to make sure Doug didn't kill you."

"I'm fine." Reed reached his hand over and took hold of hers.

She jerked away from his touch. Even thought about slapping him. "I don't know what you are or who you are."

"That's what I was trying to figure out when he hit me

with the door," Doug grumbled under his breath and engaged in a good bit of head shaking while he did.

"This *is* my house and you did sneak in."

"He did not make a damn sound when he came in." Doug shook his head in something akin to awe. "No way he sits at a desk playing with computers all day."

"I believe we've established that much," Sondra said.

Reed shifted positions until he leaned over Gabby and blocked her view of Sondra and Doug. The move was as close as he could come to a private conversation in the small, crowded room.

"Gabby, say something."

"I hate you." In that second, she did. Despised him with every ounce of energy inside her.

He winced, but kept trying to cover his tracks. "We should talk this out."

Gabby held out her hand. "Give me your gun."

He moved it farther out of reach. "I don't think so."

The man was a big fat liar, but a smart big fat liar.

"He has mine, too. Maybe I can find a knife in the kitchen for you to use." Doug started to stand up.

"Sit down." Sondra delivered the order without breaking off the scowl she sent in Reed's direction.

If Sondra had the power to make another human implode just from her frown, Reed would be in tiny pieces on the floor at this minute. Which made Gabby wonder where superpowers were when you really needed them.

"Before we all choose our weapons, why don't you explain your last statement about being her bodyguard." Sondra's voice vibrated with fury.

Gabby walked over and joined her friends on the other side of the room.

"I am," Reed said.

That was it. No explanation. No apologies. Gabby wondered if she would even need a gun to inflict pain on Reed.

"Care to give a few details?" Doug asked.

"To Gabby." Reed smoothed his hand over his gun. Did not show one sign that he had been caught in a lie or that he should be begging for forgiveness.

"There is no way I'm going to be alone with you. Not now. Not ever again." Gabby's stomach heaved as she said the words.

The disappointment, the betrayal. She felt it all. Last time anger swamped her. This time the fury lingered but the sadness kept creeping in.

Instead of dwelling on the pain, she tried to hide behind that anger. Later, when she was all alone in her condo, she would dredge up their breakup, and this moment, and . . . bawl her eyes out.

She would mourn the loss of something she believed to be special. Then she'd burn her sheets and make a vow never again to be lured in by men bearing food. Until then she would concentrate on the hundred best ways to murder Reed.

"We don't need an audience or, in Doug's case, a circus. I talk with Gabby alone, or I don't talk."

Make that the hundred and fifty best ways to murder him. "No one is going anywhere."

"Three against one, nerd. Start talking." Doug rubbed his hands together. Probably getting ready to land a punch.

Gabby had no intention of stopping Doug this time. He could beat on Reed all day if he wanted to.

Reed sighed. "Gabby, I'm sorry."

"No."

His eyebrow kicked up in question. "No?"

"You do not get to apologize. Not this time."

"But I want to." He had the nerve to look hurt.

"I don't care what you want."

"What can I say to make you believe me?"

"Look, you already did the whole forgive-me scene. I

stupidly bought your act once, and now I'm here. Screwed again."

"I didn't—"

"Talk or I find a knife." Gabby talked tough, but her adrenaline surge started fading. All she wanted was to go home, curl up and forget the last month and a half.

"Now there's an idea I can support." Doug balanced his feet on Reed's coffee table.

Gabby knew the move was meant to provoke Reed. And it worked.

"Put your feet down or I'll shoot you in the knees." Reed took aim.

"Reed." Sondra's stern voice caused them all to look in her direction. Her severe frown had them listening.

"Yeah?"

"Now is the time to come clean."

Something in Sondra's tone or demeanor broke through to Reed. Gabby watched his face morph from anger at Doug to resignation. His lips flattened, and his eyes darkened to a brewing storm. But he talked.

"I can only tell part of it."

"Start there," Sondra said.

Reed inhaled a few times before starting. "Like you, I work for the government. Not directly, but indirectly."

"Who said—"

Reed cut Sondra off to continue with his explanation. "I'm with a division of Homeland Security. My assignment is to make sure Gabby stays safe while she works for Benson."

"Since when?" Gabby tried to remember even telling Reed about working with Greg until it became a subject of pillow talk.

"Gabby, I have been watching Benson's activities for quite some time now. When you moved in and started on your assignment, my objectives changed to include keeping you safe."

"In other words, to protect me." Her hatred for the thought showed in her voice. She could hear it. Reed would be deaf to miss it.

"Yes."

"Let me kill him," Doug said.

Sondra stopped her coworker by touching her hand against his knee.

"In a second."

"Why wait?"

"Enough." This time Sondra dug her nails into Doug's leg to stop him. "You said Homeland."

Reed sat down on the couch with one arm stretched across the top of the sofa cushion and the other on his lap with the gun. "Yeah."

"You are trying to tell us you're a spy." Doug's sarcasm came through loud and clear.

Gabby would have asked a question, but she was too shell-shocked. Reed had lied to her over and over again. As the truth of that fact sank into her gut, her sadness soared.

"I prefer the term government worker," Reed said.

"And I'm Batman." Doug pointed to Sondra. "She's Wonder Woman."

"I would have guessed you were the Joker. That would explain how easy it was for me to get the jump on you." Reed smiled. "You get hit with doorknobs often?"

Sondra rushed in before the boys started rolling across the floor. "What were your objectives? The ones other than Gabby?"

"Come on, Sondra. You know I can't tell you that."

"Then let's try this. What exactly do you do for Homeland Security, and why would Benson's lobbying activities attract your attention?"

This time, Reed's sigh was deeper and longer. "Can't answer that either."

"I don't get it. If this is true, Homeland should have clued me in. I'm Gabby's supervisor. If there was some sort of joint assignment, I should have been advised."

Sondra's fury now matched Gabby's. While Gabby dealt with the personal blows, Sondra tried to understand the professional aspects of what Reed was saying.

"That information is well above my pay grade and you know it," Reed said.

"No one uses my group without my knowledge," Sondra said in a voice that suggested the situation was personal to her, too.

"I don't get to know the ins and outs. I just do what I am told." Reed did not hide his disgust at the idea.

Pain and outrage battled inside Gabby until her stomach churned. "Isn't this all a bit convenient, Reed? You tell us bits and pieces but then insist you can't tell the rest."

"Gabby's right. You are going to need to give us more." Sondra's voice stayed stern, but the flames stopped arcing off of her.

"I can only say certain things." Reed shook his head. "I have already overstepped."

For the first time, Gabby hated the rules. Despised protocol. She walked into the kitchen to burn off the extra shot of uneasiness working through her. It failed.

Without warning, something inside her blew. "Why not tell me the truth from the beginning?"

Reed's laziness disappeared in a flash. He jumped to his feet and followed Gabby into the kitchen. "Gabby, baby—"

"Do not call me that." She shoved against his chest. "And do not come any closer."

He held his hands up in surrender but never let go of the gun. "I won't, but you have to believe me. I was told to follow you. I did. After spending time with you and . . ."

"Sleeping with me. Having sex."

Reed shot a quick glance in Doug and Sondra's direction before he lowered his hands and voice.

"Gabby, it isn't what you think."

"What, Reed? You fell for me so hard that you forgot you were on a job?" She snorted in derision. "Give me a break."

"The assignment got all wrapped up with how much I wanted to be with you."

"Which, of course, explains why you dumped me three days ago."

"I want to tell you everything."

If she did not know better, she might have believed his pleading tone and the desperate darkness in his eyes. But now she knew the truth. She learned that much over the last week. Reed could turn it on and turn it off and never feel a thing in the process.

"You are a liar. You have made a fool of me from the beginning. And, you know what? I'm done. No storming. No scene. Just goodbye." She shoved past him, avoiding his outstretched hand and ignoring the concerned look on Sondra's face.

Gabby kept on going until she hit the front door. At that point, she did look back. She wanted to see Reed one more time so she could remember this moment. In the future when her instincts told her to give a guy who hurt her a chance, she would force her mind to conjure up this scene.

And run like hell.

Chapter 24

Reed stood outside Greg Benson's glassed-in office and stared at the closed miniblinds. His insides felt flat and empty, as if someone had scooped him out hollow and left only the shell.

He did not have to fight or sneak his way into Benson's secure high-rise building today. Courtesy of DSP with a little help from Homeland Security, he had an engraved invitation in the form of having his name on the approved visitor list.

Gabby knew the truth about him. Hiding and subterfuge were no longer necessary on that score. He could walk right in wearing his gun and hover over Gabby if he wanted to.

That part of his job remained.

The boyfriend part had ended.

He should have been relieved, even grateful, that the lies had come to an end. Now he could get back to work and focus on getting his career on track and his butt off probation.

All of that should have been true, but if the gnawing on his stomach lining and sleepless night constituted relief, he preferred a life of lying.

Right now he needed to get back to the protecting part

of his job. He rapped his knuckles against the glass, then walked in before anyone could suggest he stay outside.

At his surprise entry, the file in Gabby's hand dropped to the floor and her mouth hung open. "What the hell are you doing here?"

"Working."

She clenched the remaining papers in a tight fist until they folded into an accordion. "This is a private office. You cannot be here."

"It happens to be my job to be here."

"Not if Greg doesn't approve." Satisfaction lit her eyes when she said the other man's name.

Reed realized he was too raw to feel anything. "Your dear Greg did not have a choice."

From her sweet floral smell to her pressed light gray suit and bright pink blouse, her presence screamed calm professionalism. Seeing her smile as if nothing more than a handshake had ever passed between them knocked into Reed with the force of an oncoming car. If she was brokenhearted or even a bit upset, she hid it well.

Him, well, that was another story. Every bone and muscle inside him ached. He had never felt as unwelcome and out of place as he did standing there in his navy suit and unshaven face.

"I have work to do." She dropped into the conference room chair on the opposite of the twenty-foot glass table and scooped her file off the floor.

"That's why I'm here."

She sat back in slow motion. "Excuse me?"

"Whether you like it or not, I'm here to watch over you."

"I choose not."

"You think you get a vote?"

"Go to hell."

A place he had entered twenty-four hours ago and could

not find his way back out of. "You act as if I have a choice in any of this. I did not pick this assignment."

"Not quite. See, the way I now understand it, you overstepped your initial assignment and used me in the process. Unless you're saying you were ordered to sleep with me."

"You are the only one saying that."

"Then you have no one to blame but yourself for the position you are in now." She swiveled in her chair, looking far too comfortable with this scene for Reed's sanity.

"You're upset."

She tucked her shiny brown hair behind her ears. "Don't flatter yourself."

"I'm fine with us not talking." If she stayed silent, she could not yell or accuse.

"But I want to." She picked up her pen and twisted it back and flipped the lid on and off as she talked. "See, I'm wondering what would make a guy take a job like yours."

"A need to eat and pay the mortgage. You know, the luxuries in life." He leaned against the glass wall. Getting any closer to Gabby was not an option.

If he tried to touch her, she would likely lob off one of his limbs. And he could not venture any closer without wanting to touch her, so that left distance.

"So, then, you weren't actually in it for all the free sex?"

"Being with you was a separate thing."

Despite what Charlotte implied and the lengths he had gone to for cases in the past, sex with Gabby was different. He felt something. Wanted it to last. For the first time in his life, something took precedence over his need to get the job done.

"Come on, Reed. We're grownups. You do not need to give me the you're-special speech."

Her nastiness only added to his guilt. "I get it. You are immune to me."

"Believe it or not, I understand how you work. You

have an objective and must reach it no matter who or what crosses your path. It's part of the business."

"Looks as if you have all the answers." He wished she would listen to her explanation and realize the life she sought led to nowhere but emptiness.

"Not all."

"Didn't you say something about having work to do?"

She talked over him. "For example, I don't get why you do the bodyguard stuff for a living when you are obviously skilled with weapons."

"No idea."

"I'm also stumped by your decision to dump me. Why make it harder on yourself and go through the make-up attempts?"

"I like a challenge." Since Gabby's wrath showed no signs of weakening, he moved farther into the room and took the seat directly across from her.

"All you had to do was tell me I was your assignment."

"Right. Because you would have believed me. Wouldn't have kicked my ass if I told you all that the first day in the coffee shop."

"Instead, you took the benefits, and all it cost you was a few meals."

The continued coldness of her voice shook him. Her usual sweet smile gave way to something predatory. Something more fitting with a woman entering a life of undercover work.

The thought of his world touching her made his stomach clench, so he tried one more time to convince her. "I know you don't believe me, but I care about you."

"Oh, please."

"Sex was not part of my plan. I tried to break it off before that happened, remember?"

"Are you looking for a humanitarian award?"

He laughed, even though he could not find anything funny

about the situation or about her change in demeanor from loving to spiteful. "Hardly."

"You can leave."

He drummed his fingertips on the glass top. "I have never walked out on an assignment in my life."

"There's the door." She threw out her hand in a flourish. "I won't tell a soul."

"I would know."

"What with you being so moral and all."

"As I said, we don't have to talk."

Her eyes sparkled with an emotion he could not identify. "I could call Greg. I'm sure he would be happy to be my new watchdog. To step into your shoes, so to speak."

Her intentional prick at his anger, to use his jealousy against him, took the banter to a new level. A nasty one, and he refused to play the game.

"You're smarter than to trust a guy who is working with Homeland Security in an attempt to save his own ass."

"Are you ready to tell me what Greg's finances have to do with threats to national security?" Her tone lacked the self-assurance from the rest of the conversation. For the first time, her in-control mood faltered.

"At least you're finally asking the right question."

"How about an answer."

"Just watch your back."

"Oh, trust me. You already taught me that important lesson."

Reed felt a rush of air as the door opened behind him. "Mr. Larkin. I was told you would be joining Gabby today."

Benson approached Reed's chair and held out a hand in welcome. Reed toyed with the idea of twisting the guy's arm behind his back and smashing his face against the table. That would put a wrinkle or two in that designer suit.

"Benson." Reed stood up but skipped the handshake. He had been accused of many sins over the last few hours, most of which he deserved, but he was not about to add hypocrite to the long list.

The other man's bright eyes narrowed. "I understand that you will be assisting Gabby."

"Yes."

"I prefer to meet the individuals who will be reviewing my personal and business finances in advance and approve the addition to my team."

Sure he did.

"I'm certain you understand my position. I have an obligation to look out for the best interests of my company," Benson said.

"I know I wasn't one of your handpicked choices, but you are stuck with me."

"Reed." The warning behind Gabby's use of his name was clear.

But all that was lost on Benson. He was too busy fiddling with his watch. The same expensive self-winding watch that did not require any fiddling whatsoever.

"Gabby and I met, had lunch and came to an—"

"Let me guess, an understanding?" Reed tried to sound as bored as possible.

Benson missed that part, too. "She is quite capable. I trust her neutrality. And, frankly, from what I can see, she does not need an assistant."

"Not your call."

When Benson dropped his hands to his sides and focused on the conversation, Reed knew he had made some progress. If the burning sensation on his cheek was any indication, he had Gabby's, too. The anger behind her stare melted his skin.

"Actually, since this is my office—"

"Go tell someone who cares."

"Reed!" Gabby's warning turned into a full-fledged threat.

Everyone coddled Benson's law-breaking ass. Reed refused to play that game. "Gabby and I need space to work."

"I do not appreciate your tone." Benson made the statement, then shifted positions until he stood just out of reach. "We're even."

Reed did not *appreciate* anything about Benson, his condescending tone or his pretty-boy looks. Most annoying was Gabby's propensity to stick up for the guy. That alone made Reed want to stomp the country club pretty boy into the ground.

"I would prefer if you left the premises." Benson picked up the phone as if he was calling in reinforcements to do just that.

"Take it up with my boss." Reed held out his cell phone.

"I just might."

"While you're at it, you might want to reread the government's deal with you. My memory is that you were not to interfere with the investigation."

That wiped the smirk off of Benson's face. "I never—"

"It would be a shame for you to violate the terms of the deal, but here, call." This time he flipped the phone open and pretended to dial.

Gabby gasped, but he kept on going.

"You can put that away." Benson's words were more rushed and far less sure. "I am well aware of my obligations to the government."

"Thank God," Gabby muttered.

Reed closed the phone and shoved it back in his blazer pocket. "Then unless you want to skip over helping and get right to a jail term, you should leave."

Benson shot a furious look in Gabby's direction.

"Don't look at her for help." Reed moved his hand to an inch away from his gun on his hip. "You've got a problem with me or something I've done, you take it up with me."

Gabby stood up and balanced her fists on the table. "Reed, that is more than enough of the tough guy act."

"You should listen to the beautiful lady." Anger brewed just below the surface of Benson's satisfied smile. "She is doing a fine job."

"She would do it better if you stayed in your office as agreed."

Benson looked from Gabby to Reed and back again. "Out of respect for Gabby, I will leave. For now."

"Whatever it takes to get you gone." Reed pulled out his chair and rested his hands on the back.

Benson cleared his throat. "Gabby, if you need me, please call the operator and have me paged."

"She won't." Reed stared at Gabby. "Anything you want to say?"

"Yeah. You stink as an assistant."

Chapter 25

Gabby waited until Benson left to let her wrath run free. Seeing Reed again after all he had done was difficult enough. Being trapped in a small room with him proved impossible. Watching him torch her career prospects destroyed what little reasoning ability she had left.

Her attitude of indifference crumbled around her as she stalked around the table and grabbed his upper arm.

Reed frowned in confusion. "What are you—"

"Your behavior and comments to Greg were outrageous."

"But necessary."

"If your job really is to protect me, then you can do that while standing quietly in the corner. Better yet, wait outside."

"I was not about to stand here while some lame ass told me to jump through his hoops."

"This is a testosterone thing."

"It is the way I work. Deal with it."

On the subject of his work, a thought struck her from out of the blue. "How have you been doing your job? When it comes to me, I mean."

"The only way I know how."

She pulled away from him. "That's nonresponsive."

"But true."

"And you are all about telling the truth."

"Do you have a point?"

"You haven't been with me every second since we've met."

"Again, true." His face was as telling as a blank slate.

"Or have you?" When he stood there not moving and not giving anything away, suspicions started percolating in her mind. "Well?"

"Gabby, you do not want to know this. You're angry enough as it is."

Part of her agreed with him, but she needed answers. The only way to be on her guard against the next time, or against another guy who treated her this way, was to know all of the tricks.

"I do."

"It's not pretty."

"Honestly, Reed, I could not think any less of you."

"You've made that pretty clear."

She refused to let his monotone voice get to her. "Just tell me what I want to know."

His shoulders slumped until he lost inches in height. Enough time passed in silence while he shuffled and fidgeted that she thought he had decided to leave the conversation with what he already said. Which, as far as she was concerned, was not much.

"It's a long list starting with how I waited for the right time to approach you," he said after exhausting all of his other moves.

"I figured out our initial meeting was part of the setup. What's the rest?"

"First off, I took your badge."

And she knew that much from Sondra and Doug.

Not having been back to the office since the scene at Reed's house, Gabby needed the details from him. "Why?"

"Because you had one and no one bothered to tell me. I

took the badge so I could figure out why that pertinent detail was missing from the file I had on you."

"It wasn't included in whatever briefing you had for your assignment? That doesn't make any sense."

"On that, we agree." He leaned back against the conference table and held on to the chair behind him. "Needless to say, the missing detail proved to be a significant problem."

The last thing she wanted to hear about was how hard a time Reed had in dissecting her life. "You gave it back to me at some point. I never even knew it was gone."

He frowned hard enough for her to hear his teeth crack. "I took it at the first meeting in your office, then returned it at your condo that night."

The apology, the kiss that convinced her to give him another chance, all a lie. The admission drained all remaining emotion from inside her.

"So the heartfelt 'I'm sorry' was fake. What a surprise."

"No, I—"

She did not want to hear his excuses either. "What else?"

He looked as if he wanted to defend his position, but he answered her question instead. "I knew everything that happened at your lunch with Benson because I planted a microphone on your jacket and listened in."

Every admission he uttered stabbed through her, slicing out all of her hopes and dreams and leaving nothing but scars behind.

"You're saying you heard our entire conversation." She said the words nice and slow as if hoping he would rush in and deny his explanation.

"Everything."

Gabby chalked up his break in eye contact to boredom since she doubted he understood the concept of guilt. "You're unbelievable."

He cleared his throat before continuing. "I removed the microphone when we met up later."

That explained his surprise visit to the coffee shop. The one where he professed to be so worried about her. She *knew* she had not told him the specifics of her lunch as he insisted. He knew because he basically came along for the ride.

Lies stacked upon lies. There were so many half-truths and so much scamming, she wondered if she would ever be able to tell real from unreal again.

"Is there more?"

"That's pretty much it."

Pretty much. She knew what those words meant. "Was anything you ever said or did the truth?"

"Everything else." Emotion surged through his words.

The guy should win an acting award. "Right."

She paced away from him and stared out the window of Greg's waterfront office. Across the Potomac River was Virginia. At this moment, she would rather be over there.

"If you believe nothing else, believe me when I tell you to stay away from Benson."

A laugh burned through her chest. "You don't know when to quit."

"I can't afford to."

Without a sound, he stepped up behind her, so close she could smell his crisp earthy scent, feel the tickle of his breath against the back of her neck. As if a magnet joined their bodies, her back moved toward him. When she realized the pull had taken hold, she tucked in her pelvis and pulled straight to put as much distance between them in the small space as possible.

"Don't," she whispered.

"I am trying to help you."

The tiny piece of control left inside of her shriveled into a dry, crumbling ball. "I do not want your help."

"Ignore everything else if you want."

"I intend to."

He closed the gap and let his fingers travel up her arms. "Don't ignore this warning."

Maybe it was his touch or his closeness, but something caused her to snap. She heard the sound echo in her brain, then take off on a race through the rest of her body.

She whipped around. "How dare you!"

His fingers tightened against her jacket. "Listen to me."

"No, you listen." She struggled to break free from his hold, but he did not budge. "I am no longer buying your lines."

"Think, Gabby. What do I have to lose? I answered all of your questions. Every rotten thing I did, I owned up to doing it."

"So you say." She tried once more to move back, but between his grip and the window behind her, she had nowhere to go.

"If I had an agenda, I would have lied or evaded or made what I did seem better than it was."

"You just can't turn off the justifications, can you?"

He looked at the floor for a second. When he raised his head again, gone was the innocent, apologetic sadness. In its place was a hardness that sent a tremor of discomfort shooting through her.

"Do you have any idea what you're doing?" He gave her a slight shake. "This is not playtime. This is real world, dangerous shit you're stepping in."

"Stop trying to scare me."

He caught her elbows and held her steady. "I am trying to get you to think."

"You're trying to throw the scent off your behavior."

"Benson has been dealing with some very bad men."

"He is a businessman."

"He's dirty. Knee-deep in shit just like his dad."

"Come on, Reed. You have been pushing that line from the very beginning."

"Because it's true. The only reason Benson is dealing with Homeland now is to prevent an avalanche of criminal charges." He lowered his voice to a short hiss. "What he doesn't know is that the government is on to him. He's just digging the hole deeper."

She stopped struggling to break Reed's hold. "Why are you whispering?"

"In case I'm not the only one who knows how to use a listening device."

"You are paranoid."

"Yeah, I am. This is the work you crave. You are walking into a world where there are no rules, only fuzzy lines of gray."

His words hit her like a wake-up slap across the face. "Your world."

"Which means I know what I'm saying." He eased up on his grip but did not let her go.

"At least one of us does."

"You want to know what this great excitement does to a person?"

"Reed, don't—"

"Look at me. It's all right there. You don't even have to squint to see the truth. This life kills you. Steals your soul, knocks you down and stomps until there is nothing left of the person you were before."

She had seen so many sides to this man. He could be funny and sweet. With all the lying and underhanded motives, she no longer knew what was true and what was false. But this side of him, the desperate side without any window dressing and tricks, scared the hell out of her.

"What exactly do you do for Homeland?"

"Whatever I'm asked to do. No matter who it hurts or what I lose. I obey."

She laid her hands on his biceps. "If it robs you of so much, why stay in the game?"

"Because I don't know anything else. A stint in the FBI as an expert on kidnapping turned into my current role when the world went to hell and terrorism became this country's biggest threat."

She had no idea what to say, so she stayed quiet.

"I had this naïve belief that I could make a difference. Instead, I am chasing down sewer rats like Benson." The disappointment rushed out of him.

Confidential or not, she sensed this part was the truth. No lines. No job. Just the hard ugly facts.

"I thought I'd fight the bad guys. Instead, I became one," he said more to himself than to her.

"What does that mean?"

"For starters, I looked the other way while a former partner broke the law. My goal was to help him out of the mess, but I ended up putting myself right in the middle of a nightmare that required me to give more to the office than I ever planned on giving."

"Were you suspended?"

"That would have been easier. No, my penance is getting stuck with assignments so twisted and mired in dishonesty that I can't separate my life and my work anymore. Which, I guess, is better than jail."

"It can't be that bad."

"Look where we are right now." He swept his arm out, taking in the entire room. "And, I'm giving you the pleasant version."

The job did not have to take that much. She refused to believe she would end up like him. "Sondra and Doug aren't warped. They still believe in what they're doing."

"They left this end of the business. They moved on to something different that does not include firefights and gun battles. They got out of the exact life you are begging to get into."

"Stop with the scare tactics."

"You are determined to drive your life right into the ground."

"I just want something more than what I have. Why can't you understand that?"

He crouched down until they were eye to eye. "You told me once that you didn't want the kidnapping to shape your life. Don't you see that's exactly what is happening?"

She went from holding him to pushing him away. "That is not true."

"In your rush not to be that scared, overprotected little girl, you are making decisions that put you in danger. Your entire life is ruled by that one incident. Exactly what you didn't want to happen is happening."

Her defensive shield rose. "You're a mental health professional now?"

"You know I'm right." He brushed the backs of his fingers down her cheek in a sweet touch that stole her breath. "Just like, deep down, you know what was real between us."

Before meeting Reed that may have been true. Her instincts rarely misfired. She never fell into the dating-sucky-men trap. Never picked wrong.

But all that had changed. After falling for Reed, those no-fail instincts no longer functioned on any level where she could credit them.

"You're smart. Too smart to be used by me or my office or your job," he said.

"If I am so damn amazing, why didn't I see through your act?"

"Because the parts of us being together that matter have nothing to do with acting."

Before she could argue or disagree, he swooped in and planted one of his deep, show-me-the-bedroom kisses on her mouth. Firm and in control with an underlying poignancy.

The kiss ended almost as soon as it started. She never had a chance to push him away.

The voice in her head chastised her for letting it happen.

The voice in her heart told her she would have let it go on and on. After everything, he still had the power to make her heart melt and her smart-girl genes fall into a coma.

"The decision is yours, Gabby. Go ahead and run after the exciting life of a master spy. Have it."

"I will."

"Then you are doing it without me standing by to watch over you. I'm done." This time he released her and turned toward the door.

"Where are you going?"

He hesitated with his hand on the door handle. "Home."

"What about your big role as my bodyguard? The one you didn't want but were forced to take." She watched his profile, looking for any sign of a new game.

"Walking away is killing me. But you are on this journey of yours for all of the wrong reasons." He turned his head and stared at her with dead eyes. "I don't want to be a part of it."

"I never asked you to."

"And, I won't stand around and see what this world does to you months, or even years, from now. When you realize what you've been chasing will not give you what you want."

His flat tone worried her more than his actual words, but she refused to let it show. "You expect me to believe you are walking away from your life's work, this job that's changed you in such fundamental ways, in some misguided attempt to save me from myself."

He shot her a sad smile. "I'm done with the rescuing business. And, whether you like it or not, you are a woman in need of a good rescue."

"That's not true!" She flattened her hands against the window, more to keep her body upright than for any other reason.

"Not in the way you think, but you do."

His words proved that he did not understand her at all. After all of her explanations, he still saw her as this feeble woman in need of a strong man.

He was wrong. Dead wrong.

"You don't know what you're talking about."

"Maybe, but this decision isn't all about you. I'm walking away for me. You have to decide if staying is right for you. Do it soon."

Chapter 26

"I appreciate all of you being here." Charlotte delivered the line as if anyone in the room had a choice in being anywhere except the conference room at Financial Solutions.

"It is their building," Reed mumbled under his breath in the brief time where Charlotte took one of her own.

"I recognize this emergency meeting required some of you to set aside other work. Unfortunately"—Charlotte frowned in Reed's direction—"certain recent events left me with no other recourse."

Charlotte made her snide pronouncement from the head of the conference table in the same room where Reed first stole Gabby's badge. Not Reed's favorite memory.

Not where he wanted to be right now either. Not here. Not with this crowd.

He preferred to crawl off somewhere and lick his wounds in private. He planned to do just that and then hand in his resignation. He showed up to work this morning only to see what Charlotte planned next. Knowing her next move would make watching his back much easier.

"I have been advised that there was a problem at Reed's home two days ago." Charlotte looked everywhere except at Pete.

Which confirmed Reed's theory about his faithful partner not being so faithful.

Reed had developed an exit strategy, but before he left he wanted to know where Pete stood in the fight. Now he knew. Pete was a company man. He gathered information, then ran right back to the mothership to share.

Charlotte laced her fingers together on top of her portfolio. "I am sure you can understand that I did not have any other choice than this meeting."

"Neither did we," Sondra said in a bleak reminder that she had been summoned to appear instead of being asked. "Perhaps you could fast forward and tell us what the agenda is."

Despite the deference Sondra afforded Charlotte, Reed knew Sondra seethed in secret at being perfectly upstaged on her home turf. He knew because that was exactly how he would feel if he were in Sondra's place. Someone above Sondra likely handed down the Charlotte-is-in-charge lecture, and now Sondra had to pretend to agree to the current command structure.

Doug was more transparent. He did not try to hide his anger at being called in for a meeting by a woman he did not know and to whom he did not answer. He kept spinning his coffee mug around on the glass tabletop, letting it bang and clank.

Reed assumed the goal was to tweak Charlotte's temper. He hoped that happened while he sat in the room. Seeing someone push Charlotte over the edge would be worth the pain of being in a room with Gabby while being unable to break through the hard shell that had formed around her.

When he told Gabby he would walk away from the job for his own sanity, he meant it. He could not afford to lose one more piece of himself or spend one more day wondering when Charlotte would make that one demand too many.

But he also had to leave because of Gabby. He had lied to her from day one. He had used her, manipulated her, and never blinked. Well, he was blinking now. This way of life had become normal, even acceptable, to him. In wanting to do something good, he had morphed into a man who destroyed everything around him.

His life did not start this way. He did not want it to end this way either.

Charlotte stared down the length of the table at Sondra. "As you all now know, Reed works for me. Individuals at Financial Solutions agreed to supplement our activities and provide resources for Reed's current assignment—"

"Who in my company authorized this, and why was I not told?" Sondra asked with more than a little heat under her words.

"And when did I become a resource?" Gabby asked in follow-up.

Charlotte tightened her fingers together. "I will have to ask both of you not to interrupt."

"They are asking legitimate questions." Reed leaned across Pete to smile at his boss. "It's clear no one clued them in before the assignment, which is a problem close to my heart."

"I am well aware of the facts and how this mission went off course, Reed. Since your actions have put us in this situation, it is best that you remain silent," Charlotte said.

Doug gave his mug another spin. "The way I see it, Reed here is the only reason we knew something fishy was going on. He's the only person on your side of the table who bothered to give us a head's up."

Doug sticking up for him. Reed shook his head in wonder at that turn of events over the last twenty-four hours.

Reed also noticed that his supposed computer genius partner did not open his mouth. Pete lounged in the chair to Charlotte's left. He alternated between tapping on the arms of his chair and rolling his head back as if to stretch out his neck muscles.

"If everyone will please remain silent." Charlotte waited to continue until they all gave her eye contact.

Apparently she thought that meant they respected her authority. For Reed, it meant he needed to hear more before he cut in again. He would bide his time.

"We needed an individual to make contact with Greg Benson. The contact had to be someone who was unaware of the underlying investigation of Mr. Benson's companies and financial dealings."

"In other words, a naïve patsy," Gabby said, filling in the blanks.

"Ms. Pearson, I must insist—"

"Gabby has a point. She is the contact or resource or whatever it is you're calling her at the moment." Reed could see Gabby stare at him, but he kept his focus on Charlotte. "You owe her."

Every cell in his body screamed to rush Gabby into the hall and beg her to believe something good and decent still existed inside of him. Something small that could be nurtured and restored.

He had never cared what others thought of him. He pushed ahead, did his job and moved on. But since his first day with Gabby, he realized he was speeding in the wrong direction. With her he wanted to stay, make love, take his time.

He tried to ignore the sensation. He beat back his feelings for her by insisting they arose from lust and nothing more. He knew that was wrong.

Just as he knew leaving DSP was the right thing to do.

This time Charlotte skipped the sighing and went right to yelling. "Again, Reed. I would remind you that we are in this position because of your poor choices."

"What did he do?" Doug asked.

Charlotte's head snapped back. "Excuse me?"

"He protected Gabby," Doug pointed out.

Sondra backed up Doug's defense with her own. "Wasn't that his job?"

Charlotte smoothed her hands over the sleeves of her expensive suit. "This is an internal matter."

"He's been watching Benson for you. Hell, he's the poster child for good agents, even if he is annoying as shit," Doug added.

The huge smile on Sondra's face seemed genuine for the first time. "And exactly which agency is it that you guys work for again?"

Reed glanced at Gabby out of the corner of his eye and saw she wore an impressive smile, too. Seemed the accountants of Financial Solutions could engage in some pushing and shoving of their own when needed.

Being the object of their joint protection made him dizzy with relief. No one ever rushed to his defense. Not Allen. Certainly not Pete.

Not Charlotte, despite her statements to the contrary.

"None of you are privy to that information." Charlotte's face looked as if it was frozen in stone. Only her lips moved.

"I tried to tell them the same thing, but they didn't like that answer. The whole you're-not-cleared thing makes them angry for some reason," Reed said.

Doug nodded. "He did and it does."

"Maybe I am not making myself clear." Charlotte rose from her seat. "This is serious. It is not a game."

But it was starting to feel like one. "Charlotte, they are intelligent people. Just tell them the truth."

"I will decide—"

Reed ignored her and faced the rest of the agents. "We work for the Division of Special Projects. It's a top secret offshoot of Homeland Security that tracks and investigates national security threats involving business professionals in the United States."

Charlotte banged her hand against the table. "Reed Larkin. That is privileged information."

"Fire me." Reed noticed he had Pete's attention now. All the fidgeting stopped, but his mouth stayed closed. "Anything you want to add, partner?"

"No."

Charlotte banged her coffee cup on the table. "Reed, I am ordering you—"

"And I'm disobeying." This time Reed stood up.

"I'm starting to like this nerd." Doug made the comment to Sondra, but he was not exactly quiet about it.

Reed continued over the interruption. "DSP and Homeland are using Benson to collect information on his father. At the same time, we are strengthening our case against the younger Benson. He just doesn't know it."

"He is too smart for that," Gabby said.

Reed tried to figure out if Gabby meant to prick his temper or if she was making a legitimate observation. "He thinks so. In fact, he's so intelligent that he insisted on negotiating his own immunity deal."

"Idiot," Doug muttered.

Reed enjoyed a minute of amusement. "The same deal that's full of holes and will eventually trip him up. Guess Benson didn't do so great in law school."

"The poor bastard thinks he's working on a deal, but he's really slitting his own throat." Doug clapped his hands together in a noise loud enough to make Charlotte jump. "I like it. Has a certain simplicity to it."

"I must insist that you both—"

Reed cut Charlotte off again. It felt natural the more he did it. "We needed a person on the inside. Someone Benson could provide with information while scurrying around to hide his involvement. In essence, he thinks he's fooling us, but we're fooling him."

"Benson has no idea," Gabby said with a touch of something that sounded like respect.

And she said Benson.

The more she dehumanized the guy, the happier Reed would be. "That was my sense. Are you sure?"

"He's very smug. In his view, the government needs him and he's doing us all a favor."

"Then the plan is working. With every false document Benson provides, we get one step closer to an indictment. He is within inches of voiding his immunity deal. Once that happens, everything we have discovered can be used against him."

"It's risky but smart," Sondra said.

"What it is, is confidential. Reed should not be telling you any of this." Charlotte looked down at Pete. "Are you going to do something about this?"

"Not yet."

"To get the job done, DSP looked to Financial Solutions to supply an individual who could review documents and information and keep Benson occupied. The absence of an intelligence agency in Gabby's background was perfect," Reed explained.

"Because I'm easily conned."

"Because you know what you're doing with figures and did not have the information to give away our plans for Benson."

"But now she does, which is the reason we are here." Charlotte sat back down. "We need to work out a plan to deal with this unexpected and unwanted contingency."

"Pull her out," Doug said.

"I don't want to be pulled. Benson trusts me. I can finish this project."

"Is she in danger?" Sondra asked.

"I am sitting right here and am perfectly capable of assessing a dangerous situation," Gabby insisted, but no one was listening.

Reed saw Gabby's shoulders tense and her frustration rise. He wondered how two of the people closest to her could sit in the same room and not notice.

The situation seemed obvious to him now. The reflexive jump to her defense despite the fact she was more than capable of fighting her own battles. The protectiveness came from a positive place, but he understood why that simple fact did not lessen the offense in Gabby's eyes.

"She will have someone suitable assigned to her for protection." Charlotte's smug demeanor returned as if she never lost control of the meeting. "Someone other than Reed."

"Why? Gabby works for me, and as far as I can tell, she is safe with Reed."

First Doug defended him. Now Sondra. They were either very forgiving or they really hated Charlotte. Right now, he would take either possibility so long as they stayed locked on his side.

"He's pretty handy with a gun. Believe me, I know." Doug rubbed his fingers over the bandage on his forehead.

Charlotte had the wide-eyed look of hunted prey. "There are some disciplinary issues that need to be worked out within DSP concerning Reed. His disclosures today have not helped his position."

"Truth is a bad thing?" Doug asked.

Charlotte ignored him. "Someone else will be assigned to Gabby."

"Wait a second." Gabby held up a hand. Despite her small size, she could command attention with that husky, no-nonsense voice. "What if I don't want anyone else? It *is* my safety we're talking about. I decide."

Of all the defenses batted around on his behalf in the last few minutes, Gabby's shocked Reed the most. After everything that passed between them, to hear her stand up and pledge her support filled him with a rush of warmth.

Charlotte was more hot than warm. "I am in charge of allocating my office's resources. I will decide what happens with Reed."

Reed saw an opening and took it. "Wrong. I decide."

"Damn." Doug smacked the table. "Is it just me or is he less annoying today?"

"That's probably because he's not holding a gun at your head," Sondra said.

Doug scowled.

"Or beating you with a doorknob," Gabby added.

The scowl deepened.

"Reed, what are you talking about?" Pete asked.

For the first time, Reed saw intelligence behind Pete's gaze. His usual lazy affectation gave way to something more professional, more aware. Someone who . . .

Shit. Internal Affairs. Yeah, no question about it.

Reed could not believe it took him this long to ferret out the truth. He had seen the look before. Been questioned by more IA types than he could count during Allen's investigation.

This assignment went beyond Benson. Reed knew now it was about watching his every move. Not just in the way Charlotte described. No, this was much worse. There was a full-fledged undercover IA investigation going on with him at the center. Allen's taint continued to ruin everything.

The realization gave Reed the energy he needed. "I quit."

Doug's brows snapped together. "What?"

"You are not going to quit. Sit down," Charlotte said with as much menace as Reed had ever heard in her voice.

"Reed, don't do this." Gabby stood up and walked around the table to stand next to him. "Think of your career and what you have sacrificed to get here."

"You should listen to Ms. Pearson." Charlotte fumed as she spoke.

Sondra picked that moment to challenge Charlotte's authority. "Let Gabby talk."

"He is not serious. This is a waste of time." Charlotte sounded stern, but Reed could see the uncertainty lingering on her face.

Gabby pulled him around until his back faced Charlotte. "One assignment is not worth throwing it all away. This job is part of you."

"It's all of me." He wanted to cradle her face in his hands, but settled for touching a hand against her arm. "That's the problem. My life being only about my job is not okay. I get that now."

Because of her. Gabby.

It had been years since he felt a connection to a woman. Every single day he saw the destruction and hurt people inflicted on those they supposedly loved. The illusion struck him as more dangerous than working with weapons, so he had given up on that route years ago. Then Gabby entered his life.

She made him laugh. Turned him on and left him breathless and satisfied. Challenged his beliefs and goals. She made him feel something more than guilt. The deep, thumping ache inside him at the thought of not being near her again refused to go away. Whenever he saw her or heard her voice, the intensity grew.

In his initial rush to ignore the truth, he called the feeling lust. Looking down into her deep hazel eyes, he knew. He had fallen in love with her. The emotion did not come easy to him, not after all he had seen and done. But, there it was. Bright and as clear as his decision to move on from DSP.

Knowing the truth of his feelings and knowing what to do about them were two very different things. What he could give her, she did not want. He did not have anything else.

"It's time for me to move on." The words felt good on his tongue.

"From everything?"

The look of longing on Gabby's face nearly broke him. Gave him hope. For a second he thought he might still have a chance with her. That they could somehow pull through all of this and start over.

"Reed obviously is having difficulty accepting the fact his job is in significant jeopardy. His offenses are problematic but, with training, possibly not insurmountable." Charlotte's concern vanished.

Sondra did not look convinced by anything her counterpart said. "Even though he discussed classified information?"

"Sondra, stop helping," Gabby said.

"It is true that I would hate to lose Reed. He usually follows the rules so well," Charlotte said.

Reed sensed a death blow on the horizon.

Charlotte turned her attention to Gabby. "For example, when I suggested Reed use sex to gain your trust, he did. Not many agents would go that far. For Reed, no act is beneath him."

Charlotte leveled the hit without even flinching.

Gabby did. Reed saw the tremor run through her at Charlotte's harsh comment.

"Well, shit," said Doug.

Reed thought Doug's comment summed up the situation well.

"That did not happen, and you know it, Charlotte." Reed had to say the words. His private life was none of Charlotte's business, but he could not let the insinuation hang out there without being addressed.

Charlotte feigned innocence. "Did I misunderstand? I thought you slept with Ms. Pearson after we discussed that."

Reed was not about to answer that or stick around for another bout of character assassination. The idea of seeing the crushed expression on Gabby's face kept him from looking at her.

"I'm done, Charlotte. Find someone else to do your dirty work." He gestured at Pete. "My partner can take over the bodyguard activities."

Charlotte waved him off. "We will discuss the particulars back at our office."

Reed delivered a blow of his own. "Count me out. I quit."

The rest of the gathering remained silent. He stared into Charlotte's flushed face as he reached into his inside pocket. "Here's my security card."

"Reed, wait a second—"

Reed cut off Pete. It was either that or smash his face in.

"My gun." It landed against the glass with a loud clink. "And my resignation."

"You cannot do this," Charlotte insisted.

"I just did. Blackmail someone else."

Chapter 27

The conference room fell silent the second after the door shut behind Pete. With Reed gone and Pete trailing after him, that left four of them.

Doug stopped spinning the mug in favor of staring at Charlotte. He treated her to one of those looks that suggested deep analysis. Gabby had seen the same look every time Doug studied a take-out menu.

"That was quite a show," Sondra said as she closed up the files in front of her and slid them into her briefcase.

"Reed always did have a flair for the dramatic." Charlotte cleared her throat. "Do not worry. Pete will handle that situation."

Gabby considered throwing a pen and trying to knock the satisfied smile right off Charlotte's pinched face.

Sondra settled for zipping up her bag with a loud rip. "Are we done?"

The smile slid right off Charlotte's face. "Absolutely not. We need to deal with the leak and figure out the best way to proceed."

"With what?" Gabby's fingers inched toward Sondra's pen, but Sondra stopped her with a quick shake of the head.

"Ms. Pearson," Charlotte's voice carried a false sweetness that raised Gabby's guard. "I understand that you have received some difficult news this morning concerning Reed's true intentions. You have my fullest sympathy."

Now there was something Gabby did not want.

Charlotte continued with her feigned concern. "It cannot be easy to hear that a man used you for other than honorable purposes."

"Since when does national security qualify as dishonorable?" Gabby asked.

Charlotte's tall frame stiffened. "You do not actually believe Reed had some higher purpose for his decision to take you to bed."

Gabby knew exactly why Reed took her to bed. Because she did not give him much of a choice.

"I thought you ordered him to do it." Gabby looked around for reinforcements. "Isn't that what you said a few minutes ago?"

Charlotte pretended to be confused. "Excuse me?"

"She said she thought you ordered Reed to sleep with her." Doug talked slowly and loudly.

Charlotte was too busy stuttering to notice. "Well, I . . . that is not important."

"Seems important." Gabby certainly found the other woman's floundering interesting. "If you gave him an order and he obeyed it for God and country and all that, he did have a higher purpose."

"I would have to agree." Sondra folded her hands together, mimicking Charlotte's earlier gesture. "I don't issue orders of that sort, so you will have to forgive me for asking questions. I do have a few, as you can imagine."

Charlotte recovered her voice, but her cheeks continued to glow cherry red. "This is not appropriate."

"That's what I was thinking," Doug mumbled in a tone guaranteed to be heard.

"Did you tell Reed that he was supposed to act as a bodyguard or a lover? And when you proposed this mission to my bosses at Financial Solutions, did you make it clear that Gabby would—"

Doug finished Sondra's thought. "Get a booty call."

"I'm sure the orders didn't use that term." Sondra looked at Charlotte. "Or did they?"

Charlotte visibly swallowed. "This is unnecessary."

"Do you know if booty calls are taxable or nontaxable benefits?" Doug looked around as if he expected a real answer. "I can look it up, but it would be easier if you tell me."

"I see that your office continues to view this entire situation as a game. That is regrettable." Charlotte cleared her throat. "I must say, Sondra, this behavior is a testament to your supervisory skills."

Gabby seriously thought about hiding under the desk. If she did not hate the idea of missing something, she might have done it.

"And how is that, Charlotte?" Sondra's icy tone exceeded Charlotte's.

"It is obvious. If your staff were better trained, we might be in a different position right now."

Doug and Gabby both moved their chairs back. Gabby feared flying furniture. Doug probably wanted a better view.

"What is regrettable, Charlotte, is that you saw fit to lie."

"When?"

"Interesting that you need someone to clarify the timeline so that you can figure out which lie we're talking about," Doug said.

"I'll start." Gabby's list was long, so she stuck to the highlights. "Reed did not sleep with me as a part of any assignment protocol and you know it."

"Oh, Ms. Pearson." Charlotte shook her head and gave

a look of what probably passed for concern in her world. "I am sorry to disillusion you."

The reality of what was happening hit Gabby hard enough to send her head spinning. She knew Charlotte wanted to see the fury of a woman scorned. Fireworks, yelling —something. Gabby refused to play along.

For some reason, she could not dredge up any anger. She knew the meeting with Reed was a setup. *He* was the one who told her that. Hearing Charlotte talk about Reed's lovemaking like it was part of a work scheme snapped the fuzzy picture in her mind into focus.

Gabby knew in that second that she was not the only one who understood the setup. Charlotte wanted to make Reed's life difficult. Gabby wanted to know why.

"You don't want him to leave, do you?"

Charlotte's face went blank. "Who?"

"This is about you getting a stronger hold over Reed. For the first time since he started working for you, he's not following your commands," Gabby said, growing more confident with each word.

"He violated—"

"He obeyed. He did your dirty work. But, and this is the part that's killing you, he refused to let you hold the incident with his former partner over his head."

Doug leaned over to Sondra. "I think we're missing a chapter or two of this story."

Sondra nodded. "No question."

"Obviously Reed told you a fable about Allen." Charlotte sorted through her stack of files and took one out. "It would appear Reed has grown so accustomed to lying that he is not capable of stopping."

Doug snorted. "Right. Nerd boy is the one with the truth problem."

Charlotte flicked a glance in Doug's direction, but talked right over his comment. "I am sorry you got caught up in that, but I assure you that Reed is on probation for a reason."

Doug threw his hands up. "Reed gets a gun and the girl while he's on probation? What do I have to do to get in trouble?"

"Again, this is not a joke. There are serious national security issues at stake here." Charlotte paged through the documents in front of her.

"Put your files away and talk." Gabby shot to her feet. "I won't believe anything that's in there anyway."

"I do not take orders from you, Ms. Pearson."

"Reed called your bluff." Gabby knew that was the heart of the problem.

"And you are desperate to keep him under your thumb, even if it means taking away the one thing that means anything to him." Sondra stood up, too.

"And just what would that be?" Charlotte asked as if she knew the answer. "His job?"

Sondra smiled. "Gabby."

"Her?"

Gabby was too busy being confused to feel any satisfaction from hearing Charlotte yelp in surprise. "Me?" Gabby asked.

"Damn, woman, you can't be that blind." Doug muttered something about how hard life was for the males of the species.

This time Charlotte was the one who stood up. "You are all misunderstanding the situation. Reed is in significant trouble. He will do and say anything in order to rescue his career. I am sure his partner is talking with him about that very issue right now."

"And who is this Pete guy?" Doug asked.

Sondra filled in the blank. "Internal Affairs."

"Pete's position is not your concern," Charlotte snapped out in an uncharacteristic loss of control.

Gabby watched the older woman weave small truths together with large lies until she had a big quilt of nothing. She was a pro.

And a bitch.

"Did Reed even know what the real assignment was? I mean, why did he think he was sitting at my table that first day in the coffee shop?" Gabby asked.

"Yes, Charlotte. What did he think he was doing?" Sondra asked.

"You are not—"

"Privy to this information. Yeah, we've heard that a hundred times already." Doug not only stayed seated, he leaned back with his arms folded behind his head. "Un-fucking-believable. This is why I got out of this sort of work."

"You can tell me the truth, or someone in my office will tell me. Don't forget, like you I am in management." Sondra's voice dripped with distaste.

Charlotte sat back down. "Reed is on probation. He was given simple tasks—"

"Which were?" Gabby refused to let Charlotte run off on another anti-Reed tangent.

"To discover the nature of your relationship to Benson."

"But you knew that. You said yourself . . ." All of Reed's warnings fell in on Gabby at once.

Reed got used.

She got used.

Reed was about to pay the price.

"And when he figured out you were scamming him, he tried to get you to tell me, didn't he?" Gabby knew in her heart her suspicions were right.

And Sondra joined in.

"You lied to your own agent as some demented test? Is that how your office operates?" Sondra sounded appalled by the idea. "And that's why *I* left this end of the business."

"His request to disclose certain information to Ms.

Pearson was inappropriate," Charlotte responded. "There are rules. He knows that and tried to bypass them. As I said, we have a great deal to work on with Reed before he can go on another assignment."

"Did you miss the part where he quit?" Doug asked.

"He's not coming back, you know." Gabby knew that was the case.

Charlotte barked out a laugh. "Of course he is. This is all he has."

"You're wrong. This might have been what he was once. Not anymore." Gabby knew that, too.

"Please tell me that you do not think you can change Reed Larkin. What a silly schoolgirl notion." Charlotte clicked her tongue in one of those annoying tsk-tsk sounds. "I would have thought you were smarter than that."

"She is the smartest agent I've ever worked with." Sondra winced when Doug started to protest the remark. "Sorry."

"She is foolish, and that is why she is destined to remain behind the scenes," Charlotte said with more than a little venom in her tone.

Gabby decided to cut to the heart of the problem. "Your office told me this job was my ticket into fieldwork. I'm assuming that was a lie as well."

"It would appear you are not qualified. After all, you could not hold off a man determined to sleep with you for the information you possessed. That is a basic requirement."

The slam rolled right off Gabby.

Not Doug and Sondra. They started yelling in outrage on her behalf. Gabby stayed calm.

Reed told her everything she needed to know about Charlotte and the world the woman thrived in. As much as he could say. Probably more than he should have. Spread out all the information and the facts and then stepped back so she could figure it out for herself. Armed her with the ability to protect herself.

To work for these people, Gabby knew she would have to sell a bit of her soul. Become as cold and nasty as Charlotte. No. Thank. You. Not when she could follow in Sondra's sure footsteps and act with integrity.

Not when she could get her thrills at home.

"I'm leaving," Gabby announced.

"We are not done here, Ms. Pearson."

Funny, but she felt done. "Oh, I am."

"I feel done, too." Doug turned to Sondra. "What about you?"

"Well done."

Charlotte's voice turned shrill. "You cannot leave this office."

"Yes, we can. We do not work for you. As of a few minutes ago, neither does Reed." Sondra slid her briefcase over her shoulder. "Which, from where I stand, looks like the smartest business decision the guy's ever made."

"I will call security."

Doug rolled his eyes as he ambled to his feet. "It's our office building, lady."

"In fact, I'll have someone come in and escort you out." Sondra smiled as she made the threat.

As they headed for the door, Charlotte took one last shot at staying in the loop. "Where do you think you are going?"

Gabby had an easy answer for that one. "To warn Reed about Pete. Seems to me Reed has been screwed by enough people in your office lately."

"He better not try to hit me with another doorknob," Doug grumbled.

Sondra put an arm around Doug's shoulders. "I'll protect you."

Chapter 28

Reed pinned Pete to the floor and trapped his arm behind his back. Right there in the middle of Reed's family room, he took a small piece of revenge.

"This is career suicide." The area rug muffled Pete's voice. Something about a guy having his face smashed against the floor made him less clear.

"I committed that a long time ago."

"I didn't pick this assignment. I was doing my job."

"Screwing me."

"Investigating you." Pete hesitated. "Not just you."

Reed balanced his knee in the middle of Pete's back and leaned down to hear better. "What does that mean?"

"Charlotte."

The shock knocked Reed on his backside. "No shit."

"You didn't hear it from me." Pete sat up.

"I'm just happy I heard it at all." He shook his head. "Good ol' Charlotte's gotten herself in hot water."

"You could say that."

"What did she do?"

"I can't comment on an ongoing case, but it is fair to say there are some concerns. Nothing will come of it, of course, but I get to have some fun before I'm done."

"Man, I would love to see her face when she figures that out."

Pete rubbed his arm. "Damn, you're mean."

"Part of the training."

"I'll put that in my report."

Reed jumped to his feet and then held out his hand to help Pete up. "Don't bother."

"Do not touch that horrible man's hand."

Reed felt the blood freeze in his veins at Gabby's command. He turned his head and watched her storm inside the house with Sondra and Doug right behind.

"Looks like your rescue team has arrived," Pete said, clearly impressed by the show of force.

The only emotion Reed felt was confusion. "What are you all doing here?"

"Saving you." Gabby marched over and stood between the partners.

"Really?"

"You seemed like you needed someone to throw you a safety line." Gabby made her comment and then, without a word, shoved Pete.

Being off balance, he landed on his ass on the hard floor. "What did I ever do to you, Legs?"

"Don't call her that," Reed mumbled as he came out of his stupor over the scene unfolding in front of him.

Pete reached over as if trying to get Gabby's attention by tugging on the bottom of her blazer.

"Are you crazy? She'll kill you." Doug put his hand on Pete's shoulder. "Stay down."

"I just—"

"I said, stay down." Doug pushed harder.

Reed started to understand what was happening. They had figured out Pete's true identity and come rushing over to unveil him. Reed now knew one thing these three hated more than him, and that was Charlotte and her trumped-up Internal Affairs investigation. That was the only explanation he could come up with for the show of solidarity.

"You can let Pete up," Reed said with some regret.

"He's IA." Gabby practically spit when she said it.

"I know."

"He's been investigating you."

"I know."

"He lied to you and . . ." Gabby stopped ticking off Pete's sins. "You know?"

"Figured it out during our meeting. The fact Pete failed to come to my defense or get tagged to take my place watching over you were small hints. He also leaked what I told him about our meeting here yesterday to Charlotte."

"Then there's the fact I came to your house ten minutes ago and told you I was IA." Pete rubbed his arm and shoulder on the spot where Doug pushed him.

"Okay, yeah, that helped to clear it up, too."

"Where is Charlotte?" Pete asked.

"Back in her cage." Doug finally stepped back so that Pete had room to stand. "Is it your turn to clean it?"

Pete smiled. "Hell no."

"Why were you helping Pete to stand?" Sondra asked. She did not bother waiting to be invited. She made herself at home on Reed's couch.

"I knocked him to the floor. It seemed only fair that I help him back up."

"I miss all the fun," Doug grumbled.

"Speaking of which, I'm not having any. Fun, that is." Pete brushed off his khakis. "I'm hungry—"

"What a surprise."

"—and sore, thanks to you two bruisers."

"Feel free to leave and never come back." Gabby even opened the door to help him along.

Reed almost hated for Pete to go. Being in Internal Affairs, he was less likely to let the other three commit murder in his presence. And that was how Gabby looked: Homicidal.

"I like you better when you're throwing beverages at Reed here," Pete said.

"Don't we all." Doug added a nod to show his agreement.

"Reed, one thing." Pete fought off Gabby's attempts to shove him through the door without opening it. "Consider staying on. DSP needs you."

"Maybe, but I don't need DSP."

Pete nodded and left, leaving Reed all alone with the rest of the crowd. Reed wondered if his decision to surrender his weapon back in the conference room was a good one after all.

He tried to lighten the mood before Gabby did something drastic to him. "Did I miss anything good during the rest of the meeting? It's always a risk to leave one of Charlotte's lovefests too early."

Doug dropped onto the seat next to Sondra. "Just Gabby going ballistic."

"That sounded bad. Reed knew from personal experience how difficult Charlotte could be. Having Gabby in that firing line did not make him happy. What happened?"

"She—"

Sondra stopped Doug's story. "Gabby can speak for herself."

Well, well, well. Progress.

Reed glanced over at Gabby. Her stern frown suggested that she was not a woman who felt like talking. For a second his confidence faltered. He was so sure Gabby could handle Charlotte and would not fold. The idea that the scene played out another way deflated him.

Then Gabby started to circle him like prey. She slammed the door shut and walked up until she stood right under his nose.

With her hands on her hips, she faced him down. "You have a lot of explaining to do."

"Uh, okay."

"I have a few questions, and you are going to answer them."

Reed sneaked a peek at Sondra.

"Don't look over there," Gabby said. "They aren't going to help you. In fact, if I give him the word, Doug is going to strangle you."

"The guy is afraid of doorknobs," Reed pointed out.

Doug swore. "I am not afraid of house supplies."

Reed thought he saw Gabby's lips quiver as she fought off a smile. The slight move disappeared as fast it came.

"For the record, I am afraid of Sondra." Reed saw fire in Gabby's eyes. "And you. I'm definitely afraid of you right now."

Because he was not a complete idiot.

"Did you know I was working for the government when you started your assignment?" Gabby asked.

"No."

"When you found out, did you confront Charlotte?"

Reed figured he had nothing left to lose. "Yeah. I wanted to tell you what was happening."

"That your office was using me."

He wished they could forget all of this. Talking about it was likely to raise Gabby's blood pressure, and not in a good way. "Right."

"That's what I figured." Gabby's words were sharp and her voice pinched, but her face remained emotionless throughout the interrogation.

Reed could not figure out if that was a good sign or not.

"Did Charlotte tell you to sleep with me?"

Reed glanced over to try to assess Doug's reaction.

Gabby put a hand on Reed's chin and turned his attention back to her. "Answer me. The truth. Whatever it is, I can handle it."

"I know you can."

Her features softened. "Then say it."

"I decided you were not involved in the Benson operation and broke it off with you—"

"To protect me."

"Yes." He rushed to explain the rest. "I know now you don't need anyone making decisions for you. I just hated to see you near danger and messed up with me."

Her hand fell to his chest. "Go on."

"Charlotte had a fit and told me to get back together with you." This next part could mean the difference between him living and not. "Told me to use any skill I could to win you over."

Gabby's hand tensed against his chest, but she did not remove it. "Is that why you slept with me?"

This time he did not need to look for reinforcements. This part he could handle all on his own. "I slept with you because I wanted to."

"Can we move on to another question?" Doug asked.

Not as far as Reed was concerned. "I still want to. All the time."

"Oh, man." Doug kept grumbling until Sondra smacked him on the arm.

"You can leave anytime." Reed took the risk and balanced his hands on Gabby's hips.

"Sondra won't let me," Doug said.

"But, you"—Reed looked down into Gabby's bright eyes—"I'd prefer that you stay."

"Are you going to apologize to me again?"

Her teasing tone filled him with relief. "I will say it every day, every hour, if you'll give me another chance."

"That sounds like overkill," Doug muttered.

"For once, my friend Doug is right." Gabby's second hand joined her first in resting against Reed's chest.

"I should have told you the truth and gotten out of the assignment and this job and all the confines of the top secret stuff long before now. I should have concentrated on doing what I really wanted to do."

"Which was?" Gabby's face lit up in a smile.

Reed did not understand what had changed or where her anger had gone, but he refused to waste this opportunity to tell her how he felt. "I wanted you more than my job. That should have told me something. Guess I was a bit slow."

"I understand what you were telling me about the job, Gabby said. "You were right."

She still was not getting it. She heard a mentoring lesson. He was trying to profess his love.

He needed her to understand what he felt. The pride. The respect. The love. "Gabby, you can be anything you want to be. You don't have to overcome your past or be ruled by it."

"Reed—"

He rubbed a thumb over her lips. "If you want danger and excitement, go for it. Who am I to talk you out of the life I lived for so long? I will support you, do anything I can to help and, most importantly, not get in your way."

"I like that last one."

"I mean it." Or he would try.

She traced her finger along his jawline. "You don't have to say all of this."

"I do." His gaze searched her face. "I just want you to go into this top secret life with your eyes open. You also need to know that this job is not your stepping stone. There are other ways, and you should find one that does not involve Charlotte. She plans to use you and abandon you."

"I get that, too."

Relief washed through him. He had feared that last truth would break the tenuous peace that formed between them. But, once again, he underestimated Gabby.

One day he would learn. A certain way of life was so ingrained in him. It would take time and effort to undo the damage. He vowed to put in the necessary work. Now he had to get Gabby to agree to go along with him on that ride.

"I know you do, honey." He kissed her then because he could no longer resist. Just a short, sweet peck but it quenched his thirst for her in the short term.

"I don't want to see this," Doug mumbled.

Reed ignored the snide comment and focused solely on Gabby. "You're smart and beautiful and talented. You do get it. You don't need me—or Sondra, or Doug—to talk for you. We do it because we love you."

He had said a few of the things he wanted her to know. There was so much more.

She shook his shoulders. "Reed, you are not listening to . . . What did you just say?"

Man, he did say it. The words slipped right out. So natural and right. He never had time to worry and panic.

"You heard me."

"Now can we leave?" Doug asked, but Sondra shushed him.

Gabby's eyes sparkled. "I want to hear it again."

"I know we started out wrong and we have all this stuff between us—"

"Reed Larkin, if you do not tell me you love me in the next two seconds, I am going to let Doug shoot you."

Reed felt the laugh and did not fight it. Who was he to question his luck? "I love you."

When that sparkle turned into tears, his stomach clenched. "Damn, what did I say? I didn't mean to upset you."

"These are happy tears." She alternated between hiccups and laughter.

"Uh-huh."

"No, really."

He glanced over Gabby's shoulder and saw Sondra nod in confirmation. "So, this is a good sign?"

He wiped away the wetness under Gabby's eye. Positive or not, seeing it hang there nearly killed him.

She wrapped her arms around his neck. "Much better than good."

"Doug?"

"Huh?"

"Take Sondra and get out." Reed lowered his head for another kiss. Not a small one this time. He wanted a long, drawn-out, where-is-the-bedroom kiss.

Gabby put a hand over his mouth to stop him. "Wait!"

Reed groaned. "Now what?"

She grabbed his upper arms. "Look, I have this idea."

"What did I tell you about comments that start with the word 'look'?"

"No, listen. Leaving your current job is the right thing. Charlotte is a viper."

"On her good days, yes."

"But, you need to stay in this line of work."

A rush of pride and relief hit him. Changing jobs was the right choice, but leaving law enforcement completely did not sit well with him. He had worried Gabby would not understand in light of all the other things he had said to her. She did.

"I just need to find the right thing," Reed said. "I have money saved."

He would be fine after a break.

Gabby's smile filled her whole face now. "I can help with that."

"Oh, boy." Reed knew trouble was coming.

"We should have left while we had the chance," Doug whispered to Sondra in his usual whisper tone which was anything but soft.

Gabby ignored all the comments and pressed forward with her plans. "See, I think a big problem is that you've had a bad run of partners."

Reed hated where this conversation was headed. "Honey, I will go anywhere with you except to work. We cannot be partners. I would never be able to concentrate."

She snorted and frowned and otherwise made it quite clear that was not her suggestion. "Of course not."

"Good, I thought—"

"I'm talking about Doug."

"What?"

"What?" Doug yelled the word even louder than Reed.

"You guys are perfect for each other." Gabby smiled after delivering the blow.

"I can see it." Sondra nodded her head. "It's a terrific solution. Doug needs someone to go with him on his jobs. Reed likes to baby-sit."

"We can't stand each other," Reed insisted.

Doug came up off the couch and hovered behind Gabby. "The nerd is right. Listen to him."

"And there's about a fifty percent chance he'll shoot me in the back during the first week," Reed said.

Doug nodded. "And more like eighty percent."

"Right. It's perfect." Gabby's smile turned from sweet to determined. "We'll talk about it tomorrow."

"We should discuss it now," Doug shouted again.

Reed knew how the guy felt.

"It's time for us to go." Sondra put a hand on Doug's shoulder and ushered him toward the door. "They want to be alone."

"But—"

"You'll have plenty of time to argue your point later," Sondra said.

"But—"

Sondra smiled. "Because I think Reed is going to be around for a long time."

Chapter 29

"Sondra is wrong."

The smile that broke across Reed's face despite his comment chased all of her concerns and doubts away. "How so?"

"Forever." Just that word. He stopped there.

"Should I know what that means?"

"I'm not going to be around for a week or two. I'm going to be around forever."

The idea filled Gabby with a bubbling lightness. Here she had thought she wanted excitement, that she craved this type of job that would keep her life on the edge. All she really needed was Reed.

"Oh, really?"

"I can wait, you know." He tightened his arms around her waist.

The hug made her feel secure and loved. For so much of her life, she missed those feelings. Not anymore.

"What is it you plan on waiting for?" She asked.

"You."

Did he really not see that she was right there, ready for the picking. Hell, if he did not get her naked soon, she might get violent. "Me?"

"For however long it takes. I'll wait. I am a very patient man." He did that nibbling thing on her neck.

Now he was getting with the program. She thought she would have to beg him to get physical.

The gentle caress drove her wild. "I've heard that."

"Of course, if you want to put me out of my misery and tell me sooner, that would be fine, too."

What she wanted was to take him into the bedroom for a round or two of make-up sex. Talking could wait until later as far as she was concerned. They had made up, had enough of an understanding to reconnect on another level.

"Should I know what you're talking about?"

He sighed against her bare skin. "Women."

"Aren't we adorable?"

"You are." He lifted his head. All traces of playfulness had disappeared.

"Reed?"

"I meant the words when I said them earlier. I love you." He stood there for a second, not moving and not talking. "Well?"

She laughed. A doubled-over-with-her-hand-over-her-mouth sort of laugh. She could not help it. The poor guy stood there waiting for her to make a grand admission of love, and she was planning the easiest way to get him into the bedroom and seduce him.

Yeah, she needed to work on the romance side of her life.

He frowned. "I've waited most of my life to say that to a woman. Never expected her to burst into laughter upon hearing it."

"I'm sorry." She composed herself. "Really. I thought . . . well, it doesn't matter."

"You're killing me here."

Growing serious, she took both of his hands in hers. "Reed Larkin."

"You're not going to laugh again, are you?"

"I want to laugh with joy, but not for the reason you

think. See, I love you. I have loved you for weeks. Despite everything, maybe because of everything, I fell for you. I didn't plan it. Certainly didn't like it."

"Thanks."

"But I love you. The forever kind."

A look of pure male satisfaction crossed his face. "Now you're talking."

"The idea of loving you is comfortable to me now."

He wiggled his eyebrows. "I guess the lying thing turns you on."

"About that . . ."

A pained expression crossed his face. "Awww, shit. I was kidding."

"Sit." She pushed him down on the couch.

He threw his head back and groaned. The complaining stopped when she straddled him. "Good idea."

"I wanted to get your attention."

"Honey, you have it." His hands cupped her backside. "I like this position."

She slapped his fingers away. "Enough of that."

"Nowhere near enough, actually." He put his palms back and started nuzzling her breasts with his lips and nose.

"We're starting over."

He stopped moving. "What?"

She lifted his head and forced him to look at her. "We got off to a rough start. You're right about that."

"I was wrong. Dead wrong."

"We've done this backwards." But they could set it right.

"True, but we arrived at the right place. Why mess that up? I don't want to lose the progress we've made."

"Calm down." She kissed him to keep him from jumping out of his skin. "We need to go back. Learn the basics. We know the complicated stuff. It's the simple stuff we need to know, like how to trust each other."

"I trust you."

"You know what I mean."

He groaned again. "We're not going to go back to the part where we don't have sex, right? I mean, we are good at that part."

She toyed with the idea of torturing him. But, since she enjoyed their lovemaking as much as he did, she would only be hurting herself. So, she threw that idea away.

"We are committed to forever, right?" she asked.

"Yes."

No hesitation. She loved that about him. So many things, actually. He was a good man. Somewhere along the line he forgot that fact, but she knew. She would show him.

"We need to fill in the gaps of what we know about each other. No more lies. No more trying to protect each other with half-truths."

His face went blank. "What if you don't like what you hear?"

She rushed to ease that fear. "You dumped me, lied to me and used me, and I'm still here. Do you actually think you could say something that would be worse than all of that?"

"When you put it that way . . ."

"I'm not going anywhere, but I want to know all of you, the real you. Good and bad."

He shot her a deadly serious look. "Promise you'll stick it out no matter how rough it is?"

His vulnerability gave her all the hope she needed. "I promise."

His gaze searched her face. After a few seconds the strain on his mouth faded away. It was as if the pain and mistrust of his past crumbled under the promise of their future.

"Now, you said something about giving my couch a try." He bounced a bit as if testing the springs. "We got a bit off track, what with Doug's break-in and all, but I'm still willing."

"Are you?"

"Count on it."

She loved Reed for many things. She loved him most for how free and cherished he made her feel.

"Well, big boy. I'm not getting any younger."

He pulled her closer. "And you're not getting any older without me."

"Count on it."

You've got to try
AT HER SERVICE
by Susan Johnson,
out this month from Brava . . .

"You did well to expedite your brother's release." Darley offered her his arm. "It will likely save his life."

"I must see that it does," she declared, tucking her gloved hand into the crook of his arm. "Whatever is necessary to see him well again, I will do," she firmly added as they walked away.

"I gathered as much."

She glanced up at him. "I'm not ashamed."

"Nor should you be. We all do what we must in this senseless war."

She shot him a look. A distinct antipathy had entered his voice. "Is this war any different from any other?"

"It was unnecessary," he muttered. "Religious fanatics and overweening egos brought this disaster upon us."

"Whose side are you on?" An ambiguity had suddenly colored his tone.

"No one's," he replied, careful to rectify his fleeting candor. "I just dislike war in general and this war in particular." Which was God's own truth. He smiled, a teasing glimmer in his eyes. "Perhaps it's no more than blatant selfishness on my part. I'm finding it increasingly difficult to ignore the misery and amuse myself in my usual profligate way."

"Which is?" Gazi's provocative gaze had awakened some inexplicable, heady wildness in her.

His dark brows flickered roguishly. "Nothing conventional, I assure you."

"Is that so?" A honeyed coquetry, a lush smile.

Both irresistible. "Consider the danger in tantalizing me, Miss Clement," Darley gently warned. "I am only chivalrous under duress."

"Perhaps I'm not in the market for chivalry." Her words were quite unexpected, but once spoken, she felt no compunction to retract them.

He turned to look at her, his gray-green gaze intense. "What *are* you in the market for?"

For any number of reasons, some purely selfish, others paradoxically both whimsical and survival based, all deeply bereft of reason, Aurore said, simply, "Forgetfulness."

"With me?" He was too tired to play games.

She held his gaze, direct and unblinking. "Yes."

"In spite of your brother?"

"*Because* of my brother."

"He will soon be on the mend," Darley offered, benevolent and obliging, possibly lying as well.

"I am of the same mind," Aurore replied, unlike him, resolute in her belief. "Thank you for saying so. Now tell me, Gazi," she went on in an altogether different tone, one that threw caution to the winds without any further soul-searching, "what does Zania find so enticing about you?"

"Is this a game?" he bluntly asked. "Are you and Zania competitors?"

She shot him a sideways glance. "Does it matter?"

He didn't know why he hesitated when it *was* a game

for everyone involved. "No, of course not," he finally said. "It doesn't matter in the least."

"I didn't think so. But what other than survival does at the moment?"

"Indeed," he murmured. "There's no escaping reality."

"Gazi, my sweet," she drolly murmured, "pray do not blue-devil me with such reminders, when at the moment I require only amusement from you."

"And that you shall have, darling," he said as lightly, the endearment rolling easily off his tongue. Without breaking stride, he scooped her up in his arms and moving down the street kissed her lightly, then not so lightly—and ultimately, not lightly at all. He kissed her wildly, urgently, as if there was no tomorrow—a distinct possibility for them both with the present social disorder swirling about them.

Walking swiftly toward the beckoning hospitality of Miss Clement's bed, Darley's kisses took on a burning impatience. Unlike a man who hadn't slept in days. Nor like a man who had only recently risen from Countess Tatischev's bed.

As the lights of the hotel came into view, shocked back to her senses by the imminent prospect of being seen, Aurore heatedly whispered, "Stop, stop!" She pushed against Darley's chest. "I can't do this! Put me down!"

"No." Nothing altered in his stride, not so much as a millisecond of hesitation marred his pace.

Drawing back even more, she regarded him with a hot-tempered gaze. "Put me *down* or I'll *scream!*"

"Scream away." His gait remained unchanged.

How dare he speak so calmly. "Dammit, I *will!*"

He actually looked at her then, his gaze in contrast to hers, unsullied by high emotion. "I don't know you very well," he said, gently, as though he were soothing a temperamental child, "but from what I've seen, your moods are—how do I put this—highly changeable," he diplomatically finished. "Not that you don't have reason of course." His smile was indulgent. "Why don't we talk about this upstairs?"

Supernatural. And super-sexy.
Here's a sneak peek at
WILD: THE PACK OF ST. JAMES,
the first in a new series from Noelle Mack.
Available now from Brava . . .

"**Y**ou are beautiful, Vivienne. And I would have you."

Such a masculine voice, deep and rough-edged. She loved the sound of it, loved to hear him talk. She sighed. "I know that women never refuse you, Kyril. But I—"

He drew the heavy velvet curtain that hung in voluptuous folds over the window and moved with alacrity to stand in front of her, interrupting her reply. "Will you not stay with me tonight? My carriage is outside and no one will see you leave here."

"I—I cannot."

He reached up a hand to caress her cheek. Vivienne felt a hot blush suffuse her skin. "Is there no way to persuade you?" Coaxing and tender, his thumb traced the line of her chin.

"No." But the light sensation of his touch thrilled her all the same. She did not push his hand away. "I must consider my reputation. What is left of it."

"Bah. Your guests went home long ago and your servants are nowhere in sight."

"That does not matter." His determination was flattering but his presence made her uneasy.

"I would rather be in my own bed in the morning."

"Alone?" He inclined his head and pressed ardent kisses to the side of her neck. Vivienne moaned softly—the pleasurable stimulation was almost too much to bear.

"Yes, Kyril. Quite alone."

He moved down to her shoulders, kissing and stroking her bare skin until languorous, highly sensual warmth spread through her.

"It seems a very great shame."

His arms stole around her waist in a lover's embrace. His nearness was overwhelming. Vivienne arched her back, wanting and not wanting to be a little distance from the pressure of his body. She placed her hands upon his chest, feeling the strong beat of his heart through her palms.

"Ah, what you do to me . . ." Kyril kissed her neck once more and lifted his head. She could not help but meet his eyes. A dark blue, like twilight, they reflected no detail of her face or the room in which they stood—and yet they glowed.

He smiled down at her and Vivienne felt a dizzying vertigo. If not for his arms around her, she would have fallen. For no more than a moment, she had glimpsed something very odd in his eyes . . . a vision of a wild and forsaken otherworld buried in white. As if that were what he saw and not her. He blinked and the vision disappeared. But she recalled the story . . .

From the far north came men of a legendary race, born in the shadow of the blue sun that never sets. They ruled the frozen seas and rode its terrible winds . . . and they were masters of the great ice wolves that are no more . . .

The fanciful tale he had entertained her with when the servants had at last left them alone by the fire in the drawing room. A fantasy, nothing more, heard and remembered from his childhood in Russia. Suddenly, caught in his possessive, encircling embrace, Vivienne was ready to believe that the tale was something more than fantasy and something less than real. But what its meaning was, she could not say. She could not think. His warm hand had moved up her back and clasped the nape of her neck. The gesture was both calming and sensual. In an instant, her feeling of falling vanished, replaced by one of stillness and safety . . . Vivienne straightened. She was not safe. No woman was, with him. With a slight shake of her head, she dismissed the momentary vision and her wayward imaginings. Tonight's soiree had dragged on too long and she was fatigued, that was all.

He would not possess her.

Since his arrival in London two years ago, the tall, darkly handsome Kyril Taruskin had been much whispered about. His heavy-lidded eyes and full mouth hinted at a talent for passionate lovemaking—and his conquests were many. Vivienne had heard the rumors, but invited him to her soirees all the same, presuming that she, a woman of the world and the former mistress of a duke who still adored her, would be immune to his sensual charm.

Foolish of her.

"Oh!" She breathed the word, startled by what he was doing. The slight pressure of his thumb under her chin brought her face up to his.

"Well, then," he whispered. "Shall I stay a little longer?"

"N—no. Please go."

"Vivienne . . . to satisfy your intimate desires would give me the deepest delight."

It was just after midnight—she had heard the church bells toll the hour and the candles had burned low. The fireplace held a broken mass of scarlet embers that danced with shivering little flames. She closed her eyes, avoiding his intent gaze, not wanting to see his mouth so close to hers. But Kyril did not try to kiss her.

All he did was touch her once more.

Vivienne steeled herself to resist the brazen sensuality of his caress. His fingertips brushed the side of her neck that he had kissed and then moved lower, over her collarbone, causing her bared flesh to tingle. She should not have worn such deep décolletage. He was smiling down at her again, self-restrained . . . and somehow . . . ready to pounce. He embodied masculine elegance, but his dark clothes and immaculate linen only brought out his wildness. That quality too was much talked about—it was something Vivienne found overpoweringly attractive.

She prayed Kyril's hand would not move lower to the swell of her breasts . . . but it did. His exploring caress was deliciously stimulating.

Vivienne sighed without knowing it and swayed toward him. Then she came back to her senses. Kyril Taruskin would not get the better of her so easily.

Be sure to catch Shelly Laurenston's
THE BEAST IN HIM,
coming next month from Brava . . .

Sherman cleared his throat. "I'll speak with you another time, Jessica." She heard his footsteps heading back to the coffeehouse.

When Sherman opened the door, Smitty tossed out, "Just don't call her when we're having sex—which will be constantly!"

Jess waited long enough for Sherman to get inside before she yanked away from Smitty and followed up with a solid fist to his chest. The pain that radiated up her arm afterward—she ignored.

"What is wrong with you?"

"Nothin'," he said, looking confused. "Why?"

Smitty wasn't sure what he enjoyed more. Torturing that scrawny dog—and he had tortured him. The poor guy didn't know whether to be horrified or jealous of Smitty and Jessie going at it. Or had his pleasure come from torturing Jessie Ann? All that was fun, but what he enjoyed the most was having Jessie Ann plastered up against him. She nuzzled real nice, even when she didn't mean to.

At the moment, however, she looked real cranky.

"I was helping like you asked."

"You were being a dick," she said while looking down at the giant watch on her wrist. "And you were enjoying every damn second of being a—oh, my God! I've gotta go."

She ran to the corner and hailed a cab, but before she stepped inside, she ran back over to him.

"One other thing."

"Yeah?"

She slid her hand under his jacket and twisted his nipple until his eyes watered.

"Touch my tits again without permission and I'll rip this off." She glanced at her watch again. "Ach! Now I really do have to go."

Jessie turned and ran back toward the waiting cab. Sure, Smitty could have let her go, but to be honest, he'd never been so damn entertained by a woman before. "So how do I get permission?"

She spun around, jumping back when she realized he stood right behind her. "Stop sneaking up on me! And you don't get permission."

"Why not? You said I was pretty."

"Look, Smitty, while I appreciate your doglike persistence, you need to know that nothing you do or say will change my mind about this. You're part of my past and these days I'm all about my future. I don't have time or room in my life for you and your casual chats. Understand?"

"Sure."

"Good."

" 'Cause I always love a challenge."

He'd caught her with that when she was halfway in the cab. With one foot in and the other still braced against the curb, she stared at him. "What challenge?"

"You're challenging me to get you back into my life."

"No, I'm not."

"Your exact words were 'I challenge you, Bobby Ray Smith, to get me back into your life.' "

"I never said that."

"That's what I heard." The beauty of wolf hearing. You only heard what you wanted to, made up what was never said but should have been, and the rest meant little or nothing.

"Is there something wrong with you? Mentally?"

"Darlin', you met my family. You've gotta be more specific than that."

"That's it. I'm leaving. I can't have this conversation with you. I can't—"

He saw it immediately. The way her entire body tensed, her eyes focusing across the busy city street, locking on something in the distance. She went from exasperated to on point in less than five seconds.

"What's wrong, Jessie?" He followed her line of sight but didn't see anything that stuck out to him.

"Nothing," she said, her eyes still staring across the street. "I need to go." She went up on her toes and absently kissed him on his cheek. He'd bet cash she wouldn't even remember she did it.

She stepped into her cab and closed the door. She didn't look back at him, didn't acknowledge him in any way. That wasn't like her. Even if it was to give him the finger, she'd do or say something before driving off.

Smitty turned and stared at the spot Jessie'd been staring at. But he still saw nothing that made him feel tense or worried.

So what the hell had worried his little Jessie Ann?